Burning Midnight

This Large Print Book carries the Seal of Approval of N.A.V.H.

BURNING MIDNIGHT

LOREN D. ESTLEMAN

THORNDIKE PRESS
A part of Gale, Cengage Learning

Detroit • New York • San Francisco • New Haven, Conn • Waterville, Maine • London

This is a work of fiction. All of the characters, organizations, and events portrayed in this novel are either the products of the author's imagination or are used fictitiously.

Thorndike Press® Large Print Mystery.
The text of this Large Print edition is unabridged.
Other aspects of the book may vary from the original edition.
Set in 16 pt. Plantin.

IBRARY OF CONGRESS CATALOGING-IN-PUBLICATION DATA

Estleman, Loren D.
Burning midnight / by Loren D. Estleman.
pages ; cm. — (Thorndike Press large print mystery) (An Amos Walker novel)
ISBN 978-1-4104-5018-0 (hardcover) — ISBN 1-4104-5018-X (hardcover)
1. Walker, Amos (Fictitious character)—Fiction. 2. Private investigators—Michigan—Detroit—Fiction. 3. Large type books. I. Title.
PS3555.S84B87 2012b
813'.54—dc23 2012016465

Published in 2012 by arrangement with Tom Doherty Associates, LLC.

Printed in the United States of America
1 2 3 4 5 6 7 16 15 14 13 12

To Frank Wydra
(1939–2008)
A kinder, wiser soul never was.

Fire burns the match as well.

— old Spanish saying

■ ■ ■ ■

Uno:
Crown of Thorns

■ ■ ■ ■

ONE

I had a mouse in the office, a cute little seal-colored rodent with black shiny eyes like licorice drops and whiskers longer on one side than the other, so that when he worked his nose he looked like Uncle Vanya. He lived in the wall, in a hole in the baseboard, one of those Gothic arches you see in cartoons; inside he would sleep in a bed made out of a sardine can. I called him Wally. Next time he stuck out his head I was going to brain him with the stapler.

It would be the acme of my week. It was March, a muddy one with the remains of a February blizzard going like sixty in the storm drains, and all the feral spouses and politicians to let seemed to have given up their bad habits for Lent. That left me with time to shred some old files and make room in the stove-in green cabinets for the heap on the desk. It was pleasant enough work, demanding little from the faculties of reason, and the noise made by those ancient infidelities and aging runaways as they passed through the blades sounded like jet planes taking off for exotic destinations.

I was stuck in Detroit, but that was okay. Most Detroiters don't live there by choice. I'd paid off the mortgage on my house near Hamtramck and had a little money in the bank, from the spike in shady behavior that always takes place around the middle of January when the New Year's resolutions run out of gas. With luck it would hold me through Easter. You could set your calendar by the season of impiety that followed.

So I was caught off guard when the door to my shallow reception room opened from the hall, breaking a connection and setting the buzzer going. I almost never get business off the street. It comes over the telephone from my display ad in the Yellow Pages, from referrals and lawyers I've worked with in the past. Even when things are brisk I can go weeks without a heartbeat in the place except mine and the mouse's. I could just as well work from home, but that sort of thing leads to wearing a bathrobe in the afternoon and related types of sloth. I'm lazy enough without encouragement.

As luck would have it — mine, anyway — Wally's pointed snout poked out of his hole just in time for the sudden noise to scare him back inside. I put the stapler back in the drawer with the walnuts I used it to crack open and dusted the flakes of domestic upheaval off my lap just as my visitor entered the center of empire.

He was a bald man with a carroty fringe and the exaggerated features of a Toby mug, and built along those lines. A blazer that fit him the way a borrowed jacket in a ritzy restaurant fit anyone wore the logo of a local TV station on the breast pocket. His neck was red and rashy from the struggle against the tie that closed his collar with a knot as hard as a ball bearing. It was a spread collar, but getting it buttoned would be a daily challenge and put blisters on his fingers. His neck had been engineered to hold up something a lot bigger than his head, but it was a big head at that; if he wore a hat it would have had to have been custom made. He had the skim-milk complexion of the true redhead, which called attention to the scarlet lesions of the true drunkard.

But he was sober now, and came straight up to my desk without looking around. I had more than a hunch he could still have described everything in the office down to the buttons on General Custer's tunic in the framed print covering a bald patch in the wallpaper. Everyone's eyes are pretty much the same size, despite what you read, but his were lost in his face, bright and blue under bloated lids.

I got up to shake his hand. It was too small for his wrist but it had plenty of torque. "Walker? I'm —"

"I know who you are, Mr. Pearman. My TV doesn't work so well since HD, but a memory for faces goes with the job."

His name was Louis Pearman. He did stand-up for the news and had worried away at the reputation of a local investment counselor with an international portfolio until he got down to a pool of corruption as big and deep as an underground lake. The Securities and Exchange Commission was still conducting diving operations there, but Pearman had moved on to City Hall.

He was a very good reporter or they'd never have let him near a camera.

"HD." He made a porcine noise. "That little act of Congress almost put me out of work. Nobody likes to come home from a hard day on the line and look at a kisser like this. I'm considering an offer from the CBC. They're still analog in Canada, and fuzzy enough to make me look like the mannequin behind the desk." But he was pleased to have been recognized. "I didn't call for an appointment. It doesn't look like I'm interrupting much."

I was right about his powers of observation. Two file drawers hung out like dogs' tongues and the pile on the desk looked unchanged since I'd started, two hours ago. I'd only just cracked the twenty-first century.

I said, "I'm on hiatus. That's the word, right?"

"Don't ask me. I'm still a print journalist at heart. Stinking shame what's happening to newspapers."

"I know. I had to let the parakeet go."

That stumped him for half a second. Then his paunch started undulating and something he thought was a sardonic chuckle came staggering out through his nostrils. He seemed to do most of his communicating through them. "I can see we won't have to break the ice. I don't suppose you have any." His face took on a hungry look.

I opened the safe I never bothered to lock and took out a bottle of Old Smuggler and stood it on the desk. The safe came with the office. I kept a change of shirts in it and the floor plan to the Federal Reserve, but it had looked empty until I moved the Scotch there from the desk. That had made room in the deep drawer for cartons of cigarettes. I got out two souvenir shot glasses and filled them both. "No ice, sorry. When they wired this place it came by horse."

He grinned and took a sip. I'd pegged him to put it away in a single easy down payment, but you don't get far in my occupation being surprised. We sat, he in the customer's chair I'd bolted to the floor to keep the halitosis at bay, and fed quietly from our glasses. It was ten A.M. on the dot, but the sky was overcast and you couldn't see where the sun was in relation to the yardarm. I never said he was the only drunkard in the room.

"World's gone to hell," he opened, warming his hands around the little glass; they were that small. I'd have suspected polio in childhood if not for the strength of his grip.

I shook my head, smiling my secret smile.

"You don't agree?"

"I didn't say that."

"Most everybody does."

"*Al*most everybody," I said automatically.

He made a face, on top of the one God already stuck him with. "That's what forty years in broadcasting does to you. It's a wonder I can communicate at all. But you know what I meant."

"Not me. I'm in too good a mood."

"Spring in the air?"

"Cash in my wallet. Same thing."

"Doesn't look like you splash it around."

"I put one of those funny new lightbulbs in the ceiling fixture just last week."

He changed the subject. "I heard most private detectives are ex-cops."

"Some of them are still on the job. It depends on the regulations regarding moon-lighting."

"What about you?"

"I was briefly."

"What happened?"

"I broke my hand."

"They don't toss you out for that."

"I broke it on a jaw."

His eyelids lifted. Scratch a journalist, find a newshound. "Whose?"

"It's a long story, and I don't feel like being this week's human-interest feature. Anyway, I have filing to do, and you have to brush up on the metric system if you're going to work in Canada."

"To hell with Canada. They kind of let their mask slip during the Olympics. They're as big a pain in the ass as Americans. Which they are, no matter what they like to think. We don't have the deed to the entire continent."

I let my secret smile spread into a sunny

grin. “Small talk. I guess that’s how you burrow under their skins, then go for the jugular from inside.”

He thought about that, deciding whether to get mad. You could see the flush spreading under that blue-white skin like a high-pressure front moving across the Great Lakes during the weather report. Then he decided it wasn’t worth the effort, and you could see that, too, in the color-coding. My respect for him as a gatherer of information went up another notch. In his job you had to be good to overcome a handicap like that.

“I started off out of step,” he said. “You can’t impress another card-trick artist using the same deck he does. I’ll put them on the table.”

“If you want. I’d just as soon let the files wait another day. My health plan doesn’t cover paper cuts.”

He put down the rest of his drink in the fashion I felt sure he was most comfortable with, and spread his palm over his glass when I lifted the bottle. “I like to do my serious drinking alone,” he said. “They say — the scientists — that that’s the definition of a problem drinker. But science is what’s got us in the mess we’re in.”

“Mathematics is the only science. Everything else is open to interpretation.”

"Who said that?"

"Someone, probably. Does it matter?"

"Just wanted to get the attribution right. I've got a daughter-in-law."

"She's got a thing about attribution?" I wasn't even sure what the word meant.

"She's the reason I'm here instead of the City-County Building, where I'm supposed to be asking the treasurer who his bookie is. Actually, it's her brother, but that's family. They're Mexican."

"Uh-huh."

"Why 'uh-huh?' " he snapped.

"Positive reinforcement. To show I'm listening."

"Okay, if that's all. People make snap judgments about them. They're hardworking, devoted to their families. They pool their pesos to send someone up here, and as soon as he's got enough together he sends for the rest."

"That's a snap judgment too. Some of them spend it on cockfights."

"Most don't. The ones that do get more than their share of attention."

"Just their share. You're in the news business. You didn't get that Pulitzer nomination writing about honesty in high places."

"The award went to an embedded war correspondent who spent all his time in bed with a hooker in a four-star hotel in Dubai. Can I tell my story?"

"Who stopped you? All I said was 'uh-huh.' "

He grinned again. It wasn't a nice grin, but I doubt he had spares. "They told me you're an independent son of a bitch. I guess that would explain this office."

"You're forgetting that lightbulb. Tell me about the brother."

"Good enough kid — she says. He's got himself in a gang. My son came to me to get him out. I wouldn't know how to go about it. My work always starts when it's all over."

"What did the social worker say?"

"What social worker?"

"You're making the same mistake your son did. My specialty's missing persons: It's spelled out right there in my listing. I just find them, and if they let me I bring them back."

"If they *let* you?"

"I'm not a bounty hunter. The ones I know I wouldn't trust to lend a book on my library card. Come back when the brother goes missing. Until then you need to go to Family Services."

He shook his head. That operation involved a hydraulic system buried deep in that neck. "Maybe if you put as much time into accepting a job as you do into turning one down, you'd have a suite in Grosse Pointe instead of a flea hatchery downtown."

"I'd need a better car first. One I've got, I have to shoot a valet in the leg to get his attention. Then I'd need a suit to go with the car, and you can't ever get out of those places without a fight unless you buy a tie to match, and then a handkerchief to match that — shoes, too, you can't wear Hush Puppies with Italian worsted — and before you know it you're back in the flea hatchery wearing a suit that makes it look even worse."

He sat still for this, so I finished my drink and lit a cigarette. It was against the law now despite my name on the lease, but it's a three-story walk-up and I can hear the butt cops coming. I don't even bother to blow the smoke out the window. Nine decades of nicotine is what's holding up the building.

"If you people are determined to come to me with a phony cover story," I said, "you ought to stop giving interviews to your colleagues. You've had two wives and no kids, hence no daughter-in-law, Mexican or otherwise, and consequently no brother in a *cuadrilla.* Tell me who it is you're bearding for and maybe we can do business. Probably not, though. There's usually a lie at the start of every case, but working my way through one liar just to get the one who sent him is too much overtime. With your alimony you can't afford it."

He turned as red as his hair, which concerned me a little. He was lugging around too much weight for a tall man, and he wasn't tall. If he had a blowout in a major artery, he'd be a corpse before the EMS crew got him to the ground floor. Then the color faded. The hydraulics in his neck turned his head halfway around on its axis, then back.

"I told him you probably wouldn't fall for it. I came in on the end of a couple of plays you had a toe in, and you didn't strike me as the kind to go around with your flap stuck inside your coat pocket. How's the reception here?" He dug a cell phone out of his blazer.

"Lousy, but my service is based in Saginaw."

His wasn't. He got a signal right away and his party answered on the first ring. "Yeah. A bust. You want to call it a wash?" He listened. "Okay if I don't hang around?" He waited again, then swung shut the hatch, put it away, and got up without making any of the noises men in his condition usually made when they fought gravity. "No bad blood, I hope. Someday I might want to call on you on my own dime."

"No fear. Don't let the front throw you. Business isn't that good."

"Coat of paint shouldn't break you."

"Too much red tape. It's a historic building."

"Yeah?" This time he looked around, taking in the zinc radiator and the ceiling that screamed asbestos. "What happened here?"

"A water commissioner refused a bribe down in the foyer in 1919."

He made that laugh that sounded like an empty air mattress being rolled up and took himself out. I didn't ask him if the party on the other end had decided to call it a wash or not. I'm only curious when I'm on a retainer.

In a little someone started walking a stove up the stairs and then the buzzer went off a second time, a personal best. Inspector John Alderdyce of the Detroit Police Homicide Division came in and dropped two hundred pounds of muscle and polished granite into the chair Louis Pearman had quit.

"My son married a Mexican," he said. "Or can I start where he left off?"

Two

"They're a hardworking people," I said. "devoted to their families."

"Family: warm, fuzzy word. It's why we always leave the guns behind when dispatch calls us to the scene of a domestic disturbance. What's so hot about having a family, anyway? Bitches eat their pups."

I looked at my watch. "Ten-twenty. I knew it couldn't last."

"What, your liver?" He glanced at the bottle on the desk.

"My cheerful mood. Why slam my head into the masonry when all I have to do is call a cop?"

"Pearman showed up drunk at a press conference downtown a couple of months ago," Alderdyce said. "He jerked at my sleeve in the hall later, and based on the questions he asked, if he'd reported what he had the way he had it, he'd be covering openings of bowling alleys for the *Macomb*

Weekly Shopper until his Social Security kicked in. I let him sleep it off in holding down at the First, wrote it up as interfering, and made a public apology to him and his station for overreacting to a question I considered impertinent. I got a reprimand in my jacket. Today was the payoff for what he owed me."

"It doesn't sound like you."

"What? You think I wouldn't be kicking in the doors of meth labs right now if I didn't swap solids with the gentlepeople of the press from time to time?"

"I meant the show of stealth. I never knew you to come in from the side."

"It was just until I got you onto neutral ground. Homicide's worse than a Tupperware party for spreading gossip, and I didn't want to pay a call on you and answer questions from anyone who spotted me going in or coming out. It's like one of the Fords being seen going into a Kia dealership."

"Couldn't you at least make it Chrysler? A man has feelings."

He didn't bother to react to that. Lately he'd taken to cropping his hair close to the skull — he never let Mother Nature have an idea he hadn't had first — and now there was nothing about him that appeared remotely organic. His skin had lightened with middle age from a deep eggplant to indigo, but the way it was stretched over bony outcrop made him look like a project three sculptors had given up on. The suits he wore, made by a retired Greek tailor who'd brought his bolts of cashmere and silk home when he'd closed up shop, toned down the effect in his body while calling attention to the brutal head and his hands, large and squared off at the fingertips with veins as thick as baling twine on the backs.

"Gerald turned out fine. We worried about him for a long time; everything you hear about a cop's son starts with real life. He's an accountant with a bus company, which is about as far from police work as you can get, and his wife, Chata, belongs to a family with ties to Spanish aristocracy. Her great-great-something grandfather got Sonora in a grant from Philip the Second for killing a lot of Indians in his mines. That might not be what it said on the parchment, but those old royals didn't reward you for charity work. Anyway the only real estate anyone in the family owns now is a corner lot in Lathrup Village, and Gerald and Chata were generous enough to let Comerica Bank in on that little piece of heaven."

"Is this a long story?"

His face made a scowl. It didn't have far

to go to finish it. "Late for brunch?"

"No, but I charge by the day. Tell me about the brother."

"His name's Ernesto Pasada. It's an old family name, with a string of others in the middle. Ten or twelve Pasadas had it before, going back to Cortez. His friends call him Nesto. These friends run with the Maldados in Mexicantown. I see you've heard of them."

I reminded myself not to sit down with him at a poker table without a set of false whiskers. "I've done business in the neighborhood. I had to get their permission to do it. They've got a branch office in every city between here and Juarez, where they swap bullets with the Border Patrol every day but Sunday. God's the only authority they recognize, and that's on approval. I'm sorry Nesto didn't fall in with the Mafia instead. The mob won't touch a cop."

"Downtown policy is never to go into Mexicantown without backup. Unofficial policy is when in doubt, start shooting. Let the brass sort it out with the public when the smoke clears. So of course we don't go in. Their idea of sorting it out involves throwing the uniforms to the hyenas."

"I didn't know the gangs recruited in the suburbs."

"Nesto sleeps at his sister's. He *lives* on West Vernor. He's sixteen. That's when the cultural issues set in, right after the hormones. You can't get up a decent *piñata* party in Lathrup."

"How does his sister know he's ganged up?"

"The Maldados had a dustup with the Zapatistas last summer. The Zaps came out on the short end, but they inflicted a casualty. This is a detail from a crime-scene photo." He slid a four-by-six manila envelope from an inside breast pocket and flipped it across the desk.

I undid the clasp and slid out the grainy shot, printed on ordinary copy paper from a laser scanner. It showed the back of a hand in tight close-up with a tarantula tattoo nearly as big as the hand. Nothing looks deader than a body part in a police photo. I put it back in the envelope and flipped it back his way. "That's the gang insignia," I said. "I saw it wrapped around a Beretta Nine once. I take it Nesto came home with it on his hand one day."

"He tried to hide it with a gauze patch, said he'd cut himself building a table in the garage; he's good with wood. His grandfather was a master cabinetmaker, so he's the hope for the family in *Los Estados Uni-*

dos. Women don't count down there. After a couple of days Chata became suspicious and braced him on it. He tore off the bandage and got snotty. Stayed away overnight. She was about to set the juvies on him when he came in the door. They haven't done a lot of talking since. I got sent for. I tried that tough-love deal, but the spiders brainwashed him pretty good. Cops don't scare him."

"I'm supposed to?"

"You're not ugly enough. Stop interrupting. I went against conventional wisdom and had the Early Response boys send a squad into Maldado territory to shake them up, tell 'em Nesto's off-limits, but these characters have seen cops crucified in Durango: I'm talking literally, nails and crosses. Some of them may even have spelled those *mestizos* on the hammer. They know we can only go so far. Jail time for them is a rite of passage, like First Communion, and since none of them expects to reach thirty, they just laugh when you offer to bust a cap in their ass. The job needs somebody who isn't trussed up by the system."

"The job needs Bruce Willis. I can't help you, John."

"I'm not suggesting you bring down the gang. Just make hanging onto Nesto not worth the trouble."

"They've got the DEA and RICO on their necks. They eat and drink trouble. They don't scare; you said it yourself. A day without a death threat for them is a day lost."

Another breast pocket delivered another envelope. I looked at a face I'd seen before, on that occasion without numbers underneath it. The long crease on his left cheek had been inflicted at birth, by forceps in the hands of a careless OB-GYN. The scar on his right was more recent and came from a box cutter, the twenty-first century's answer to the straight razor. It was a young face despite the rough handling, handsome if you liked the undernourished type, with black hair tousling down on the forehead and an arrogant Elvis twist in the upper lip.

"Luís Guerrera," I said. "The quiet half of the Guerrera brothers. Or he was until Jesus got shot out from under his baseball cap by a police round. We've had some words. He doesn't run the gang, but the one who does listens to him when he's got something to say. He the one you want me to drop the hammer on?"

"He's your excuse for being in the neighborhood. Luís dropped out of sight last week. He didn't really, but who's to know?

The Maldados think the Zapatistas took him, so they're polishing up their box cutters for a fresh round. You've been hired by his family in Mexico to find him before blood gets shed and maybe some of it Guerrera's. While you're at it you can spot a mess of grass lying around and maybe some crack, give us probable cause to come in and tear the street apart and tie them in with the smugglers on the border. That's federal. They might come out the other end clean and they might not, but it'll take months, long enough for Nesto to lose interest and concentrate on his carpentry."

"And just in case I don't spot any dope, I carry it in on my back?"

"The evidence room can use some clearing out."

"Suppose Guerrera shows up before I start asking questions?"

"He won't."

"Where are you holding him?"

"You don't need to know any more than what I've told you."

I poured myself a drink. He watched me finish it in four swallows.

"Now that you've thought it over," he said when I didn't resume the conversation.

"I know my answer. I was just wondering how many schemes you drew up and threw out before you came up with this one."

"You think I'd put my pension on the line if it weren't the last resort?"

"You love this kid that much?"

"I only saw him the one time. Gerald and I don't exactly take each other to lunch. I said he was a handful once. I took the wrong tack. After he moved out of the house he had his name legally changed so people wouldn't keep asking him if he was related to a police inspector who stands in front of a camera now and then. He doesn't know I'm in this. It was Chata who came to me."

This was all news, including the fact that the two boys I'd seen in the family picture on the desk in his office had outgrown youth soccer. I'd known John since we were younger than that, but socially we were strangers. We'd spent too much time with that desk between us to pine over the purity of boyhood friendship.

"Let Guerrera go," I said.

He nodded. Cops seldom ask a question they don't already know the answer to, but that doesn't stop them from going ahead and asking anyway. "Your credit downtown's a long way in the red," he said. "You could fix that with one word."

"If I gave it to you, every time I tried to cash in on it you'd hate me worse than you hated yourself. And, brother, that's hate."

"I'm not your brother."

"I wasn't trying to bridge the racial gap."

"I don't use it in that sense either. It ought to be retired from the language, buried in effigy like the *N* word. I guess we're through here."

"Don't get your Kevlar in a twist. I wasn't turning down the job, just the shot at a conspiracy rap and altering my good opinion of myself. I'll take a crack at what you should've tried at the beginning."

"What's that? I lost track."

"If talking ever hurt anyone, I'd be in traction. I'll start with the adults and work my way up to the child."

"Gerald won't let you past the front door. His opinion is it's a problem he can handle himself. He thinks just because I bungled the job with him, the other way will work better. He's got a lot to learn, but he sure as hell won't learn it from me even if I had anything worthwhile to contribute."

"Then I'll go over his head."

What he put on his face would be a smile on any other. When he tugged the corners of his mouth that direction it was usually to let out bad air. "Waste of time and money; but it's my money." He went back into the first pocket and gaffed a checkbook bound in brown pebbled leather. "Is it still fifteen hundred?"

"That covers three days, more than enough for most jobs. But I'd rather work on that credit problem you mentioned."

"*I'd* rather you took the money."

"No deal, John. Expenses only."

He hesitated with the book open and gold pen in hand; it looked like a toothpick between that thumb and forefinger. Then he put them away.

I said, "Just for the record, we've been talking about the weather all this morning. People in Michigan get plenty of mileage out of that this time of year."

"You didn't have to say it. I've learned from bitter experience you wouldn't open your mouth to yell help if you were on fire. Not if a client asked you not to."

"Bitterer for me than you."

"The same goes for what I said about Lou Pearman. He lost someone close that day, his mother or someone. One of those occasions they invented liquor for."

"I read somewhere it was an accidental invention."

"So was nitro." He looked at his watch, a simple gold circle on a plain band. He'd gotten as far up in the department as he had through merit, but good taste in his personal furnishings hadn't held him back. "I could stand such an accident. Got another glass?"

I wiped the dust off a third glass with a fresh tissue from the dispenser on the desk and leveled off his and mine. That made two personal bests in one morning.

He took a healthy gulp and made his face less handsome. "Just where do you find this stuff?"

"Different places, just like the Ten Most Wanted. It stands to reason it doesn't want to be found. Another hit?"

"Better not. The chief we got after we bounced the last one wouldn't approve." As he said it he pushed his glass my way. I took a hit off mine and bought another round. "How far were you prepared to go with that little passion play?"

"Not much farther. I'm a little worried I put it out there to begin with."

"Luís isn't really in custody, is he?"

"Doesn't matter. We know where to find him. They've got a little Casbah going there in Mexicantown. One block east or west, he's just another immigrant with a green card just a little off the right shade. We snared him with the rest of the fish in a rooster roust a couple of months ago. Shook him back out. Who really cares if a chicken goes down with his spurs on or in a pot pie?"

"The chicken, probably."

"We got heat from PETA. Who said people who care so much about animals don't have anything left for their fellow human beings?"

"Hemingway. He was talking about bullfights."

He looked around. "This isn't such a bad setup. At least the walls go all the way to the ceiling. Anything in it?"

"Just what you see. Looking for a change of scenery?"

"Not just yet. Maybe after the next election. Did you know no successful reform ticket has ever succeeded itself? Voters get a dose of integrity and it doesn't go down as well as they thought. Then the rats get back in and lock it up for eight years minimum. I almost lost my billet last time. If you're still around, the new crowd thinks you had to have played with the same dirty ball. That, or you're too competent and might show them up. You get so you can't take a drink on the house in case it'll find its way into your jacket. One little slip, that's all it takes."

"You can put a buck on the desk if it makes you feel any better."

He picked up his glass and swirled the contents. "That's one hell of a markup."

"So sorry. Next time I'll break out the Johnny Walker Blue. I'm due for a bonus. Ten trips to Detroit Receiving and the next one's free."

"You want to compare scars?"

"Extra points if they're in front?"

"Hell, no. A cop that never ran away from a fight is a cop I don't want in my division. They're always standing next to the guy who gets to be guest of honor at the next department funeral." He emptied his glass, thunked it down like a tankard somewhere in France, and launched himself to his feet. "I'll send over a khaki with all the contact information you'll need. I'm guessing you don't have a fax machine."

"They tell me they come in handy when you're expecting a communication from 1993."

"I don't see how you do it. My *grand*son has a laptop, and he still wears rubber drawers."

"I like to be the smartest thing in a room I pay rent on."

"You're still aiming for the moon."

I let him keep that one. It wasn't so bad at that.

"Don't call me with what you *don't* know," he said. "Understand?"

"Plan I'm on, I don't have that many

minutes."

After he went out I poured what was left in my glass back into the bottle. Any case that involved Mexicantown needed a clear head and good reflexes.

THREE

The house was a ranch style with fresh pale-yellow siding and probably a filled-in bomb shelter in the backyard. It had a two-car garage — if you knew how to get two twenty-five-pound turkeys into a toaster oven. Someone had planted a dense juniper hedge along one side to cut down on the glare of headlights coming around the corner and there was what promised to be a really spectacular floral display on either side of the concrete walk. I assigned the credit to the mistress of the house. Some women can grow flowers on sheet metal.

"Yes?" She was a plump, pretty brunette with hair to her shoulders and probably halfway down her back, in a yellow sundress and sandals on her bare feet. She wore no makeup except for vivid red lipstick that brought out the olive tone of her skin. Her eyes were a warm shade of hickory, rimmed with black lashes.

I gave her one of my cards and asked her if she was Chata Pasada.

"Conchata, actually. Chata is a family nickname. As a girl I couldn't pronounce the whole thing. Are you the man John told me about?" Her light accent softened the *J.*

I hadn't heard anyone refer to Alderdyce by his first name in years. I did it myself just to get his goat. "Yes. Are you alone?"

When she hesitated I got out my leatherette folder and showed her the state license with my picture and the star that said I was an honorary deputy with the Wayne County Sheriff's Department. "The badge is a toy," I said. "Cost me three hundred tickets at Chuck E. Cheese's."

"Come in. Yes, it's just me here. Jerry's at work and Ernesto is in school. Shop class right now, so I know he's there." Her smile was meant to be ironic, but eyes that color have difficulty hiding pain.

I stepped into a living room done in bright colors with a spray of cut flowers in a terracotta vase on the coffee table. It was too early in the season for them to belong to the display out front but they'd been arranged by someone who knew something about the art. A copper-sepia Christ in His crown of thorns looked pensive in a print about the size of a postcard in a white mat the size of a TV tray hung above a gas hearth. It was the first thing of its kind I'd seen in a private home that didn't make me want to turn away in embarrassment.

She offered me coffee and I said yes. With the social contract out of the way we sat down in facing chairs with our cups. "You speak very good English," I said.

"Thank you. So do you." She smiled again, this time without pain. "I was born in Arizona. I have a bachelor's degree from the state university in Tempe."

"Blew it right off the bat, didn't I?"

"Don't be embarrassed. Almost everyone makes the mistake. How do you know my father-in-law? He didn't say much about you, only that you might be able to help us."

"I can't remember a time when I didn't know him. Our fathers were business partners. We were in the same training class at the police department."

"He didn't say you'd been a police officer."

"I wasn't one long enough to put it on my resume. I quit and joined the army. When I got out he was already a sergeant with the detective division."

"I can't imagine him as a young man. What was he like?"

"Less wrinkled."

She laughed, a low chuckle with bells in it. Over her coffee she said, "Jerry never talks about his father. I thought he was an orphan until our wedding. That's where I met his brother and asked him why he had a different last name. Jerry walked away while I was getting the answer."

"John's a good cop. I don't know what kind of father he was. We don't hang out."

"Such a lonely man."

I didn't know which one of us she was talking about, so I said, "Tell me about Ernesto."

"I raised him after our parents died. I thought I was doing a good job, but last year he became sullen. Jerry said I shouldn't worry, it was all part of being a teenager; the important thing was to let him work it out for himself. He was so serious about it that I have to think it had something to do with the rift between him and John."

"John said something like that."

"Well, that wasn't the answer either, apparently. Ernesto's grades fell off and I found out he wasn't going to school some days. If it weren't for shop I think he'd drop out entirely. He's a wonderful carpenter."

"Is that when he started hanging around Mexicantown?"

"Yes. He's saving up to buy a used car out of what he earns fixing houses and doing other projects for people, but for now he hitches rides with friends into town on weekends. I didn't think there was anything wrong in that at first; most of his fellow students are Anglos, and a boy becomes curious about his heritage. His new friends were teaching him Spanish. I'm ashamed to admit I don't speak it so well myself anymore. Maybe if I'd concentrated less on being American I wouldn't be so naïve. I assumed a Mexican would be safe in a Hispanic neighborhood. I knew nothing about gangs until Ernesto came home with that horrible tattoo." She shuddered and drank coffee. It didn't seem to warm her up.

"How much do you know about the Maldados?"

"I never heard of them until he admitted — boasted — that he was a member. Now I'm an authority. According to the Internet they're connected with the animals responsible for most of the bloodshed on both sides of the Mexican border over the past several years. They smuggle Colombian cocaine, Mexican heroin, and illegal aliens into the U.S. and have murdered more Mexican and American police officers, including at least four Border Patrol agents, than any of their competitors. They chose the tarantula for their emblem because it's believed to have been the personal totem of Montezuma. He's supposed to have had it carved into the foreheads of rebellious Aztecs and captured Conquistadors. Most historians have been unable to find evidence to confirm it, but spreading myths is the least of their crimes.

"A lot of other stuff on various sites," she went on, "including hideous photographs of corpses. But I couldn't find anything about them in Detroit."

I'd seen some of those pictures: men missing heads and limbs and assorted other appendages, others dragged to jelly behind Jeeps and Hummers.

I said, "They're fairly new here. Most Mexicantown residents came from the same area a couple of hundred miles below the border. Little Detroit, it's called. The Big Three built some auto factories down there back in the eighties. Then some of the assembly workers got the Yankee bug and transferred here. The Maldados came with the third wave, like tarantulas stowing away in crates of bananas. Maybe that's where they got the idea for their emblem and made up the rest. Even instant tradition's important when you don't have anything else going for you but *pistolas.* The Zapatistas were already here. That bunch took the name from Mexican rebels. If we don't nail them for anything more serious, the originals can sue them for infringement of copyright."

"You know so much about them. That must be why John recommended you."

"All I know is what I hear. As to why the referral, my name has a way of popping up like spam whenever a job looks dirty."

"Ernesto won't be home for several hours — if he really went to school. I'm assuming you'll want to talk to him."

"Before I play Dutch uncle, I think I'll drop by Mexicantown and see what I can see. It might not be quite as bad as you think. So far as I can tell, neither the Maldados nor the Zapatistas are officially affiliated with the originals. A youth gang is hard to start from scratch without a ballsy name to make them seem tougher than they are. If my language is too frank, I apologize."

She smiled for the first time. No one wears one better than a pretty *señora* in her twenties. "John may have told you how far my family goes back in Spanish history. My father insisted that only English be spoken in our house, but that didn't stop him from slipping when he got upset. Anglos are rank amateurs when it comes to turning the air blue. In profanity at least, I'm bilingual." The smile slid away. "I hope you can find out more there than I did reading the Mexicantown International Welcome Center Web site. I learned more than I needed to know about customs and traditional dress and nothing about criminal behavior among my people."

"The Community Development Corporation set up the center to attract Chicanos, not scare the pants off them. I've got a contact on West Vernor, Emiliano Zorborón. *El Tigre del Norte,* they call him. I'm guessing it was just *El Tigre* when he was running guns to the Zapatistas rebels. If anyone can give me a rundown on the Maldados, it's him."

"He sounds worse than the people you're investigating."

"These days he's a semireformed character. When I met him he had a thumb in every dirty pie in the community, but now he's more of a general contractor. If you want to organize a local cockfight or arrange a job for your cousin who won't pass muster with Immigration, he's your *hombre.* The colors on a green card you get through him are guaranteed not to run."

She shook her head. " 'A hardworking

people,' that's what they call us."

"Burros work hard, too, but they don't put much thought into it. You're all smarter than that, or at least no dumber than the rest of us. Zorborón would've been rat food years ago if he didn't have the best head on his shoulders of anyone in the underworld."

"My God, if you do talk to Ernesto, I hope you'll keep that to yourself. The last thing he needs from that crowd is a role model."

"If he's been spending as much time there as you say, he already knows it." I drank coffee. It had gone tepid. She got up, smoothing her skirt, and reached for my cup — she claimed to be an assimilated American, but chromosomes don't always go along — but I shook my head and motioned for her to sit back down, setting it aside. "This will go easier if you tell your husband I'm in the picture."

"I'd rather not. He says it's a family matter, and he doesn't consider his father family. A complete stranger would really set him off. Just from my brief meeting with John, I know where he got his mulish streak, but I'd never tell him that. As you said, we're not all as dumb as burros."

"If that's what you think I said, I can see why Nesto is so hard to talk to."

"Please call him Ernesto. None of the

Pasadas who bore that name would thank you for vulgarizing it."

"I'll try to remember that when you're listening. If he prefers it the other way, that's the foot I have to start out on when we talk."

"And you won't say anything to Jerry?"

"The client's always right — until he's wrong. Do you have a picture of your brother I can show around?"

She popped up again with that same motion involving her skirt and took a stand-up photo frame from a forest of them on the mantel under Jesus. "Jerry won't notice it's missing. He married into a very large family." She opened the back and handed me a color shot of a willowy youth with longish black hair all unbrushed the way they're wearing it now and the usual high opinion of himself in the expression. I stood and slid it into my inside breast pocket. "When can I call to report without going through your husband?"

"Not before eight, and not after six weekdays." The smile ambushed her face. " 'If a man answers, hang up'; isn't that how it goes?"

"So they tell me. I never go woman-hunting without a license. I'll keep you posted."

She went back to solemn. "Money's tight

right now. How much is this going to cost?"

"More than you can handle. John Alderdyce's pride."

When change comes to our city — I'm not talking about the slow rot that is always taking place — it comes fast. Thirty years ago, the old Hungarian neighborhood in the southwest section was called DelRay, but I doubt there are a dozen people living there who ever heard the name. All the Lazlos and Horoznys had vanished from the signs on the shops, replaced by Gonzaleses and Mendozas; where you put the *Z*'s makes all the difference. It takes a trained detective to find a dish cooked with paprika, but cilantro and rice are available by the long ton.

It's not necessarily a bad thing, unless like me you're part gypsy and prefer strudel to fried ice cream. The Hungarians had been gone a long time before the Mexicans came, and in between, the area crossed by West Vernor Avenue (named after the ginger ale plant that used to stand there) had fallen into compost, with new strata of soot arriving daily by way of the old Great Lakes Steel and Allied Chemical plants on nearby Zug Island, and green sky reflected from the toxic waste flowing downriver from there. The plants are shuttered now, and a generation of anti-litter and clean air and water campaigns has scooped up what they left behind. The Mexicans sold or donated the vehicles abandoned at the curbs for scrap, replaced broken windows, lobbied to tear down the crack houses built with the good intentions of a dim former governor, painted the buildings in bright colors, and put their strong backs and manual skills on the market so that their children wouldn't have to. A Hunky wouldn't recognize the place now.

Still, it's not all margaritas and *caballeros* strumming guitars under balconies. A cosmopolitan population imports its own variety of violent crime, and you learned to stay out of certain blocks after dark.

I hadn't visited the place since Jackie Brill's head had rolled out of a Hefty Steel-Sak in an alley behind a restaurant a couple of years ago. He was a grifter from an old founding family who'd nosed into the cockfighting racket, which smart Anglos steer clear of, and gone around with Emiliano Zorborón's daughter Carmelita, just to add another spicy pepper to the mix. *Tigre* Zorborón had been arrested for his murder — Downtown had been eager to tag him for something for years — but it had turned out to be the work of an old *compadre* for motives of his own. Because I had had something to do with bringing that to light, I was welcome there any hour day or night, and I could leave the revolver at home.

Then again, the Maldados and Zapatistas had been too busy establishing themselves then to paint the place with their own colors. On the chance my visa had expired, I stopped by the office to trade out the stale cartridges in the Chief's Special for fresh ones and clipped it to my belt under my coat.

It was earmuff weather despite the thaw, with piles of gravel raked up by privately owned snowplows and the crusty brown remains of extinct snowmen turning even the best-kept lawns into slop buckets. Leprous gray ice clung in patches of shade and someone had done his best to crumple the brown-and-orange branches of a Christmas tree into a trash bin, but the sanitation crew wasn't having any of that, because the truck had passed it by to idle in front of a neighbor's house two doors down. The season for it had expired the first week of January. Then I crossed the border into Mexicantown, where the sky was still the color of filthy linen but the sidewalks were swept and last year's annuals uprooted from the flower boxes and replaced with fresh loam.

Emiliano Zorborón operated a garage where on occasion pairs of well-trained fowl challenged one another in a circle drawn with chalk. There were generally bags of feathers and the odd torn carcass in the Dumpster beside the building, and inside you couldn't tell whether the reddish stains on the floor were blood or transmission fluid. A mechanic there built like Pancho Villa with a round Basque face stood kneading a greasy rag in his black-nailed hands and didn't know a word of English until I showed him my card. He recognized the name and said, "You know Suiz's?"

"The restaurant?" Nolo Suiz, Zorborón's cousin, ran the best Mexican kitchen in town. A dismembered body could show up anywhere, and the place's reputation was too good to let a little thing like that put a hitch in business.

"*Sí. La Riata.* Go in the back, ask for Ronaldo."

"Who's he?"

"He is nobody. But you don't ask for him, maybe you do not come out in so good shape as you go in. It is not for Anglos to go in the back."

"Why don't I just go in the front?"

"In the front they do not know Ronaldo."

I shook out a cigarette and tapped it on the pack. "Is there a secret handshake?"

"No. Just Ronaldo." There was no irony in the round face. Getting a Mexican to appreciate your humor is like persuading a Parisian to understand your French.

FOUR

La Riata is where we get lariat, so the low-key neon in the restaurant's front window made a blue-green lasso, with no name spelled out. The subliminal message was if you didn't know at least a little Spanish, your business wasn't wanted. Mexicans rarely insult you to your face outside their own country.

The lunch crush was under way. Groups and couples loitered on the sidewalk, listening for their names on the PA. It was one of the liveliest sections in the city at that hour. After dark the throngs reassembled for baklava and blackjack in Greektown, in the shadow of police headquarters. People also think that a bunch of eighteen-wheelers in the parking lot means a good place to eat. But sometimes you can get decent ham and eggs in a roadside joint, and crowds provided their own protection. The food and service in *La Riata* lived up to the hype. A good band was playing, interrupted from time to time by a seating announcement; something about true love and murder, with a merry marimba beat.

I went around back into an alley that was as tidy as the main drag now that there were no coroner's cases in the Dumpster and pushed the buzzer beside a plain brown steel door without a knob or a handle on the outside. In a little while it opened, letting out a haze of caramelized onion and fried peppers that would bring tears to the eye on the back of the dollar bill. A tall burly *mestizo* in a white wife-beater undershirt and his hair in a net stared at me through the eight-inch gap with a cleaver in his hand. The undershirt was stained with what looked like blood but was probably salsa. His face was brick-colored, with little triangles of moustache clinging to the corners of his mouth and a straggle of three-day beard hanging three inches below his chin. He was more than half American Indian, but he wouldn't have looked out of place in sheepskins riding behind Genghis Khan.

"Ronaldo," I said.

"No sé."

I'd never met a secret code that survived its first encounter with the enemy.

The door started to close. I leaned my shoulder against it, and when the cleaver moved back an inch for the downswing I stuck the card I had ready through the gap. While that was distracting him I took my shoulder out of his business. A thumb and forefinger equally thick and stubby closed on the card and the door snapped shut.

I finished the cigarette I'd started in the garage, and then the *mestizo* swung the door wide.

I squeezed in past him and he followed me down a narrow hallway that went past a stainless-steel eight-burner range and all the rest of the usual kitchen stuff, where two more brick-colored men were stirring hissing skillets while a third slid something steaming out of a chest-high oven on a wooden paddle. Everything shimmered behind a stinging mist of peppers and onions. At the end of the passage I stopped to wipe my eyes and blow my nose into my handkerchief.

"*Señor* Walker." A light baritone voice, accustomed to the lower registers where you had to lean in to hear the words. *"Hace tiempo que no te veo."*

"Sí. Tengo un lapiz rojo." I shook the hand offered me by the compact man in the black T-shirt.

Puzzlement stirred his polished features. " 'I have a red pencil'; this is an expression, yes?"

"It is an expression, no. It's the extent of my conversational Spanish."

In casual dress, he looked more like the owner of a successful auto-repair shop than a member in good standing of the Mexican Mafia. He was small for a tiger, fine-boned, but built like a bantamweight, with little flesh between muscle and bone. He didn't smile; *bandidos* are serious men and leer only in movies. There were steel splinters at his temples now, but apart from them he could pass for thirty. Since he had a grown daughter I put him closer to fifty. I asked about the daughter.

"Carmelita is an old married lady now: *Dos niños.*" He held up two slim brown fingers with a thunderbird tattooed between. It was a tribal symbol, not associated with a gang. "They live in Royal Oak."

I liked the way he rolled the *R* when it fell at the beginning of a proper noun. I supposed it was a grammatical rule of some kind. His family was nowhere near as old as the Pasadas — a hundred years ago it had traded its picks and shovels for bandoleers and robbed Spanish aristocrats first of their gold, then of their governorship — but he was as careful in both languages as he was in his habits, at least in the presence of outsiders. I'd heard stories of amputations and ritual scorings when someone from his own culture had displeased him, but that was all in the past. So the theory went.

I said, "You won't mind if I don't call you Grampa. Who's Ronaldo?"

"My pet goat, when I was ten. My father butchered him and I ate three ribs before I found out. I am bound to say I finished. Who was to say when we would eat again?"

"The golem at the door never heard of him."

"Miguelito is overprotective. You have not had lunch, I hope."

"Never when I'm going to be in Mexicantown."

"Come dine with me. I have no business to discuss at present and since my daughter deserted me, I eat alone, and that is merely feeding."

I followed him into a private room separated from the rest of the establishment by heavy brocade curtains. Here were none of the Mexican movie posters or paintings of bullfighters that attracted the general population outside, just paneled walls and bright ceramic tiles and a certificate in a silver frame attesting to the fact that Emiliano

Francisco Sorno was a naturalized citizen of the United States. Zorborón was an Anglo corruption of his surname, which translated as "cunning"; *El Tigre* himself seemed to prefer the one that had been hung on him by accident. A long time ago he'd fought under it professionally, until he'd found out the money end never entered the ring. He was a quick study, and his sense of timing was dead on. Police informants said he'd gotten out of gambling just before casinos were legalized and thrown over the dope racket when it fell under the jurisdiction of Homeland Security.

For whatever underworld information was worth; that pipeline went both ways.

"You know Nolo."

Manuel Suiz — Manolo, Nolo; which name you used depended on where you stood in the community — paused in the midst of laying out the flatware to turn his head my way and decline it a tenth of an inch. He bore no resemblance to the Tiger, and I'd never learned if they called each other cousin for reasons of family or friendship. He was pear shaped, soft through the middle, but the fat didn't reach his face. He was completely bald. His eyes were large and liquid, with long silken lashes. It was a feminine sort of face except for the black beard beneath the skin. That made him more potentially dangerous than his macho countrymen, because it combined the more dreaded qualities of both sexes.

That was too much to get out of appearances. Suiz ran one of the few four-star restaurants in town. For all I knew, pullets were the only ones who had any reason to fear him. So far, the stickup artists and shakedown crews left him alone because of his connection to Zorborón, but these new gangs weren't long on respecting inherited traditions. That was an angle to take if I needed one.

Zorborón did the ordering. I was pretty sure he was ordering off the menu, not because he didn't have one — he'd have memorized it by then — but because that's what you did when you knew the owner and you had a guest. My Spanish was a little better than I made out, just in case I felt like overhearing something he'd sooner I missed, but it was going at 78 rpm and I'm strictly 33 1/3. I got *pollo* and *rellenos* and nothing else until he got to *cervezas*; when it comes to beer and strong spirits I'm a polyglot. "I think you will like this beer," he said, when Suiz left. "I import it from a very old friend whose family started the brewery during your — our — Prohibition. You can get it nowhere else in this country."

"Sounds fine. I always heard bootleggers were good company."

"Not this one. He is vain without reason and sensitive about his many faults. But none of us really chooses his friends. A tumbleweed has no say which fence he will come to rest against."

"It's even worse with relatives. They're why *tu me ves ahora.*"

He arched his brows, splendid black ones plucked as neat as inverted commas. I'd tipped my hand as to Spanish, but if I didn't get his attention we'd kill the afternoon making pleasantries and building metaphors. A Grand Jury had given up on him when he met every question with a homely platitude. *"Tu familia?"*

"Not mine. Someone else's. *Sabe los Pasadas?*"

Which was a mistake. The brows came down and collided and he whittled off a long curl of vowels and consonants that zinged past my ear without grazing it.

"English," I interrupted. *"Por favor."* I demolished the accent.

"Forgive me. Spanglish is the local dialect. I despise it and become carried away when someone even attempts Castilian. Yes, I know of the Pasadas. In the pueblo where I was born, whenever one approached, you took off your hat and stepped aside from the pavement. If you stepped into horseshit, that was your misfortune."

"That was in the old country. The Pasada I met today is all about democracy. There's a brother involved. He wears the tarantula." I touched the back of my hand with a finger.

He lifted a quarter-inch of lip. "I know of these as well. *Hijos de putas.*"

"They may be sons of whores, but let's not blame the *putas* just yet. He's sixteen, the ideal age for carrion. The family thinks there's hope for him."

"Please continue."

"They may have carried the melting-pot idea a little too far. Place he lives, the only Mexicans he sees are cutting grass and delivering takeout. So he skips school and comes here to explore his heritage."

"I came here to escape mine."

"That's the story, except for one detail. His brother-in-law's the son of a cop."

"How big of a cop?"

"An inspector."

"Detroit?" When I nodded, he nodded. "This clears up a mystery for me. I'd wondered about the police presence here one day recently. It seemed unnecessary. The gangs have been quiet lately."

"Not so quiet. I saw a crime-scene photo taken on the field of battle."

"That was many months ago. The so-called Zapatistas came out on the short end. I did not disapprove of this outcome. Every time they parade around under that name they defile the movement."

I digressed. Delicate negotiations are zigzag affairs when cultural differences exist. "I saw a picture twenty years ago, a man with a bandanna on his face hoisting a rifle above his head. Someone told me it was you."

"It might have been. I never saw it."

"It was taken in Chihuahua, near the caves where the Villistas hid out from Pershing in 1916. Ring a bell?"

"One tires of hearing about Villa. A bandit with a cause is still a bandit. We named ourselves for Emiliano Zapata — my own namesake, I add proudly — an illiterate peasant born to *la causa.* Do you know what that was?"

"I'm pretty sure it had something to do with liberty."

"An abstract concept, impossible to grasp the meaning of when you have never seen it in practice. He fought for land. Not conquest, not vast tracts to govern, but patches for growing beans and grazing milch cows, with proper deeds in the names of citizens of the Republic of Mexico — farm plots of eighty to one hundred acres, out of a land mass the size of Western Europe. For this he was called a Marxist. In one hundred years, nothing has changed. The land still belongs to the wealthy, and those of us who oppose the status quo are called terrorists. It is enough we have that to deal with without a band of psychotic children shedding the blood of their own and calling themselves Zapatistas."

I had a thought. "Are you by any chance bankrolling the Maldados?"

Our food came, borne on a tray by a light-skinned youth in a green apron, who uncovered the dishes and set them before us, cautioning us not to touch the plates. Strips of rare steak sizzled and steamed furiously on beds of rice, tomatoes, and peppers, and a platter of tortillas kneaded and baked on the premises gave off their warmth through towels covering them. The boy filled our glasses with a long showy stream of water from a pitcher and set out frosted mugs and squat green bottles with an armadillo on the label. He asked if there was anything else. I shook my head at Zorborón, who dismissed him with a wave.

"No. I do not subsidize activity that

encourages police invasion. In older days I would purge the neighborhood of these gangs, but I am as they say a reformed character. A grandfather has too much at stake to risk bringing further scorn upon his name. If Carmelita were a man and did not take a new name upon marrying, I would counsel him to use Sorno. I myself cannot after all this time. It would be like Nolo deciding to start wearing a toupee on top of years of baldness. Questions would be raised."

We ate for a while in silence. Mexican food prepared by Mexicans the way they prepare it in Mexico is a rare thing, even in many places in Mexico. Each village has its own cuisine, and the big cities serve up theirs the way the tourists are accustomed to. What we were eating might have been locked in an airtight clay pot in some mud pueblo unknown to maps, shipped to the nearest airport on the back of a mule, and flown directly to *La Riata* without going through Customs, still steaming when it arrived. I didn't worry about what kind of parasites it may have contained; the *cerveza* from the stubby green bottles would have stopped an epidemic in full cry. It was as bitter as burnt cordite and there were hops floating on top. At least I hoped they were hops. The alcohol went up my sinuses like ammonia and filled my head with helium.

"Try the *rellenos,*" said my host. "I turned down a princely offer to distribute them in cans."

"What did NASA offer you for the beer? Twelve ounces would put us on Mars."

Serious men ignore rhetoricals. "I have no influence with this spawn, if that is what you have come to ask for. They do not fear the police, and they certainly do not fear an old cock-fighter."

I wiped my hands with a napkin and brought out Ernesto Pasada's picture. I'd stopped at a Staples on the way and had copies made. "Ask your people to show this around, tell them the boy's a runaway. *Sabe* Amber Alert? If he can't stay here, he'll go home. In theory."

"Perhaps you should stop trying to speak Spanish. Your atrocious usage is distracting."

I waved a hand and picked up my fork, grateful for the release. I couldn't concentrate on conjugations and still enjoy the fajitas.

"*Es verdad,* this Amber Alert?"

"No, that decision comes from high up. His family expects him home today when school lets out. In theory. But I doubt even the Maldados would want to mess with a dragnet that big. That is, if they buy it."

He shook his head. "They will waylay the boy and offer to turn him in for a reward."

"Kidnap and ransom, they'd do that?"

"They are animals. I need hardly spell out in what condition the boy will be returned once their demands are met. If they are not, he will simply have vanished. *Desaparece.*" He pursed his lips and blew a puff of air, gracefully dispersing it with the hand holding the picture.

"Anyone can point out a problem. I'm looking for the solution."

"Is your job, no?" He was fluent in pidgin. "I will show this around. Anyone who spots the boy and reports it to me will find himself in good graces with *El Tigre del Norte.* Some of the older residents will consider that coin of the realm."

"You're not a *Tío Taco* yet."

"You do not know us as well as you think. I sacrificed more than money when I went legit. Legit, this is a word?"

"It is if you're legit. I'll see you semi and raise you notorious."

"I have heard this term applied to me and I am puzzled by it. Our nearest equivalent means 'obvious,' and yet I pride myself on my subtlety."

"It started out as another word for 'famous,' but it kept getting trampled over and turned into something else, like 'alibi' and 'discrimination.' "

"Such a difficult tongue."

"Isn't it? I think the government's in charge." I drank some beer. I was starting to get used to it. "Have things changed that much in the neighborhood?"

He sat back and stripped the cellophane off a black cigar with a portrait of a geezer in white side whiskers and a rusty black coat on the band; the founder of the tobacco company, or maybe just an early president of the Republic. He bit off the end and deposited it in an ashtray shaped like a pagan god who looked like Mickey Rourke. Even the presence of an ashtray violated state law. "Everything here is zoom-zoom. In the village where I was born, the water wheel is considered a great technological advance. You will hear from me regardless. Your address and telephone number, they have not changed?"

"Nope. I'm saving up for a water wheel."

He chuckled in the midst of lighting up. I didn't think the joke was that good. Another time I might not have gotten a reaction at all. He was still as easy to read as the temple of Quetzalcoatl.

FIVE

"What can you tell me about the Maldados?"

Zorborón frowned and blew on his cigar tip, making it glow bright red. "The bull is merely out to pasture. He has not been made a steer."

"I thought you were a tiger."

He ignored that. I didn't blame him; it was a pointless direction to go in. The Latin way of conducting business seemed roundabout, but it always circled back to the main thrust. I did the same.

"Snitches are a glut on the market," I said. "I'm not looking to make a citizen's arrest. I just want to know what I'm up against."

He shrugged, a gesture with as many meanings as his language has dialects. "You know *El Hermano?*"

I shrugged; in my case a gesture with only one meaning.

"Luís Guerrera," he said. "They call him

the Brother now that he has none."

"I know Jesus got smoked by the cops and that Luís is now the brains of the outfit, such as they are. Domingo Siete gives the orders, but that's only because the rest of the gang is afraid of him. His parents must have been smoking Acapulco Gold when they named him Seventh Sunday. Guerrera's the boy you go to when you want to do any sort of business here."

"It used to be me; but one does not stand in the path of a train that has gone out of control. Domingo's a burning fuse. If Luís wasn't handy with a bucket of water when it's needed, the streets would be a river of blood. It was the same with Jesus; younger brothers are frequently of cooler temperament. I was one myself. I think *El Hermano* was down with the chicken pox when that fight took place with the Zaps." He had difficulty calling them Zapatistas. "Luís can be reasoned with, if you show him the respect he thinks is proper. It is all respect with these *muchachos*; they profane its purpose with their insistence. A little humility benefits us all."

"*Hermano*'s new," I said. "Keeping up with nicknames is a full-time job. I knew the rest. What about the others?"

"Punks. Pushers. *Cojones* big as artichokes, which diverts circulation from the brain. What is true about all the other gangs in this city is true of them."

"With a salsa beat. Anything else?"

He thought. "You know a new tattoo when you see one?"

"All scabs. One look and the customer would bolt."

He showed me his thunderbird. "A despicably filthy parlor in Saltillo, behind a whorehouse. I thought when the scab fell off there would be nothing but brown skin beneath. I had been cheated out of twenty-five pesos, so I thought. But it is merely part of the process. It is a scarring after all, underscored with ink. When you see that particular ugliness on the back of a young hand, beware."

I waited. Impatience never got you far with a tiger.

"It means they are new: not yet men, and not quite beasts, but eager to prove themselves as both. *Hombre y lobo.* You know this?"

"Man and wolf. Wolfman. Werewolf."

"*Sí.* Beware the werewolf. Tread lightly when you see that mark, red and raw. It is the mark of the beast."

I grinned. He shrugged again.

"I am melodramatic to make my point.

Entiende?"

"I understand, thanks."

He laid the cigar in the copper tray to smoke itself out and drank from a cup of coffee brewed the way you seldom found it north of the border. Anyone can make it strong enough to float a Beretta. The trick is to keep it from being bitter. "Where to next, amigo?"

I blew on mine and parboiled my tongue anyway. "I thought I'd drop in on Sister Delia. She still around?"

"She must be. Someone tried to set fire to the garage last week."

"It wasn't her. Arson isn't her style."

"Rabble-rousing is; and destruction always was the way of rabble."

"I thought you two might have kissed and made up after you got religion."

"I never did not have it. Because a man misses Mass a few thousand times does not make him an infidel."

"I meant went straight. Semi-straight, anyway."

"With her it is all or nothing. The world in which she lives is *blanco y negro.* I fear we shall never see things eye to eye."

"She's not wrong. It's the people who say the world isn't black and white who got us in this mess."

"If such is your view I very much doubt you and I will see things *ojo a ojo* either."

"I can live with that. *Usted?*"

"También." When he gestured with his hand, the thunderbird flapped its wings.

I thanked him for the meal and left. In the public area, the conversation was building to an ecstatic high. You can measure the popularity of a dining establishment by the decibel level at high tide. Nolo Suiz stood at attention by the passage leading to the back door, his liquid brown eyes prowling the room for diners who'd lost their waiters and employees who wiped their noses in view of the clientele. I was invisible. I hadn't added a *centavo* to the till. He was just a hash-slinger after all, not a tiger or a werewolf.

In the old days, when DelRay was still Del-Ray, you could cross the Mexican part of the city in a few minutes on foot — faster if you ran, which was the recommended gait for Anglos in the Murder City years — but that was before Little Detroit and the exchange program that followed. Now, to get from the business heart of the community to the place where it worshipped, I had to burn dinosaur bones the way the locals did when they attended Mass. I fired up the Cutlass and fumed behind a UPS truck until it turned off, then found a thirty-minute spot around the corner from my destination. The population fell below one million a long time ago, but there seemed to be five cars to the person.

Holy Redeemer is best known outside the Hispanic community for its Pewabic pottery tiles crafted by Mary Chase Perry Stratton, one of a pair of local institutions, whose workshop is still operating after more than a century. I doubt the tiles, fashioned from the same clay that fed the rich copper deposits in the Upper Peninsula, get much attention from the regulars. The same old sins get confessed in the booths, but in Spanish, not Hungarian, and the aesthetics can wait.

If your head was full of the pitch you planned to make to the Lord, you might not have noticed the iron-front building across from the church and a little down the street. It was a hardware store once, and before that a tailor's where the Tammany crowd bought its full-dress suits for the mayor's inauguration. Before that it was an auto dealership, with chromework gleaming in rows behind plate glass and Chief Pontiac's head in profile mounted above the door. Back further my history is weak: a stove foundry or Studebaker works — the covered wagon, not the automobile. The squat structure had the out-of-proportion look of a place that had been originally built to support more stories.

It looked empty, like a place waiting its turn at vandalization or arson, but if you looked closer you saw the steel awning rigged to roll down over the entire front and lock with sliding bolts to the base, and here and there the glowing red eye of a surveillance camera. In just about any other town you'd think it was a pawnshop or an electronics store, maybe a cut-rate jewelry outlet, some place containing items that could readily be turned to cash if you knew a fence; and who didn't, in that neighborhood? But if you jumped to that conclusion, and you were a certain type of person and decided to pull on a ski mask and take a crowbar to the fire door in back, inside you would find a pit bull waiting. Her name is Sister Delia.

If you went by reputation alone, you'd expect a caricature of a parochial school nun with dewlaps and a weapons-grade ruler grafted to her fist. What you got was tall and stately, with red hair cut boyishly short and the general look of a woman who would not be out of place wearing a riding habit. She wore an unstructured jacket over a mannish white shirt and a pleated skirt that showed her muscular calves. I rescued my paw from her hickory grip and took a seat opposite her in a reclaimed armchair in a patch of sunlight coming through the plate glass behind. The overcast was breaking up for the first time in weeks.

"The Tiger thinks you tried to burn down his garage," I said by way of opening the conversation.

Her smile was as tight. "Someone keyed my car a few days ago. Now I know who."

"Not his style."

"His kind has no style."

"I wish I knew the story of you two."

"It's no mystery. I've devoted half my life to the people of this community, first with the Church, then on my own dime. He's devoted half of his to tearing down what I've tried to do. Everything he does, everything he stands for, reinforces every stereotype that's been applied to these people."

"Except sloth."

"Our definitions differ. If he had an ounce of industry he wouldn't have taken the lazy way."

She'd left the order after the Vatican had instructed her to lower her profile. She'd been arrested once for trespassing — an organized demonstration to turn spectators away from a cockfight in Zorborón's garage — and used the death of the old pope as an excuse to enter the laity, which was a neat way to obey the order and tell Rome to go shinny up a candle at the same time. Her expenses were paid through charitable donations. In her time she'd twisted more arms than Strangler Lewis.

"He's gone straight, sort of."

"A line that's sort of straight is still crooked. Is he the reason for this visit? I helped you spring him from a bad rap once. That's one more good turn than he rates."

I got out another print of the boy's picture and gave it to her. "Name's Ernesto Pasada. He's been bitten by a tarantula and his family wants him back."

"The last thing this neighborhood needs is a litter of Tigers. I went down to their hangout once to give them the motherly talk. I was lucky not to get raped."

"From what I hear, luck's no defense."

"Neither is faith." She swung open one side of her jacket and let it fall shut. I glimpsed a checked walnut grip curving out of a chamois underarm holster. "Parting gift from the bishop. The papers are in order. I don't know the boy." She held out the photo.

"Keep it and let me know if he shows up. He's not missing — yet. The job's to keep him from winding up that way, or worse."

"What's worse?"

"Earning his tattoo. What's the story on the Maldados? All I could get out of Zorborón was a history lesson."

"He has a selective memory, like the people who know all the wrong Bible passages. As it stands, they're just insurance salesmen. You know: a grease fire in the kitchen, half the staff calls in sick, a dead skunk wanders in through a dryer vent and spoils the customers' laundry. No threats of physical violence yet, but that's the logical next step. So far no one's opted out of their payment plan. I assume they're peddling dope; that's a given."

"Any connection with the home office in Mexico?"

"Not that I know of, but the Maldados down there wouldn't mind opening a branch this far north. They killed a reporter a month or so back. Lopped off his head with a machete and sent it to his widow. Considering the quality of the Mexican postal system, it must have been plenty ripe when she took delivery." Very little of life's uglier side shocked Sister Delia. Nuns don't hear confessions, but the seal of the priesthood didn't prevent anonymous gossip. Some of what they heard would raise blisters on the ears of a veteran cop.

"Not a U.S. reporter, I'm guessing."

"If he was, you'd have seen it on page one of *USA Today.* But it wouldn't have slowed them down. The gangs down there are at war with each other and authority. Anyone with dry ink on his law degree has a shot at being a judge in Mexico. There are plenty of vacancies due to death and very few takers. Roman emperors had a better shot at life insurance."

"If a Detroit Maldado wanted to tie up with the border variety, would that person be named Domingo Siete?"

"That little beast would butcher his mother just to get the cops to vacuum his rug for free. But he's too stupid to be dangerous for long. He thinks he's indestructible, which is as destructible as it gets. He takes too many chances, and I hear he's his own best customer in the narcotics trade. If we're still talking about him this time next year except in the past tense, I'll re-up and wash the feet of the Archbishop of Canterbury."

That wasn't likely to happen, so I moved Seventh Sunday down a notch on my list of Things to Fear Today. Not all the way to the bottom; I didn't want to be his one chance too many. "What about Luís Guerrera? Another indestructible?"

"No, and that's what makes him dangerous. Being the power behind the throne suits him. He got pinched just once for possession of a concealed weapon, did six months for that in the Boys Training School in Whitmore Lake; he was a juvenile offender then. Nothing since. These days he lets another Maldado do his carrying. His goal is to be invisible. If he makes it, *El Tigre del Norte* will be a kitten by comparison."

What she'd said about mysterious grease fires had put an idea in my head. "Any chance that key job on your car and Zorborón's fire are connected?"

"I can't answer for him, but no one's tried to sell me protection. Kind of a wienie way for a bunch of *hombres malos* to do business, wouldn't you think?"

"They're just getting established. Trouble is, kids are fast learners. If they wanted to make a push, taking out the two biggest influences in the community would be a place to start."

"I'll let you know when they graduate to water balloons."

I gave it up as a waste of time. If anyone

knew the dangers, she would. "Maldados still hanging out at the mission?"

Her well-bred face grew furrows. "Please don't call it that. I gave up the oath, not the Church. It's just another crack house in waiting since the brothers abandoned it."

The Jesuits had set up a soup kitchen and salvation parlor in an Edwardian showplace a couple of blocks north of West Vernor. It hadn't been a showplace since McKinley was shot, but it was too pretty to condemn in spite of paint deprivation and a beehive behind the lath-and-plaster walls that was solid enough to pass zoning regulations regarding construction. The brothers had moved out to save souls in Grosse Pointe; sold out, some said, for central air and a roof that didn't leak, but if souls ever needed saving, the carriage trade in the Pointes would have no trouble electing a poster child.

I looked at my watch. It was siesta time — if not for transplanted Mexicans, then certainly for an aging PI with a bum leg due to lead poisoning. "I'll drop in on them bright and early tomorrow. What kind of ordnance are they packing these days?"

"The usual. Sig-Sauers, some war surplus forty-fives — they never wear out, damn Sam Colt — a MAC-10 or two. The box cutters scare me the most. I'd rather take a nice clean round in the chest than show up at Receiving with my lower intestines in a bucket. This kid worth it?" She tapped the photo in her lap.

"You tell me. You're the sister of mercy."

She shook her head. There was a bitter snap to it. "I'm burning out. My worst fear. Some days I'd just as soon take a flamethrower to that mess of turrets and gimcrack and throw myself into a tank of Jack Daniel's."

"My advice? Jack Daniel's first."

She smiled; a real smile, not the inch and a half she measured out when the situation called for it. Then she got up and unlocked the file cabinet where she kept the records for the IRS. I couldn't think of a better place for a bottle.

Back on the street I called Chata and asked if Ernesto had come home from school.

"He didn't go." She sounded tired. "His principal called. It's the third time this month. I'd hoped if you're in Mexicantown you might have seen him."

"It's not that small a place and it's well-populated. I salted it with his picture. If he shows I'll hear about it."

"Did you find out what you needed to know?"

"I found out what everyone here seems to know, which is next to *nada.* The Maldados in Detroit are connected with the Old Country Maldados, or they're not. They're into the dope trade up to their sombreros, or they're running a protection racket, or they're practicing for their knot-tying badge from the Guadalajara Boy Scouts. Tomorrow I'll talk to the source and strain out the rumors."

"That sounds dangerous."

"I'll start early and be out by nightfall." The secret to hunting werewolves is to finish up before the moon rises.

SIX

Bright and early I walked around Rosecranz, the building troll, waxing the linoleum in the foyer and carried a Sausage McMuffin and 1,000 degrees of caffeine upstairs. I had a visitor in the private office, but there wasn't a job in it. I'd set a trap for Wally the mouse and he'd tripped it and broken his neck. He was small enough to flush, so I did that in the little water closet, washed my hands, stuffed his hole with paper, and sealed it with duct tape from the professional detective's kit I keep in the desk. After that the Sausage McMuffin wasn't appetizing. I chucked it in the wastebasket and waited for my coffee to cool.

It was just about fit to drink when the mail slot in the outer office squeaked on its hinges and a small bundle hit the floor. I went out and got it, but my rich uncle hadn't died and there was nothing happening with my ten shares in whale oil futures, so I dragged over the telephone and went to work. John Alderdyce's son had just left for the office.

Ernesto hadn't come home last night. That had happened before, so I told his sister not to waste time on worry and said I'd shoo him along if I came across him.

Next I tried Barry Stackpole, my go-to guy for the latest on organized crime in America, but he wasn't answering and I remembered he'd said something about Alaska in the spring, something to do with a Justice Department scheme to smuggle in members of the Russian Mafia to consult with on matters of Homeland Security; how a solo journalist got the drift of things that the State Department didn't know about was a mystery no one was paying me to solve. I finished my coffee and left, listing a little toward my right hip where the gun rode.

A lumber baron had built the place, they said, using harder wood than the old-growth pine he'd made his killing cutting in the Upper Peninsula and shipping the logs down to the furniture factories in Grand Rapids. The virgin stands are long gone, and the coffee tables and bedroom sets they sell on the western side of the state are made in

China for assembly in the home, but Lars Larson's frame castle still stood that day, needing shingles and paint and glass panes where the plywood blocked out the sun. The surviving original shingles were rounded like chain mail links atop the turrets, and a front porch hung on by its fingernails, just big enough for a resident to sit in a rocker and spit tobacco at the rats in the shaggy yard. The place looked like you could knock it down by blowing a kiss at it, but those old Swedes knew their mortises and tenons. It had survived a dozen Deco sky-scratchers put up during the boom days of Prohibition and just about everything from the 1970s. A street gang and before them the Jesuits with their nonexistent maintenance fund hadn't done it any more damage than stone-chuckers and Michigan weather.

Just for fun I grasped a bronze oval knurled with embossed oak leaves and gave it a twist. The bell actually rang, a raspy falsetto tinkle, like an old lady laughing over a scrapbook. No one answered. I tried again. Halfway through, the old lady choked, something snapped and jangled with a falling-away sound, and after that I couldn't raise a thing. I was probably the first visitor to use the bell in ten years. It had been waiting all this time to let go.

I snapped my cigarette butt at a can lying on its side in the yard and tried the thumb latch. The door wasn't locked. I went on in with my gun still on my hip, which was dumb. But instead of a muzzle waiting on the other side I saw an empty entry hall with a scratched floor made of narrow strips of tongue-and-groove oak and patches of old varnish the color and finish of peanut brittle still visible outside the traffic area. A rug with no pattern left had snuggled itself into the cracks between the boards and there was one of those iron-spined hedgehogs to scrape your boots on with a dumb neglected look on its tiny rusted face.

I smelled dry rot and marijuana, neither of which was new to the building by a long shot. Apart from the scorched weed, the place contained none of the odors associated with a residence of any kind. It might have stood empty since the mission closed, but that couldn't be, because Detroit abhors a vacuum. Sooner or later any sort of shelter attracts a meth lab or a spot to score crack or just to practice the oldest profession, by some of the oldest professionals who can still wriggle their brittle bones into a miniskirt. There's a woman on Michigan Avenue named Ukrainian Audrey who claims her pelvis is on the National Register of Historic Places.

I waited, but the only sign of life was a muffled humming where the third-generation colony of bees continued building its hive between lath-and-plaster walls that provided shelter year-round.

"Hola?" My voice rang back my way from the curving panels at the base of the ceiling, mocking my accent.

A foot scraped the staircase, a lazy *S* framed by a mahogany banister missing several spindles leading to an open second-floor hallway. I looked up at five and a half feet of clear brown skin in white shorts and a pink halter top that fell short of her navel and a longer way short of her collarbone, with piles of shimmering blue-black hair and toenails too pink for her natural coloring, in cork sandals. Her makeup was all wrong, too, her lips a candy-corn shade of orange. She'd used a spray gun to put on a perfume that probably came in a drum. She was all of fourteen years old.

She was chewing gum, and damn if she hadn't matched it to her pink nails; I had a good view of it all the way to where it lost its flavor and she took it out and stuck it on top of the newel post. There she rested a hand on the banister with the other splayed on her hip, a pose straight from the manual.

"Está policía, verdad?" she said. "*O* DEA?"

"No está uno o otro, señorita. Está materia privada. Dónde están los muchachos?"

She giggled, a loopy sound. She didn't need the stairs. She could float from one level to the other all on her own. "Who taught you Spanish?"

"An old friend. Speedy Gonzales was the name."

"I don' know him."

"You'll never get the chance. He broke his neck in a trap at my office sometime between midnight and seven A.M. Boys around?"

Another giggle. It went straight up my spine. She turned her head an inch toward her left shoulder and yelled. *"Domingo! Tíenes un visitante. Un puerco."*

I had a cigarette in the corner of my mouth and both hands on the matchbook. "You shouldn't go around calling strangers pigs. Especially when they told you as politely as they could they're not cops."

"You're lying."

"If I were, you'd be halfway to juvie by now, and everyone in this dump over the age of eighteen in County."

She spat something in border Spanish I just caught by the back handles. That culture is overconcerned with the mating habits of mothers. *"Domingo! Muy pronto!"*

"Why don't I go up and give him a shake? If he doesn't get up soon he'll miss siesta."

She rolled a bare shoulder. Her left halter strap slid down her arm. She left it there, switched her hips down the three steps remaining, and put plenty of Spanish on it on her way out the front door.

I put the cigarette back in the pack and climbed up, unbuttoning my coat and loosening the revolver in its holster. The humming grew louder as I climbed; when I touched the staircase wall to steady myself I could feel the heat generated by all that insect activity.

It didn't take a detective to find out which door was Domingo Siete's. He was snoring loud enough to drown out the bees and loosen the panels. It was unlocked. Resting my hand on the butt nudging my kidney I turned the knob and opened it. I got a faceful of locker-room air overlaid with more marijuana and a Homeric case of morning mouth that had spread to fill the room.

The place was as dim as a tropical jungle. Newspapers had been taped over the windows, and as I groped my way toward the lump on the bed my toe struck something that rolled across the floor and came to rest against another object with a clink. Empty tequila bottles make a handy alarm system, but it was lost on the lump. The snoring stopped abruptly at the end of an intake, but the pause was only a second before the air came back out with a little whistle. After that it got louder.

I circled the end of the bed and tore the sports section off the nearest window. Sunlight poured in.

Domingo lay on his back in cruciform, wearing a green army undershirt and boxer briefs, nothing else. He hadn't much body hair for a Hispanic male. I remembered him as small for his age though sinewy, but his muscles had gone flabby and his face looked bloated and middle-aged. He had thick black hair growing far down on his forehead, mowed close to the scalp, a burr cut, and coarse features blurred by the first beard of youth, cobwebby patches of fine down. His mouth was a black hole in its center, rimmed with meaty red lips. A thread of spittle led from the right corner to a puddle on the mattress. No sheet covered it. It was marbled all over with stains, some of which had probably already been present when it was dragged in from someone's curb. Standing over him I found myself breathing through my mouth. Not eating that Sausage

McMuffin had been my wisest decision of the day so far.

I shook him by the shoulder. All that got me was a rattling snort and more snoring in a different key. You didn't get that depth of sleep from just a bottle and a joint.

I had a brainstorm. I got out the book of matches, struck one, and held the flame to a curl of beard. It went up on that side of his face like wildfire up a dead pine. The room was filled with the stench before he came awake with a lurch, swatted at that side of his face — and came up off the bed all in one piece, roaring and swinging with both fists. But by then I had a grip on the hollow metal frame and flipped it up and over to the side, dumping him to the floor.

That made him surly. He scrambled onto his hands and knees and bit me on the leg. I kicked out of instinct, caught him under the chin with the toe of my shoe, clapping his mouth shut with his tongue caught between his teeth. Blood trickled out both sides of his mouth, but he wasn't through yet. His arms went around my legs in a kneeling bear hug. I jumped out of that noose, a fancy rope trick I didn't know I had in my repertory, came down with my feet spread, and laced my fingers in a double fist to bring it down square on top of his head.

"I think you're done, amigo."

This was a new voice. I stopped short of my target, almost losing my balance in the follow-through, and turned my head toward the door to the hall. Luís Guerrera stood on the threshold holding a nine-millimeter Sig-Sauer pointed at my mid-section.

I straightened and pulled apart my fists. "I'm done," I said. "Question is, is he?"

He was. When I'd jumped his trap, Domingo's momentum had carried him forward onto his face. He was kneeling on the floor with his rump in the air, snoring as energetically as ever.

"We'll let him be. He's an angel when he sleeps. Where do you keep it?"

"Behind my right hip."

Guerrera closed the distance in cat's stride and relieved me of the gun's weight. He reversed himself just as quickly, stuck it under his belt, and gestured with the semi-automatic. I went out into the hall ahead of him.

He drew the door shut, took the Sig off cock, and parked it under his belt on the other side. Wild Bill Hickok wore his brace of Navies the same way, with the butts twisted forward. We were facing each other.

His long hair curled around his ears and fell down on his forehead, a broad intelligent brow that seemed too much for the rest of his undernourished features to support. His skin was bad, sallow and pockmarked, and the forceps scar on his left cheek and more recent slash on his right underscored the *V* made by his cheeks and chin. He wore a denim Cesar Chavez jacket over a gray T-shirt with a stylized sunrise screen-printed on it, khaki cargo pants two sizes too large but cinched tightly with a broad leather belt, and two-hundred-dollar Nikes that looked freshly swiped from the store. No tarantula tattoo: But I think I'd heard somewhere that that was for members who had to prove they were worthy of belonging. The founders were exempt.

I said, "I thought someone else was carrying your gun these days."

"You here to arrest me?" He had almost no accent.

"I leave that kind of thing to the cops. They've got the manpower to do it all over again when someone takes your place." I tilted my head toward the door behind him. "That's a heroin nap. It's not good business to raid your own stock."

"Cut him some slack. Today's his eighteenth birthday. Not a small thing to know your life's almost over."

"Doesn't have to be."

"You don't know what you're talking about." One of his caved-in cheeks poked out, bulged by his tongue. "Walker, right?"

"Sí, está correcto."

He shook his head. "It makes me puke when Anglos try to speak Spanish."

I moved a shoulder. "You can't be far from eighteen yourself."

"I'm twenty. Just about used up. You're trespassing. Why?"

I doubted anyone but the Jesuits had clear title to the place, but I let that one ride. "In a minute. I saw Little Miss Mexico on the stairs. She ought to be playing jacks."

"Jacks, Petes, she's not choosy. If you want a fix-up, talk to her. I'm not in that racket."

"Every word, every little move, straight from the script. Don't you boys watch anything but *Scarface*?"

"*Carlito's Way.* Less clowning, more plot."

"Listen to Rex Reed. I'm doing you a favor. Girl like her could put you both in the joint and save you the trouble of dying in the street."

He smiled. He had good teeth. "I guess where you come from jail's a really bad thing."

"I'm going to reach inside my coat. For a

picture. Okay?"

"Describe it to me."

"Sixteen, five-ten, but about your weight. His name's Ernesto Pasada."

"I don't know him."

"Too thin. The neighborhood isn't that big, and you don't really all look alike."

"Maybe I've seen him. What's your end?"

"His sister wants him back."

"Why tell me?"

"You're the man to see in Mexicantown."

"Domingo's the man to see. I'm just a peon."

"I can't wait around for him to sober up. I work by the day."

"Talk to Nesto. He's old enough to wipe his own ass."

"Tell me where he is and I'll give it a whirl."

"I haven't seen him in months."

"No good. His tarantula hasn't had time to heal."

"Anyone can get a tattoo."

"If he doesn't mind leaving that hand behind when he goes home. No ink artist in town would touch the job without gang endorsement. Come on, Luís. Your type never forgets a wrong or an insult. Last I knew there was a thousand bucks riding on the head of the cop who put down your brother."

"That's a lie. I wouldn't pay anyone else to do my work."

"Sure you would. You're as yellow as Siete. He's afraid he won't live long enough to buy a drink legally."

That shot him right out of his expensive sneakers, that did. His smile didn't flicker. "Time to go, amigo. You get a free pass today, it being today."

"Sure. Tell him happy birthday. I hear he celebrated early by setting fire to the Tiger's garage."

"Did Zorborón tell you that? He's an old lady."

"He can take care of himself. I'm more concerned about Sister Delia. A little automobile vandalism is nothing new, but the timing worries me. That last sweep by the cops was just practice. If anything happens to her they'll come back with the marines."

"I'll give Domingo the message." He took out my Chief's Special, swung the cylinder, shook loose the cartridges, swung it back, and held the revolver out to me butt-first, all one-handed. "Tell John Alderdyce *El Hermano* said hello."

The little girl who should have been dressing Barbies was talking on the corner with a group of youths who looked like freshly opened jackknives, all lean lines and angles in Red Wings jackets and a porkpie hat or two. Her motor never stopped; shifting her weight from one foot to the other, shooting her hips, adjusting her halter strap when it looked like the negotiations weren't going so well. It was an admirable performance until you realized she'd only grown breasts since your last oil change.

Leaning on my car watching her I almost missed seeing Ernesto Pasada trotting up the front steps to the former mission.

SEVEN

"Nesto!"

That was a mistake. I should have put less than the width of a sidewalk between us before I called his name.

He had the reflexes of a cat on coke. Without even glancing my way he vaulted over the side railing of the porch and swung around the corner of the house through the strip of dead grass that separated it from the apartment house next door and vanished. I'd gotten a glimpse of plaid flannel shirttail and narrow hips in faded Wranglers and then it was as if he'd never been there at all.

I ran that way, across the grass and halfway up a six-foot board fence where the yard ended. That got me a palmful of splinters and a bruise on my left hip when I hit the ground.

I got up, plucked out the splinters, repeating the lesson I'd learned with each one:

You can't argue with two seconds' head start and an old bullet wound in the leg.

When I had it committed to memory I stood there for half a minute, deciding whether I should go back in and pump Luis Guerrera some more, but my time was worth something even if I wasn't charging for it. Anyone can climb a porch, and Nesto wasn't officially a runaway, so there wasn't any leverage. I went back to the car, stirred up the motor, and drove around a few blocks, but he'd gone to ground.

Waiting for a light change on the way back to the office I called Nesto's sister, just to tell her he hadn't fallen down any rabbit holes.

"Why did he run?" she asked. "I'm sure he doesn't know you're looking for him."

"I startled him. I shouldn't have called his name. I try to make all my mistakes the first day, but some days just aren't long enough."

"It just isn't like him. He's not timid."

"Not at home, maybe, or school. Mexicantown can make a jumping bean out of anyone. His picture's made all the rounds by now. Zorborón can't use the trouble and Sister Delia hasn't given up hope yet on his generation. When I get a call I'll play it smarter next time. So far, you have to admit you're getting every penny's worth."

"But you're not — Oh." Air moved in and out on her end of the line. "I don't blame you, Mr. Walker. I'm really very grateful to you. Jerry will be, too, when he has all the information."

"Not if he's as much like his old man as you say."

"What now?"

"Now I wait for the phone to ring."

"That's all?"

"The work doesn't get any harder."

"I didn't mean that the way it sounded," she said. "I just keep thinking of myself at sixteen, if I were lost in a strange place."

"Not so strange to him." Which could make things worse, but that was more information than she needed. I said good-bye and punched off.

I had nothing waiting for me back at the office but a bunch of elderly files, not even a mouse to outsmart. When the light changed I made a broad U-turn in the middle of the intersection and drove back to Zorborón's garage. If I told him Nesto had been seen in the neighborhood he might know where he would be likely to land.

The same Basque mechanic was sitting on a cement block in front of the open bay with a tire iron in his hand, prying a blowout away from the rim. The sleeves of his greasy coveralls were cut off at the shoulders and his biceps were as big as tether balls. When I asked for the boss he took a hand away from his chore long enough to jerk a thumb back over his shoulder in the direction of the office.

On the way to the room in back I passed a Mexican with an air wrench spinning lugs off the wheels of a VW beetle on a rack and another who looked like his identical twin at a bench pounding the bend out of a driveshaft with a ballpeen hammer. I could make more noise driving a truckload of cymbals through the wall of a steel foundry, but I wouldn't be able to keep it up. The air was thick with grease and blue with the haze of scorched metal.

Glass partitions enclosed a corner, plastered with posters advertising discounts on brake inspections and tune-ups. The dates had expired on all of them, but they were mostly there for privacy. The office was inside the partitions.

The doors to offices in commercial garages are rarely closed; some don't even have doors. Zorborón's was an exception. The business he conducted, in personal meetings and over the telephone, seldom involved transmissions and repair estimates, and everyone else was too busy to pay much attention to who might be wandering about with his ears open. I knocked, but if he heard it and answered, the whine of the wrench and the ringing of steel on steel drowned him out. The knob turned freely. I let myself in.

I didn't pay any particular attention to the smell at first. I still had traces of Domingo Siete's charred beard in my nostrils, and the odors aren't dissimilar. Whoever decorates those places doesn't tamper with the convention. Miss March Muffler posed in a bikini and high heels holding an exhaust system on a calendar on the block wall at the back and there was the usual message board shingled over with yellow Post-its. Zorborón's desk was made of sheet metal and black Formica. On it stood a flat-screen computer monitor surrounded by stacks of papers: insurance reports, work orders, and bills of lading. The Tiger sat at an angle to it in a hydraulic office swivel, wearing what looked like the same black T-shirt and gray slacks he'd had on the day before. He was in a slouch. The back of his head rested on the back of the chair, with his eyes closed and his lips parted. He wasn't the siesta type. He had a black mole two inches under his left eye. It hadn't been there before, and it wasn't a mole.

Eight

I noticed the smell then. In a room that small, smokeless powder is as smokeless as silencers silent, and although the smoke had cleared, the stench was strong enough to be fresh. I confirmed it when I searched Zorborón's neck for a pulse. There wasn't any, but the flesh was still warm.

I went back and locked the door, but there wasn't much to see. He carried his cash in a gold-and-black-enamel clip with a tiger on it; nothing else in his pockets, not even keys. He had a driver, so no driver's license, and that party or a bodyguard would open all his locks for him and likely carry his weapons. Eighteen hundred twenty-six dollars in crisp folded bills: walking-around money, if you cared to walk around that neighborhood with a roll that size. Zorborón's reputation would have demanded no less. It eliminated robbery as a motive.

I went through the desk drawers, but there

was no time to be thorough. Anyone could come to the door any time and jump to a conclusion that could only add to the body count. The papers on the desk might have included forged Compuware stock or a suicide note elegantly worded in Old Castilian, but there wasn't time to go through them. Anyway I eliminated suicide, too, unless he'd held the gun far enough away to prevent powder burns and hid the gun when he was finished. It was a smallish hole, no larger than a .22 or a .25 would make, but even if the shooter had fired from the doorway the range would still be lethal.

That was the extent of my knowledge of forensics. I unlocked the door and went out past the mechanic who had the wheels off the VW now and his twin still banging away on the driveshaft and stood in front of the Basque working on the tire out front, watching him with my hands in my pockets. When after ten seconds he didn't look up, I said, "I thought you had a machine for that."

"*Está roto.* Busted." He went on moving his chisel around the inside of the rim, tapping the handle with a clawhammer to get a purchase.

I said, "Man could work all day on that."

"*Sí.*" Tap, tap, tap.

"What's it, ten-buck job?"

"*Veinte.* Twenty dollars, this job."

"Even so. Garage must be doing good."

"*Por favor,* no? Is Detroit."

I was running out of small talk.

"Your boss isn't available," I said.

"Sí?" He had a star-shaped bald spot on his crown.

"Permanent condition, looks like."

"Sí?"

Either I was being too clever or his English was as bad as my Spanish. I dusted it off anyway.

"Está muerto."

The hand holding the hammer went still. His face came up like a chunk of submerged driftwood floating to the surface. The pouches under his eyes were like wallets. A bead of sweat had slid down his nose, but the shift in angle had prevented it from falling off the end. It quivered there, the only thing about him that was in motion.

"Asesinato." I took my right hand out of my pocket, pointed the index finger at him, and worked the thumb; tapped my left cheek with the same finger.

Deep beneath the fat that cushioned skin from bone, a nerve twitched in his own cheek. The skin fluttered once and was still.

Before he could move, I whipped the Chief's Special out of its holster and did a border spin, twirling it by its trigger guard around my finger so that the butt was pointed toward him. He jumped, made a quick motion toward the hip pocket of his filthy coveralls, but stopped when I'd finished spinning. He hesitated, then took hold of the butt when I removed my finger from the trigger.

I shook my head when he pointed the revolver at me, touched my nose, pointed at the muzzle, touched my nose again. He got the message and sniffed the barrel. All he would smell was oil. He grunted and lowered it to his lap. His other hand rested on the tire and wheel leaning against his shins. He shoved at it and stood while it struck the asphalt and wobbled to a stop. He made a motion with the gun — not a threatening one; it was just a gesture that happened to include the object he was holding. I nodded and went ahead of him into the garage.

The man at the rack was air-wrenching the wheels back on, but the one at the bench wouldn't give up on that shaft. His ear drums must have been as thick as the hammer. We entered the office and the big man shut the door on the noise. He didn't approach the dead man behind the desk. He crossed himself and said, "Holy shit." A devout people.

I reached inside my coat. The revolver twitched upward. I showed him the cell. *"Nueve-uno-uno. Sabe policía?"*

A lower lip got chewed. It was as big as a slice of prime rib and took a while. Finally he nodded.

I jabbed at the keys and snapped my fingers at the mechanic while I was waiting. He gave me back my gun. I think he'd forgotten he was still holding it.

A woman came on the line. "Nine-one-one, what is your emergency?"

"Define *emergency.*"

The garage was quiet at last. A couple of plainclothesmen I'd seen around 1300 Beaubien, the cop house, were in one corner talking with the air-wrench jockey, one of the first uniforms on the scene was writing in a notebook while the twin brother with the hammer was talking, and John Alderdyce had the big man all to himself. Outside, the yellow tape and barricades were up and a mixed crowd of Hispanics, blacks, and whites had gathered on the other side. A helicopter shuddered overhead, first TV news scout on the scene. The police cruisers sat with their motors purring and their juke lights blinking on the roofs. I smoked a cigarette and read a fan belt display.

John came over, flipping shut his leather-bound memorandum book. He wore a chocolate-colored Palm Beach suit with a gay yellow necktie. It was like hanging a ribbon on a coffin. "You'll have to start the conversation," he said. "Usually I get the ball rolling by asking who's your client."

"Who am I talking to, you or the department?"

"Oh, hell. How do you work it? Ask permission, what?"

"For starters. Then I decide whether I do anything with it."

"Okay. Client first. Report."

"Not till you put away that damn notebook."

"I changed my mind. Give me the official version." But he returned it to his inside breast pocket.

I spoke as if I were talking to a different cop. "I'm working for the family of a kid who's in a Mexican gang. They want him out, but they don't know how to go about it. I came here yesterday and today to find out what I could about the gang." I gave him what I'd learned about the Maldados, named my local sources. It was all pretty silly but it kept the interview professional.

Alderdyce was all cop on the job. He jumped on the arson attempt at the garage.

"He blamed Sister Delia?"

"I think he was joking. With him it was hard to tell."

"Her style's to set up a picket line, maybe spend a couple hours in jail for disorderly conduct. It sure isn't arson."

"It has to be Maldados. They're making a power play."

"You said Zorborón said he was semiretired."

"He's still a symbol. It's a culture that likes broad strokes. I'd put a detail on Sister Delia."

"She'll like that — not. But we have to make the offer. These guys don't know anything. Buy that?

"Could be. It's a busy place and the door's open all day. What about a bodyguard?"

"We'll check Unemployment." He put a hand on my arm and led me away from the other interview groups. His voice dropped. "Give me the rest."

"Ask your daughter-in-law. I've reported to her already."

"Jesus. I'm your client!"

"Not when you're inside police tape."

"I thought you were a pain in the ass before." But he got his party on his cell and asked her what he'd asked me. He said nothing about Zorborón. The rest of the conversation he spent listening. He flipped the phone shut.

"Why'd he run when you called his name?"

I shook my head. "Could be the neighborhood. If they're gunning for you they make sure it's you first. On the other hand, I don't know why anyone would be gunning for him."

"I can think of a reason."

"Yeah, I thought about that, too. I don't like him for it."

"The mission's what, a five-minute walk from here?"

"The body was still warm. I didn't say he couldn't have done it. Pretty big leap for a kid from the suburbs."

"Not so big here. It's like on the moon."

"He just got his tarantula."

"He has to earn it."

"You don't try for Eagle just out of Cub Scouts."

"I'm a worst-case scenario kind of guy," Alderdyce said. "Comes with the shield."

"I'd start with that arson attempt."

"You think?"

I let that slide off and shook out a cigarette.

He said, "I'll take one, since you didn't offer."

"I thought you quit."

"I thought you quit saying you thought I quit."

I lit us both up. "Okay if I do some nosing around?"

"You asking me or a cop?"

"Doesn't matter. I'll nose around anyway. I was just being polite."

"Try not to get dead. All the neighborhood needs to blow its top is an Anglo with a knife in his belly." He took the last of three drags, threw the rest outside the bay doors, and went over to start in on the twins.

I walked around the outside of the building. It was an American original. There aren't many of those white glazed-brick shops from the fifties still doing the same kind of business. The gas pumps had been hauled away and the underground tanks filled with earth and fresh concrete poured on top of them, but it was one of the few places left where you could have a dent bumped out and a new drive train installed all on the same premises. Even the dealerships farm out body work. The low riders and aging muscle cars that thundered along West Vernor all came to roost there sooner or later.

The scene of the fire wasn't hard to spot: a black stain on the wall behind the building, fresh plywood nailed over an empty window frame, and a Dumpster that had provided the kindling. The burn pattern didn't look as if accelerants had been used. An amateur job, using the materials that happened to be at hand, probably on impulse. It lacked seriousness, smacked of malicious mischief or a halfhearted warning of some kind. There wasn't a thing promising about it; but until I found Nesto, it was all I had to work with.

An undamaged window at the other end of the wall wore a red-and-silver decal reading:

THIS PROPERTY PROTECTED BY
H&M SECURITY
YOU ARE UNDER SURVEILLANCE

A slim video camera clung to the overhang of the roof near the corner with a red light glowing above the lens.

If the firebug was caught on tape or disc, the cops would have it. Zorborón's insurance carrier would have insisted the incident be reported. But Alderdyce couldn't risk giving me access. Records are kept in those situations, and inquiries made.

I didn't need him. I had an in at H&M. Finding out what the cops already know is a lousy place to start, but it was a lousy case.

On the way I called Chata.

"I had a call from John," she said. "Do you know what that was about?"

I told her about Zorborón. She took in a sharp breath. "He doesn't think Ernesto is involved with *that.*"

"He thinks like a cop."

"Do you?"

"I don't know what I think. I haven't met your brother. But you're going to have to tell Jerry everything before he hears from the police."

There was a short silence. "Could you tell him?"

"I have to run some things down. It has to be you."

"God. Yes, of course you're right. He'll want you off the case. Are you still on it?"

"Yeah. He'll have to take that up with his father; he's the client."

"He won't. John won't. I don't know him at all, but I know that much." A second of silence passed. "They won't hurt Ernesto, will they?"

"That's up to him."

"He's headstrong, but he's not violent. The fight we had over the tattoo wasn't really a fight."

I didn't tell her that running away when he was approached was just as bad. It didn't serve any purpose anyway.

"Thank you, Mr. Walker. I know he had nothing to do with this — thing."

I told her I'd let her know when I found out anything, and we were through talking to each other.

H&M stands for *Hugin* and *Munin,* ancient Norse for Thought and Memory. In mythology they were the names of the ravens that flew about the world gathering information on mortals and perched on Odin's shoulders at nightfall to report. Fredrik Nordenborg, the company founder, had served in a top security position with the state military archives in Stockholm before emigrating to America. He'd been sacked after several of Greta Garbo's letters disappeared from the files. No one bothered to explain what the scribbles of a dead movie star had been doing there among the battle plans and citations of valor, but someone had to be thrown to the sharks. Nordenborg was ripe because he'd joined a religious movement that wanted to restore the old gods to current belief; Lutheranism is the state religion of Sweden, and unconventional behavior carries the same official suspicion everywhere in the world.

I didn't know him from a plate of Swedish meatballs. Abel Osterling ran the uniformed security force that responded to alarms at the businesses and residences H&M served. He'd hired me once to gather evidence on a company dispatcher suspected of selling alarm codes and passwords to burglars, and I'd managed to do it without drawing fire from the press. The dispatcher was canned, the circumstances were wired to all Nordenborg's competitors to prevent him from finding employment anywhere else in the business, and Nordenborg himself was said to have been satisfied with the way things had turned out. My credit was good with Osterling.

H&M hung out high in the American Building in Southfield, a Mies van der Rohe knockoff poking dozens of stories above the horizontal community with enough glass to wipe out the migratory bird population in all of southeast Michigan. I hadn't been there since old Sam Lucy, who had kept an office there, had reported to the big slot machine in the sky. The Chamber of Commerce had celebrated his passing as the end of organized crime in Detroit. Anyone can say anything.

A wall of smoked glass separated the offices from the elevator bank, with the name of the firm etched on it in platinum along with the company logo: the stylized heads of two ravens looking east and west. In the waiting area, leather-and-chrome sling chairs invited you to sit down and read recent numbers of *Hour Detroit* and *Metropolitan Home* in clear plastic covers. An oil painting of Nordenborg hung on the wall behind the reception desk. He was holding a lance, with his bony shoulders covered by a red velvet cloak and a pair of tawny handlebars tickling his earlobes under a brass hat with horns on it. Swear to God.

The woman at the polished-granite desk wore her white-blond hair piled high and secured with braids like woven gold. Her complexion was rose gold and a gold pendant nestled in the hollow of her throat. She took my name, spoke to her headset, and asked me to have a seat. Her voice was like golden bells.

I paged through a photo layout in *Hour Detroit* of best-dressed local celebrities — I'd missed out again — then got up to shake Osterling's hand. He'd swept from a corridor behind the desk, five-foot-eight-inches of dusky Finlander with black hair in bangs and a suit cut short in the coat to call attention from his short legs. Nordenborg never recruited south of Greenland, but a Finnish employee was a mark of rare regard; they're Huns by heredity, hated by Swedes and Norwegians alike.

"Welcome to Ikea." He winked at me and started back down the corridor. I followed.

His office was a neat rectangle with a gray pile carpet, sleek desk, and blue steel shelves holding up books loaded with umlauts. The back wall was glass with a view clear to Canada. Laptop on the desk. *Minimalist* was too long a word to describe it.

I mouthed a silent word: "Bugged?"

He shook his head. "Paranoia's the only delusion the old clown doesn't suffer from. Did you check out the picture in reception? The Western Order of the Sons of Asgard Lodge elected him Lord of Thunder for a third term last month."

"What makes you stick?"

He waved a hand at family pictures taking turns in a digital frame on the desk.

We sat. "I'm here about one of your clients," I said. "Emiliano Zorborón."

He worked the laptop. His brow furrowed. "My, my. I thought we were more choosy."

"Times are hard. He reported an arson recently. You should have something on video."

"We shared it with the police, of course. Company policy says that's where it stops."

"I suspected that, but I didn't think I'd hear it from you."

"It was a statement of fact, not opinion. You'll have it, of course. I need a reason, just for my files. No one has to see it unless it becomes a serious criminal case. Right now it's just vandalism."

"Not anymore. You'll hear about it at six o'clock, unless terrorists take out the Coleman Young Municipal Center before air time."

"Heaven forbid; although they'd just put up another one under the same name." He waited.

"You can strike Zorborón off your client list. Someone shot him in the face today. I don't know if it has anything to do with the fire, but I'm running it out."

"Fatal?"

"I said it was in the face."

"Not conclusive. This job's in my blood. My old man traced assassination threats for the government in Helsinki. His stories would surprise even a hardened character like you."

"Trust me. He's strictly Accounts Uncollectable."

"When did you start working murder cases?"

"They have a way of working me. It started out as a runaway."

Keys rattled. He turned the laptop my way and I watched a felony in progress.

Dos: Lake of Fire

Nine

It was as useful as those things ever are. When you mount a camera overhead, the top of the head is what you get. The infrared lens bleached out the shadows, but from the moment the arsonist showed up and rooted in the Dumpster for combustible materials until he touched them off with a cigarette lighter I had only the impression of dark hair, a slender build, and a flannel shirt over a dark T-shirt that may or may not have been the outfit I'd spotted on Nesto Pasada that day. I had to assume he changed clothes now and then. Whoever it was never looked up at the camera once, and when the blaze caught the wooden window frame he turned and strode away. The fire burned long enough to burst the panes, then died out for lack of fuel. I'd seen more successful arsons on doorsteps at Halloween.

"Hardly worth reporting," I said, when

Osterling paused the image.

"I've been after Nordenborg for months to add a second camera and mount it low, catch 'em in the crossfire. He says it would raise rates and drive away clients. He'd rather spend the budget on Viking relics at Pottery Barn. At least we know it's male."

"Maybe. Girls come in every shape and size. Can you zoom in on details?"

"Name the detail."

"Back up and stop when I holler."

He tickled some keys. The fire rekindled itself, burning backward down from the window. The starter backed into the frame, turned around, watched the result of his work, took the lighter from his pocket, and knelt to start it all over again. I told Osterling to stop it. The image froze and stayed rock-steady. I pointed at the hand holding the lighter. He tapped the same key three times. The hand filled the screen. It wore a dark dime-store jersey glove; no tarantula in sight. I said as much.

Osterling knew a bit about gangs. "So that's your interest. I heard the Maldados are as bad as they come. This is just one step up from a T.P. job. Disappointing, if it's them."

"I'm looking for a kid who just joined up. Ink's still wet on his tattoo."

"There'd be plenty of red in it in that case, scabs and bleeding from scratching the itch. Couldn't tell any of that by infrared, even without the glove."

"I expected a tattoo, and that it wouldn't tell us much. I wanted a closer look at the lighter."

He hit some more keys, shifting the angle to include the object in the hand. It was an ordinary kerosene lighter, tombstone-shaped and shiny, with a symbol I'd seen before engraved on the bottom part: a stylized raptor with spread wings.

"Eagle?" Osterling said.

"Thunderbird. Zorborón had one tattooed between his fingers."

"The little shit probably stole the lighter from him just so he could use it against him. He forgot to plant it at the scene."

"This wasn't planned. If he really wanted to make him bleed he'd have brought a Molotov cocktail and tossed it through the window."

"I can do an Internet search on the symbol. It must mean something. The Tiger wasn't the gaudy type."

"The Net knows too much and makes the rest up. I'd never sort through it all. Can you print out this shot? I'll show it around, see who recognizes that lighter."

His telephone rang. He looked at the lighted button. "That's the inside line."

"Communication from Valhalla?"

"Walk in my shoes. My oldest has her heart set on Princeton." He reached for the receiver. "I'll messenger the print to your office."

I thanked him and left while he was talking to the Lord of Thunder.

I went to the office and spent ten minutes dumping all the files, current and obsolete, back into their drawers. A disordered mind in a disordered room was a double negative I was better off doing without. I looked at the duct tape stuck on the baseboard across from the desk. I missed Wally. He might have had a new angle on the job.

But there were worse places to run to ground. When a city dies the jungle takes over, and the only reason *jungle* has a bad rap is people keep projecting all the uncivilized tendencies of the race on something that was pure at the beginning. The street was quiet between the mad rush to get to work and the madder one to get away from it, but not so dead you didn't get a little buzz from the odd loose tappet or beep-beep-beep of a dump truck backing up to fill a pothole the size of Crater Lake with gravel and spit, and taking all week at it because the mayor was footing the bill and nobody had told him that paying by the hour was a bad idea on its face. No family photos on the desk to remind you of your obligations, no TV to distract you with stale sitcoms and sex-starved hospital dramas and paid programming that didn't necessarily reflect the views of the station that nevertheless cashed the checks. No Internet, with its tired jokes and urban legends and Photoshopped porn. A brain factory, that room, pure and simple. What you did with the brain was your own damn business.

I drew out the leaf from the desk and rested my foot on it. The leg had started to hurt. It was just a dull throb now — in earlier times it had taken the top off my head — but persistent. Breaking the Vicodin habit had been more expensive than physical therapy when my liquor bill went up. Not that I didn't miss the little white pills.

My cell rang. While I was groping for it the telephone on the desk rang. The LED on the cell showed the initials of the Detroit Police Department. I answered it and left the landline to voice mail.

"What's new?" Alderdyce asked.

I told him about the surveillance video. There was no reason not to, as the Arson Squad would have a copy. He hadn't had a chance to look at it yet.

"Could be anything," he said. "He stole the lighter, or Zorborón dropped it and he found it. Kids are magpies, snap up anything shiny."

"What do you know about the thunderbird?"

"It's just about the worst wine in a bottle. Offhand I can't think of a gang that uses it for an insignia. The Zapatistas lack imagination: Theirs is a *Z* with a line through it. I'll run it past the Youth Bureau."

"Any news on a bodyguard?"

"We found Zorborón's driver shacked up with his girlfriend in her apartment, across from Holy Cross Cemetery. They said neither of them has been out of the place since day before yesterday. Building super backed them up; he had to go up there three times to tell them to pipe down. They like to bat each other around and sing all the standards in between, at the top of their lungs. Not *American Idol* material, according to the supe. Place smelled like they smoked it with pot and scrubbed it down with gin. Cheez-It dust two inches deep on the floor; the Eucharist of munchies.

Warren Zevon playing over and over on the stereo."

" 'Werewolves of London.' Subtle folk, Latins."

"Say what?"

"Something Zorborón said. Not pertinent. Sweet alibi for the driver."

"We tanked them both for D-and-D and domestic assault, and him for CCW. Needless to say neither of them will press on the assault, but when the *piñata* busts you scoop up what spills out. He lugged around the Tiger's gun for him, but with his record he couldn't get a permit in Tijuana if he showed up at the police station with a bushel of pesos. They might crack and they might not, but it wouldn't be the first time a human shield called in sick just when he was most needed."

"That would let out Nesto. A sixteen-year-old from Lathrup Village doesn't have the attention span to rig a conspiracy."

"The punk who pulls the trigger is almost never the one who wrote the playbook."

I looked to Wally's ghost for advice, but my foot blocked my view of his hole. "Do you *want* it to be him?"

"I have to work extra hard to fit him to it so I can eliminate him. The tag's out. If he shows his face at home or anywhere in the area he's downtown meat. Faster if he shows it in Mexicantown."

"Suspicion of homicide?"

"Right now it's just runaway; but I let the department know the relationship. That way it's high priority, but if he tries to run, the pieces will stay in the holsters."

"You're all heart, Gramps."

"Fuck you. I don't know the kid from Charlie Brown."

"Then why am I even part of this?"

"We got to create jobs, the president says."

I rubbed my eyes. They were cured in secondhand pot and strained from staring at videos. "We through here?"

"I guess so. How's expenses?"

"I'm still working on my last carton. I'll let you know when I need to tap the Swiss accounts."

"You're going to milk this thing for all it's worth, aren't you?"

"He's just a kid, John. You used to be one, as I recall."

He blew air. There was smoke in it as surely as if I smelled it. "I wish to hell *I* could."

After we were done I lit a cigarette, but the exhaust made my eyes sting even worse and I screwed it out in the tray. I remembered to check voice mail on the desk phone. The message was from Chata. Nesto had called.

"What'd he say?"

" 'Hello.' "

"That was polite of him. What else?"

"Nothing. I should've been more clear. I didn't actually speak to him. Jerry called from work, and when I hung up I found out Nesto had left a message because the line was busy."

I let out a plume of smoke in a weary sigh. It was getting to be possible to hear from everyone in the civilized world without ever establishing direct contact. I'd had to call twice before she answered; she'd been on the line with Gerald, her husband. "Are you sure it was Nesto?"

"I know my brother's voice. He started to leave a message, then changed his mind."

"Maybe he was interrupted."

"I don't think so. I heard background noises for a couple of seconds, then he hung up. He must've been trying to make up his mind whether to say anything more."

"What kind of noises?"

"I'm not sure. A train, I think; I heard that horn that sounds like a train whistle. Some other things."

"What other things?"

"Noises. Nothing human. I'm sorry I can't be of more help."

"You didn't erase it?"

"I'm not a fool."

"I didn't say you were. Don't take everything as an insult. Did you tell Jerry what's going on?"

"I didn't get the chance. He said he'd be working late; some kind of emergency at the bus office. He was in a hurry, so I didn't think it was the —"

"Can you hang around until I get there?"

"Of course. I haven't budged from the house since I found out he'd skipped school. I have a cell, but —"

"I don't trust them either. I'll see you in twenty minutes."

It was a little longer than that. I slid over to make room for an EMS unit with all its equipment going and got hung up on I-96 behind a procession of gawkers crawling past an overturned semi. After that, more construction. At the end of the ramp I ignored the NO TURN ON RIGHT sign. Right away I passed two squad cars stopped in a Park-and-Ride, but the drivers were too busy talking to each other to notice. I took advantage of the situation to pour on the coal. In the driveway I was out of the car in time to eat my own dust drifting from my rear wheels.

I don't know what the hurry was, except there was a tag out on Nesto; cops are people and I don't entirely trust every gun to stay in its holster when a citizen fails to heed the voice of authority.

She led me into the living room with Jesus wearing His thorn hat. Today she had on a thin pale blue sweater and a pair of pleated slacks, loafers on her feet. I hoped, with no agenda connected, that she wouldn't fall for the fitness craze and lose those extra pounds. There is a narrow line between thin and haggard. The message was on voice mail. I stood in the center of the carpet and held a slim cordless receiver to my ear while she worked the buttons.

There was a little hissing silence before he said, "Hello," then the receiver on his end made fumbling noises. It was an adolescent voice, shallow and uncertain. I heard the asthmatic whistle of the Amtrak and a growling that sounded like the lion house at the Detroit Zoo when the keepers were twenty minutes behind feeding time. It wasn't the zoo; the trains don't pass that close.

I had her play it again, then once more while I separated all the ambient noises. They have computers to do that at 1300, but you can become too dependent on technology if you have constant access to it. That made me the most independent detective in the 313 area code.

"The Michigan Central Depot." I replaced the receiver in its cradle.

"What makes you so certain?"

"They don't stop there anymore, but the tracks are still there and the trains have to use them. They blow the horn out of respect. It could be a crossing, but that roaring sound cinches it. There's a parking garage across the street; that's the noise, cars going up and down the ramp. What came up on caller ID?"

" 'Out of Area,' I'm afraid."

"Don't be. Most pay phones come up that way. I know where he called from."

"Are you sure?"

"I've only had the cell a little while. Before that I memorized all the places in the area where you could make a call from a public phone. The Wayne County Historical Commission ought to put this one on its list before AT&T shuts it down."

"Surely you won't find him still there."

"Every missing-persons case needs a place to start." Actually I had a specific idea, but nothing's to be gained by scaring a client out of her wits.

TEN

The Pacman dozers and earthmovers that are eating up the cityscape and dropping rubble haven't gotten to the Michigan Central Depot yet, but it's on the list. For a while the police department had considered moving from the elegant Deco rot of 1300, a 1922 construction, into the decaying pile at Fourteenth and Vernor, erected in 1913; but then it had taken a deep breath and abandoned that plan in favor of parting out its divisions into old precinct buildings. That placed them outside the chief's supervision. The department was returning to its feudal origins, with each squad self-contained and answering to no one but the inspector on the premises.

The depot's an echoing hangar built of brick and girders and native granite, with stained-glass windows and most of the other doodads of Edwardian architecture prominently in place. Pigeons, sparrows, and jays roost in the rafters, using nests built by earlier generations and interrupting their songs of truculence to listen to the hooting of Amtrak whistles as the cars chuckle past; their splatter had formed stalactites under the roof and stalagmites on the floor at the base of the walls. It's a long haul down Vernor from the part of Mexicantown where he'd been hanging out, almost in the heart of Corktown, where the migration had begun; but a kid like Ernesto Pasada, who didn't know the neighborhood so well, would be likely to run in a straight line rather than risk getting lost in a zigzag.

That was the working theory. The train sounds and automobile noises on Chata's voice mail bore it out, but only on a contingency basis. Cars turned into the parking garage entrance through the Fourteenth Street entrance, paused to take their tickets, and climbed the spiraling ramp to the higher levels, the sound of their motors thundering off reinforced concrete and spilling out the open sides louder than they had been going in. I found a spot near the roof and rode down in an elevator that smelled like an overheated radiator and wheezed and rattled like loose particles in an old lung.

A pay phone stood across from the garage

on a post with a metal cowl that protected the instrument while leaving the user to the mercy of our weather. No one was using it. I laid a hand on the receiver for a few seconds, trolling for psychic vibes left behind by Nesto when he'd called his sister. But the place was fished out. Or just possibly I'm not psychic.

The place I'd thought of when I figured out where he'd called from was an old frame apartment building that belonged to no particular school of architecture. Some opportunistic realtor had slapped it together in 1942 to shelter some of the horde of crackers, Tarheels, Kentucks, and Mississippi blacks who had swarmed north to build ships and planes and tanks to hammer Europe and the South Pacific. More lately it had been a hippie commune and a hotel for transients, with a combination meth lab and crack emporium overlapping that and its current incarnation. It had actually come up in the world, if you considered the cockfight trade less harmful than dope. The cops had to have known what was going on there, but likely had left it for seed so they knew where to go when it came time to arrest someone for questioning. The stink came out the front door and through the broken windows and squatted in the middle of the block like a broken-down honey wagon.

On the way there I'd stopped at a CVS and hit the expense account for a jar of Vicks. In the car I'd smeared a handkerchief with some of the contents and just before I went inside I ringed my nostrils with the strong eucalyptus mixture. It burned the membranes, but it beat what came out from under the tail feathers of chickens.

In the residency days a shoebox-size foyer had contained a counter where the clerk collected and gave out the keys, sorted mail into cubbyholes, misdirected the police, and escorted junkies into the street. The desk was gone and so were the interior partitions, making room for steel utility shelves on all sides, stacked with crate-size cages sided with chicken wire, each containing a haughty-looking rooster or a fat brood hen pecking lice from its feathers and scratching at the floor of its cell. The stench of droppings inserted a lever under my stomach and tried to roll it over. I wasn't sure the Vicks could hold it off for long. I heard clucking and avian sneezing. The neighbors said when the sun came up or a car swept around the corner at night raking the place with its lights, the crowing could be heard clear to the river.

The place was the champion cock capital of the Midwest. All the best scrappers were bred there, the Seabiscuits of fighting fowl, and if it looked sordid at first glance — it certainly smelled that way — the animals were well fed, the cages cleaned regularly, and all their medical needs attended to by a veterinarian in the breeders' employ. Ventilation fans whirred in all the windows, a good circulating system kept the residents warm, and a crew scrubbed the floors with industrial-strength disinfectant on a regular basis. The organic odor belonged to generations of evacuated bird colons. It went clear down to bedrock.

It all had nothing to do with me. I'd seen a cockfight and didn't want to see another, but there are people who feel the same way about prizefights and baseball. Whether the birds died in combat or had their beaks blunted and their bodies pumped full of growth hormones and their heads and feet chopped off and the rest sold in supermarkets was probably all the same to someone.

The keeper of the zoo stood up from a metal folding chair and came over, legs bent, feet pointing sideways, back rounded in a permanent stoop. His hair hung in black strings to his collar and on either side of his forehead. A gold tooth winked in an idiot's smile. He carried a shotgun nearly as short as a pistol, his finger curled around the trigger and his other hand holding the barrels steady. He stopped well inside range; I'd stopped the moment the weapon made its appearance. A scattergun sawed off that far back would open me up like a *piñata.*

"Cuidado, amigo," I said. "Some of the shot might hit the merchandise."

I couldn't tell if I'd gotten through in either language. The whites of his eyes between creased lids were startling against the deep red-brown skin. It went like hell with his outfit: pink polyester shirt with pearl snaps, stiff blue jeans, and lizard boots with pointed toes. In certain nameless villages well below the border, that was formal attire. He might have been a full-blooded Yaqui, unversed in any lingo not used in the mines.

Boards squeaked under the linoleum behind me. I didn't want to turn away from the shotgun, pointless caution; did I care to see what a charge of buckshot looked like as it cut me in half? Anyway I hesitated long enough for someone to yank my right arm behind my back and up between my shoulder blades by the wrist and prick the side of my neck under my left ear with a point that broke the skin on contact. Blood raced down inside my collar.

"Any more guns, son?" asked a voice in my ear; a high-pitched twang. He might have been left over from the northern exodus.

He had me pressed up against him and would have felt the revolver behind my hip. "Just the one, Dad."

He withdrew the knife. The blade folded back into the handle with a click and in another second I was lighter by a pound and a half. That piece was harder to hold onto than a good pair of sunglasses. He let go of my arm and stepped back. I unbent it and shook circulation back into my fingers. He didn't tell me to stay still, so I took a step that would keep them both in my sight and turned. He was sixty, lean and rangy in a green work shirt tucked into an old pair of suit pants held up with dingy gray suspenders. His face was a skull with the skin sprayed on, with wattles on his neck that made him look as if whatever flesh the face had had once had melted. There was a scabrous patch on his left temple where the skin had been gouged out as with a router. A man with skin burned as brown as a brogan was a prime candidate for a melanoma. He was bald, but he'd solved that problem by smearing fifteen or sixteen white hairs across the scalp and tying them around his left ear. He'd pocketed his knife and was admiring the stainless steel Smith & Wesson in his left hand.

"Nice," he said. "I like the four-inch barrel better."

"You wouldn't if you had to carry it around all day. I'm going for my wallet."

"Turn a little that way before you do. I don't want to take a chance on Django missing you with some pellets and hitting livestock."

"Django?"

"What he calls himself, if I make it out right. He watches the birds, I watch him, make sure he don't sacrifice any of 'em to some one-eyed jasper in spic-injun heaven."

I put a vacant corner at my back and got out my ID folder, watching the Yaqui watching me with the shotgun motionless in his hands. I flipped it toward the hillbilly, who caught it in his right hand. His lips sounded out my name and occupation, showing plenty of long yellow tooth and black gum. He glanced at the sheriff's star without interest and flipped the folder back my way. He pointed a chin as prickly as cactus toward the folding metal chair and Django lowered his street sweeper and went back and sat down. The shotgun rested across his lap and he stared off into nothing as if his shift hadn't been interrupted.

"We got to be careful," his partner said. "You'd be surprised how much jack we got tied up in these birds."

"I'm not here for the birds. I'm tracking a runaway kid. He called his family from that phone outside a while ago and this is just the kind of place he might burrow into."

"Why's that, son?"

"He's a Maldado. Brand new."

"One of them spiders shows his face in here, Django'd shoot him low. He left the Sierras because the gangs down there tried to draft him into the dope trade. The gangs up here are a joke next to them, but Django don't like dope and he don't like gangs. Here you go, son. I got to be careful. I'm on parole." He offered me the handle of the Chief's Special.

I took it and put it back. "What's your p.o. say about your hanging out here?"

"Strictly speaking he'd be agin it. He thinks the chicken farm where I'm working is down by Toledo. That's what my pay stubs say."

"This is a Zorborón operation, isn't it?"

He poked at a cheek with his tongue, making it bulge. Said nothing.

"I don't care myself," I said. "You might want to be a little closer to Toledo when the cops come."

"You fixing to call 'em?"

"They don't need the invitation. *El Tigre* got dead this morning and I figure they'll be shaking all the trees in his orchard."

He scratched the top of his head, used the same finger to replace the hair he'd disturbed. That would be a hysterical fit for him. "Who done it, your runaway?"

"He's on the list. I'm not sure he belongs there. I'd like to ask him."

"What's he look like?"

I handed him Nesto's picture. He looked at it about as long as he'd looked at my prop badge, handed it back. "Ain't seen him."

"Okay if I show it to Django?"

"If you can make him understand. He speaks only heathen, and ten words of it's all's I ever heard from him."

I went over to where the Indian was sitting and held the picture in front of his blank gaze. Light glimmered in it, then died. He went back to contemplating the cosmos.

"I think that means no. I ain't just sure."

An empty crate stood next to the metal chair holding up a squat brown bottle of Dos Equis. I laid the picture on the crate. "I'll just leave it here. There's cash in it if you see him and call me." I put my card on top of the picture.

"It better cover the toll from Toledo." The old hillbilly sounded bitter for the first time. "You wasn't just funning me about that."

"It'll be on the news. You might not want to wait around for it."

"Wonder what's to become of the birds."

"Destroyed, probably. What about Django?"

"Him, too, if I can't get through to him not to be here with that stumpy shotgun when they show up."

I left the building and mopped the sweat off the back of my neck with a handkerchief, getting a little blood on it from the nick I'd forgotten about; they close quickly when the blade's ground to a finer point than comes from the factory. I used a dry corner to scrape the Vicks from my nostrils. It would take half a pack of Winstons to burn off the rest of it.

I got the car out of the parking garage, drove clear around the block, and found a spot on the street where I could keep an eye on the entrance of the rooster mill. The only other way in from the street was a steel fire door, chained and padlocked from inside. If Nesto came out, it would have to be through the front.

The 1970 Cutlass is a smorgasbord on wheels. I never know at the beginning of a job how long I might be living in it, so it's stocked with survival food: jerky, dried figs, tins of this and that, and Twinkies, which will give the roaches something to munch on after the rest of us are extinct. Bottles of water, to be used sparingly. The big empty coffee can eliminates most rest stops, but you can be arrested for exposure if you aren't careful.

Chata answered on the first ring. I asked if her brother had come home or called again.

"No. I was hoping you had news."

"Not yet. Talk to Jerry?"

"I called him at work. I hope never to have that kind of conversation again. He blew up. He told me to call the whole thing off, just as I said he would. It didn't make him any happier when I said that decision belonged to his father."

"What did he say about Zorborón?"

"He agrees with me that Ernesto had nothing to do with that. He said the best way to bring him home was to make it official: Report him as a runaway and let the police take care of it."

"Alderdyce is already on it. The way he's doing it breaks rules, so any conflict in the story would snarl things up bigtime. He'll survive the heat, but anything can happen when cops become confused."

"I told him it would just make the situation worse. He said he'd hold off, but he didn't say for how long. Could you talk to Jerry when he comes home? You may be the only person he can trust at this point, a disinterested third party."

"It might be late. I don't have much control over the angle I'm working."

She said she understood, although of course she couldn't. We agreed to call each other when something was definite. My low battery indicator came on when I hit End. I didn't have a dashboard charger, but I'd been in worse places before I had a cell. The damn things start out as a convenience and before you know it they're a vital organ.

I hadn't eaten since breakfast, and come to think of it I hadn't eaten that, so I tore open the package of figs. I had no idea if I'd guessed right about Nesto taking cover among the fighting fowl. He must've known about the place, the time he'd spent in Mexicantown, or else drawn the obvious conclusion from the smell. Calling from just outside the building couldn't have been a coincidence. But Jed Clampett and Django weren't the innkeeping type, so he might have slipped past them and gone up the back stairs to a higher floor where they stored the feed and veterinary supplies. He'd wait for nightfall to slip back out.

I hoped I was wrong, even if it meant a long wait for nothing. If he knew well enough to be cagey it meant he knew something most of the world had yet to hear about.

In the afternoon the air got warm enough to open a window. We were working on one of those false springs that make you want to break out the backyard grill just in time for another blizzard. Whoever said April was the cruelest month never saw a Michigan March.

Nobody went into or came out of the former apartment house. They don't throw out the first cock of the season until after Easter — for considerations of climate, not religion — so there was no reason for anyone in the game to risk arrest by coming around to inspect the stables. If the Zorborón investigation turned that direction I'd have to break off the stakeout. I had a hunch it wouldn't that day, despite what I'd told the caretaker or whatever he was; the number of blocks separating the old part of the Hispanic inner city from the new, where the murder had taken place, removed it from the high-priority list. The caretaker or whatever he was thought the same thing, apparently, because he didn't seem to be in any hurry to leave either. What Django thought was open to interpretation. At his level of civilization most of his decisions would be organic.

Either that, or he was busy working out the fifth proposition of Euclid. For all I knew he was there on sabbatical.

I was thinking along these lines, and about how many things about them were probably wrong, when a shotgun went off inside the building. The deep unmistakable bellow made me choke on a fig.

ELEVEN

I coughed it loose finally, spat it into my handkerchief, and paused with my hand on the door handle; but nobody came running from any direction. Activity at the parking garage had gone flat in the middle of the business day, and no train had come by in a while, not that anyone inside would have heard even so loud a report over the rattle of wheels and blast of the courtesy whistle while passing the old station, or cared if he did. Pedestrian traffic there was thin at the busiest of times; at the moment it was non-existent.

The revolver went into my right side pocket with my hand on it. I got out, leaned on the door until it shut without much noise, and went up to a window for a peek. That got me nothing, because someone had masked it with brown paper, just like all the others at ground level, to disappoint busy-bodies like me or just to cut down on bright lights from outside and untimely crowing from inside. On the front stoop I turned the doorknob without rattling it, then swung the door open and leapt inside all in one movement, ducking around the wall to avoid being outlined in the doorway. I had the gun out now.

Nobody appreciated the acrobatics, not even the chickens. The ones that were awake glanced my way, then returned to their scratching and grooming.

The first thing I noticed was there weren't nearly as many as there had been. All the lower shelves had been cleared of their portable pens up to the level where a man could comfortably stand and remove them without using a stepladder. That made it a hurry-up operation, or else the shotgun blast had brought it to an abrupt end. They'd concentrated their efforts on the roosters, which represented most of the investment. How it had been done without my suspecting stopped being a mystery when I looked in the direction of the fire door. Its chain hung loose, the padlock open and dangling at the end. They'd simply driven a truck or a van into the alley in back and loaded it from there. The hillbilly must have called to say the cops were coming, and whoever was on the other end hadn't let any grass grow when it came to salvaging most of the merchandise. One of the caretakers would have unlocked the door for the cleanup crew. I hadn't thought about any of that, because I'd been too busy thinking about Nesto Pasada.

Just to be thorough I went to the door and opened it and looked out. The alley was empty now, with the blank wall of another building staring at me from the other side. There were no surveillance cameras.

I closed the door and went back to look at the rest.

The second thing I'd noticed, after the missing roosters, was the old hillbilly lying on the floor with most of his middle torn away. His pale blue eyes were open, but they weren't doing him any good. His entrails and what they'd contained trumped the animal waste and disinfectant for stench. Under that I caught a whiff of roast pork; the shotgun had gone off close enough to scorch flesh. That closeness had prevented the pellets from spreading. A pattern the size and density of a baseball had plowed into his solar plexus, obliterating it and throwing him three feet from the point of impact.

His knife, a stag-handled Buck with the blade open, lay in his calloused palm, stained red back to the hinge.

Django was sitting on the metal folding chair where I'd left him. The shotgun was on the floor between his outward-turning feet in their pinch-toe boots and his chin rested on his chest. His shirt wasn't pink anymore. It was drenched with blood all the way down to the waistband of his jeans. His throat had been cut clear across.

I excused myself to visit an uninhabited corner, but all I managed to bring up were the dry heaves. The tragic fate of Wally the mouse had put me off breakfast, a favor I would never be able to return.

After that ritual came the heavy thinking.

The knife attack had to have come first. Even when the jugular is severed, it takes a man a few seconds longer to bleed out than when most of his digestive system has been destroyed by a shotgun at close range, and then there was the shock of the sudden impact that paralyzes the muscles; in any case the impact itself had driven him out of swinging reach. So Grandpa Duke had slit Django's throat and the Yaqui had reacted from animal instinct. His reflexes were better than his attacker had anticipated, catching him before he could duck out of the line of fire.

That's what someone wanted me to think, anyway.

■ ■ ■ ■

I stood there for a little while with the Smith dangling at the end of my arm, then got to work. It was still a missing-person case, for all the fancy trappings.

There was no place to hide on the ground floor, with all the partitions gone and the steel shelves against the walls. I took the stairs and checked out all the rooms on the next floor and the one after that.

Nothing was locked, not with a couple of highly capable watchdogs like Django and his friend from Dixie on guard. The place smelled musty here, like damp canvas stored in a boat house, and the air was dank and not as warm as outside. Wayne County had ordered the building to be demolished, but it was a long way down on a very long list. Narrow hallways with spongy boards under moldy bits of carpet runner separated the old rental rooms, some of which had been opened up for storage by tearing down the walls between. Doors were missing, electrical wiring and copper plumbing scavenged for scrap, leaving jagged black holes in the plaster, none big enough for even a slender boy to crawl into and hide. I saw stacks of cracked corn in sacks, more sacks of high-quality feed for mixing in, cartons containing antibiotics, wormers, and other pharmaceuticals whose labels didn't carry the name of the vet who'd prescribed them, a cot where the two men who'd looked after the place had slept in shifts. A flat pint three-quarters full of Southern Comfort stood on the floor beside the cot and an antique portable black-and-white TV and converter were set up on an up-ended rooster pen at the foot. Empty fast-food containers waited to welcome the first ants of spring. A flat can of Copenhagen and a pasteboard box held some cigars that looked like twists of black rope. Popocatepetl — I was pretty sure it wasn't Mt. St. Helens — smoldered in a painting reproduced on the lid.

No photographs or documents, no doodles, nothing personal to identify the occupants. They would wash and relieve themselves in the men's room in the parking garage. A camping-out affair, to be left behind at the first sound of a siren swooping into the block. *Una casa de salir,* the Spanish call it: A place to bolt from.

I holstered the gun, untwisted the cap from the bottle, and sniffed at the mouth. No smell of bitter almonds, which was as far as my toxicology training went. Poison would be redundant in that scenario. I rubbed the mouth with the heel of my hand and took a swig. It tasted normal, like peaches fermented in hydrochloric acid, with a kick like rubbing alcohol. The label isn't even classified as whiskey. But it improved my mood. I wiped the mouth again, this time with my sleeve, sealed it back up, rubbed both sides against the gray pillowcase on the cot, and put it back where I'd found it. I unleathered the revolver again.

The last flight of steps led to a narrow kiosk with a door that opened out onto the roof. A gust of icy antiseptic air from the river numbed my face and brightened my outlook further. It smelled of a change in atmospheric pressure, and with it either an early taste of spring or another hefty helping of winter. Either one was an improvement over what I'd left on the ground floor.

Here a litter of Marlboro butts had been smashed underfoot on the gravel and tar. The management would have been sticklers about not lighting up inside and breaking the fighters' training with secondhand smoke. Farmer Zeke — it would be his brand — would stand there burning tobacco, stropping his blade on his old suit pants, and looking out at the sprawl of low buildings and spray of skyscrapers glowering under the smoke from the stacks of the River Rouge plant, where his daddy had riveted M4 tanks for Mr. Ford. He'd belong to that generation. When the time came for his watch, he'd go downstairs and chew snuff when the habit gnawed at him and spit in a can. When Django spelled him he'd watch rolling billboards buzzing around an oval track at the end of the cot, mouth Bible verses along with a character in a twenty-dollar hairpiece and a thousand-dollar suit, and rock himself to sleep with Southern Comfort, dreaming of Jim Crow. I knew everything about him except his name.

Django was harder to peg. A compost heap of dead black cigar butts spoke of a man who preferred to stand still in one spot, maybe comparing the spectacular sunsets in Baja to the sooty glow of Detroit at dusk, but apart from that there was nothing to tell me what he did when he wasn't minding the store. No books or magazines or newspapers suggested one man who didn't like to read and another who'd never learned how. That was a bald guess and probably racist, but there wasn't much demand for literature in the Sierra Madres, and I had no reason to rule out what his partner had told me about his origins. Nothing about the man was remotely Hispanic or Caucasian. That rugged, sinister range contained the last pure races on earth — if your definition of "pure" stood up to their part in feeding America's dope habit. They packed the stuff over the mountains on the backs of mules and burros, sometimes on their own in rucksacks, and guarded it with AK-47s. If his compadre hadn't been kidding me about Django's hatred for gangs, that would be one reason why he'd *salir*ed north.

Why that mattered at all was anybody's guess. I hadn't a crossword puzzle handy to order my thoughts.

No Nesto. I even rapped on walls and stamped on floors, listening for hollows, but the no-nonsense builders who had thrown the place together for what a lot of experts had predicted would be a short war couldn't spare the time or material to make priest holes.

Back on the crime scene I put the gun away, for good this time, I hoped; I was wearing off the plate just taking it out and putting it back.

Anything I did after that would be busywork. A really dedicated detective, of course, would frisk the bodies for ID. I didn't fit that description. Blood's bad enough, but continence is largely a matter of concentration, something the dead aren't known for. Anyway that was a job for specialists. I didn't need trouble with the union.

I looked at the beige rotary phone on the floor in a corner, patently an illegal hookup — mobiles and cordlesses were out in that racket, with any scanner capable of picking up a conversation over the air — but I let what prints might be on it stay where they were and used my cell. It might have been the same 911 dispatcher I got before, but this time I didn't play with her. I knew, when the location was reported, who would respond.

Twelve

"Seventy by the end of the week, the weather wizards say." John Alderdyce took a deep drag and blew smoke at the windshield. It flattened out against the glass and drifted toward the open window on my side of the car. "Snow Monday. Believe it?"

"Where do we live?" I sat with one hand resting on the wheel. I wasn't smoking. I'd burned a quarter of a pack answering questions for the first cops on the scene and my throat felt like an uncured hide. When he'd asked to bum a butt I'd tossed the rest of it into his lap.

"I hate it. Weather sucks, economy sucks, my basement's got a crack in it I can stick my thumb in. I need a new roof before next winter. My third."

"I know a guy who'll do it for five percent above cost, if he makes parole next month."

He wasn't listening. "I've got my thirty in and change. My wife keeps talking about

Miami Beach, but I say Phoenix, where it's dry. That salt air's hell on chrome. I've got my eye on a '72 Vette with ninety-two thousand on the odometer, add ten thousand while it was disconnected. My third midlife crisis in five years."

"I wish you'd stick around. I wouldn't know how to begin breaking in this new breed."

"Learn to text."

"I'm not kidding. I just got Mary Ann Thaler broke in to take your place and then she went over to the U.S. Marshals."

"If you miss her that much, go stick your nose in something federal. Only tell me when you do: I wouldn't want to miss that. What made you think the kid would pick this place to fort up?"

We were sitting in my Cutlass where I'd parked it outside the rooster rookery, Alderdyce in the front passenger's seat with it slid all the way back and tilted, the back of his head against the headrest and his ankles in brown-and-yellow argyles crossed on the dash. Inside, the science guys were scraping up skin cells and playing with spatter.

"Leap of faith," I said. "He called from that phone and there's no place to hide in the train station."

"Number came up?"

"Nope. Plain old-fashioned detective work. The rest was theory."

"Thin."

"Threads always are."

"Hillbilly's name is Roscoe, no shit, Berdoo. Ypsilanti native, parents from Kentucky, both deceased. Inherited his old man's job at Rouge until they replaced him with R2-D2. Rode the high country after that. In his blood; all those Ypsituckians claim lineage back to the original Sons of the Whiskey Rebellion. Did ten years in Jackson for Robbery Armed, the whole deal because he got caught sodomizing an inmate without mutual consent."

"He didn't strike me as the type."

"They don't all turn out for Liza Minelli onstage. Anyway, it's a power play in stir, not a life choice. No sex crimes of a similar nature on his record outside the House of Doors."

"How long was he out?"

"Ten months. That's almost six years in people years. His p.o. had him down as shoveling chicken shit on eighty acres outside Dundee. As these dodges go that was almost honest.

"Used a knife in the robbery," he went on. "Some penny-dreadful stuff apart from that, B-and-E, shoplifting — pint of Crown

Royal under his coat at a Costco — solicitation; he was a bouncer in a cockshop on Michigan Avenue, got six months in County for pulling a knife on a john who was dumb enough to file a complaint. That divorce is still dragging through the courts. I don't think he ever killed anyone before this, but some of his friends did, so he was a fixture at the show-up every time a corpse needed an explanation."

"It's the Berdoo part I have trouble buying. Sounds like a bad haircut." I watched a uniform sneaking a smoke outside the door of the old hotel: three drags and then he went back inside. "I can't say much for his taste in liquor, but that's no reason to blast him into two body bags. You think he killed the Indian?"

"You don't?"

The sun was glowing hunter orange beyond Dearborn. Daylight Savings Time hadn't kicked in. The subject wasn't ripe yet, apparently. I changed it. "What about Django?"

"Don't know him. My guess is after we run him through the computer downtown and the one up in Lansing and then the FBI and Home Security and INS do the same we'll be just as well informed as we are now. He's got ILLEGAL stamped on his forehead.

Undocumented aliens, they call 'em now." The smell of burning rubber filled the car. He made a face and snapped the scorched filter out the window on his side. "If Berdoo killed this Django, he borrowed the shotgun, used it on himself, and stretched out on the floor with the knife tidy in his hand. You know goddamn well he'd've dropped it when the blast took him off his feet."

"If he didn't, it would be because his hand spasmed into a fist. The M.E. would've had to break his fingers to get it loose. So someone put it there. How do you think it went down really?"

"Right now I'm more interested in who put it down and how whoever it was made a couple or three dozen prime fighting cocks disappear while you were watching the front door."

"The second part's easy. I wasn't watching the back because I didn't care about the birds. I do now, because whoever took them killed Berdoo and Django or both — Zorboron too, probably — and Nesto might be a witness to Zorboron. That makes him a liability to someone."

"I like the big mechanic at the garage for Zorborón. Pedro Mendoza's the name. He didn't have to take an alias because Mexico exports more Pedro Mendozas than corn tortillas. He's wanted in Sonora for killing two *rurales* in a firefight over a load of Colombian; he had it, the cops wanted it. Not for evidence. Country's a cesspool. The pricks in Narcotics like him for every kilo that starts out in Juarez and winds up in Grosse Pointe. He's had more fingers up his ass than Kermit the Frog."

"What about the twins?" I remembered the man on the air wrench and his look-alike pounding on a driveshaft.

"Juan and José Pino, of the Guadalajara Pinos. No record, criminal or Immigration. Autistic, the both of them; we got that from another employee who's off today, his alibi checks. Give 'em time, he said, they'll turn a Volvo into a Maserati, but if you send 'em out for the paper they'll come back with a handful of magic beans. When we know who treated them, if anyone did, we'll get a court order for their medical records. Savants have superhuman powers of concentration. When they say they didn't see or hear anything beyond what they were doing inside the garage, and if their history checks out, I believe it."

"Find the gun?"

He shook his head without lifting it from the back of the seat. "Thirty-two, Ballistics says, jacketed round. If he heaved it, we'll find it, and if we don't, we'll collect it when whoever did uses it and we find him, and if we don't, we'll nail Mendoza without it."

"Why'd he kill the Tiger?"

"Zorborón played around with the dope racket for a while, didn't like it and got out. Narcs tossed the garage and his house a couple of times, came up empty. DEA had a go, so far as their attention span stretches. Zip. He was happy with his garage and his roosters. Mendoza wasn't, but his boss wouldn't let him quit and throw in with the Maldados or the Zapatistas. Means, motive, opportunity. The trifecta."

"Mendoza gave you all that?"

"Mendoza gave us *nada.* That's the theory. All we need now's the facts to support it."

"You've got it backwards."

"It's Mexicantown. Black's white, Pat Boone's Elvis. You throw away the book the minute you cross the border."

"Thin."

"This conversation's going in a circle." He sat up, bringing the seat up with him, grabbed the door handle. "Oh, I forgot to say we Googled that thunderbird symbol Zorboron wore, the same one the firebug who touched off his garage had on his lighter. It's Mayan, old as the temples of

Yucatan. Sidebar: Emiliano Zapata adopted it as his personal totem when he rose up against Porfirio Díaz in 1915. The Zapatistas down there still use it, and they protect the copyright. If anyone who isn't bona fide — meaning you fought the government in Mexico City twenty years ago — if he's caught with it on his hide or on something he carries around, it's an instant death sentence."

"What about the ones who call themselves Zapatistas up here?"

"Especially them, and they don't mess with it. That's why they use a *Z* with a bar through it."

"It makes no sense a genuine Zapatista would target Zorborón. He was the real deal."

"That's why we can rule it out. The firebug knew he was on camera; why else would he make sure it never got a good angle at his face? He made sure it got a shot of the lighter, in a hand with a glove on it to hide a tattoo."

"There are other reasons to wear gloves this time of year."

He let that pass. "He wasn't built anything like Mendoza, so Mendoza fixed it up with him to make it look like the Old Country Zaps had fallen out with Zorborón. Probably he stole the lighter from the Tiger himself. He was planning the murder that far back."

"Yeah, he looks like a deep plotter."

"You want a perfect case, watch TV."

"So who's the bug?"

"Well, if my hunch checks and he wasn't wearing that glove to keep his lily-white hands from chapping, he's a Maldado. None of the other gangs in the city wears a tattoo there. We knew they'd make their move against the old guard sooner or later; it's what these walking scrotums do. And he doesn't not look like Nesto."

"Your flesh and blood."

"Chata's. But if he comes forth and we don't have to spend the taxpayers' hard-earned dollars in this economy to drag his narrow butt up Beaubien, he'll get the same break we give all the other punk scum who spare us gasoline."

He opened the door and got out.

I sat there until dusk chased the sun into its hole and the air began to turn frigid; we were headed well below forty for the ninetieth night in a row. I wasn't counting single digits. Then I cranked up both windows and stepped out to stretch my legs, limping a little on the bad one until the circulation found its way as far as the knee.

The neighborhood was settling back into its mulch of boredom. The yellow tape had provided color for a while, but the novelty had worn off. The coroner's van had gone with what was left of Django and Roscoe Berdoo — a country song ought to be written with those names tucked into it — but the resurrectionists were still busy inside the building and would be until the ASPCA showed up to collect the fowl.

The TV satellite trucks pulled out, and the exodus was on. A sergeant with the Early Response Team hung up his mike and drove off. The spectators who always come to rest against the drift fence of police barricades began to lose interest. As I wandered, life tingling with heat in my femoral artery, the diehards turned away one by one and committed themselves to the current.

A lot had happened in a short time. Thirty-four hours ago the biggest thing on my mind was a mouse in my office wall.

The only positive note was what Alderdyce had said about someone framing the original Zapatistas for the arson at the garage. The originals were hardcore and no good news locally if they were moving that far north. On the other hand, if the Maldados were crowding in on the Tiger's turf, the homegrown Zaps wouldn't sit on their haunches and risk losing ground and face. It would be a war of the werewolves, and the phrase "innocent bystanders" had been coined for the people who strayed into the paths of stray bullets.

I had everything that had happened in the chicken coop, but it was too complicated to work through standing still. Whoever had the roosters had the answer.

My cell rang, surprising me; there must have been a sunspot or something to give it some juice. It was Abel Osterling, calling to report what he'd found out about the thunderbird symbol.

"Old Country Zapatistas," I said, before he got too far into office hours. "Cops beat you to it."

"They usually do, despite what you read. Any luck on your runaway?"

"Developments. I wouldn't call them luck."

"You okay? You sound like you've been hitting the bottle and lost on points."

I paused. My well of wit was sucking clay. "You can always make it up in the next round. What do I owe you for the fact-check?"

I didn't know if he heard the question. The phone beeped again, rolled over, and stuck its feet in the air. The line was as dead as downtown.

Last year's grass covered the empty lot I'd parked beside, bent over and broken by months of snow. Something stirred there with a dry rustle. I'd have missed it if I were still on the phone. There was no wind to explain it.

I had one foot inside the car, and now I took it out and folded my arms on the roof and watched the little movement. A historic building of some kind had stood there for a century or so until someone bought it and knocked it down, apparently for no other purpose than to provide the city with another place for rapists to bait their traps and lie in wait. It wasn't dark enough yet for that, so I suspected an urban pheasant or a rat the size of a bobcat. Then I heard something that sounded like a cross between a dry cough and a wet sneeze.

Winter was a long way from over, but the allergy season starts earlier every year. I left the driver's door hanging open and waded out into the weeds, watching for snakes, until I came within a few yards of where I'd seen the tops swaying. I had my revolver out. I didn't think I'd need it, but the last time I'd thought that, I'd paid for it with five weeks in the hospital and two years in physical therapy.

"Come out, come out, Nesto," I said. "Your sister's waiting supper."

THIRTEEN

He was a kid. We tend to forget that, when they're almost fully grown and their voices have changed, and it's always a serious mistake, because when you expect too much of someone there is always resentment, and in his case it was at an age when he had the energy and strength to do something about it and no judgment to balance it. He might lash out or run away. If some kind of weapon is too handy he might do something lethal. Seasoned felons are easier to predict, and you can always shoot them when you guess wrong and take your chances with the authorities. But I didn't put up the gun. That would be taking a chance I couldn't afford.

For a few seconds after I'd called out to him he lay motionless in the grass, a child hoping to confound the monster in his bedroom by becoming invisible under the covers. But I could see his narrow back now in the same flannel shirt and the stingy curve of his rump in loose jeans faded almost white. Then he stirred again and got up in one movement, thrusting himself to his feet without first climbing onto his knees. I envied him his flexibility, but it's a dumb thing to do when the person who called you out is armed. I kept my reflexes on a leash and didn't fire.

"Who are you?"

"The Easter Bunny. Find any eggs?"

"What?"

"Wrong room. Forget it. Who are you hiding from?"

He was in between growth spurts. He looked taller than he was because the last one had outdistanced his body fat, but he hadn't yet caught up with his large hands and feet. He was going to be tall for a Mexican, if they were any kind of clue. A good-looking kid, once he took a bath and changed clothes. His dark hair, defiantly unbrushed, curled over his ears and his face was narrow and dirty and feral-looking, the full lips set tight and the pupils shrunken in his sister's hickory-colored eyes. The sun was at ground level behind me, in his eyes, and he didn't like what he was seeing; narrowed pupils didn't have to mean he was on drugs. But I kept the muzzle trained on his slender middle.

"I wasn't doing anything," he said. His accent was Middle Western, no trace of Spanish.

"Not what I asked."

"Who are you?"

"This isn't *Jeopardy.* I want answers, not questions. Let's go again. See the show?"

He thought about that. "What show?"

"Seriously; again? Okay. Detroit's Finest. They're here all week. Stop wasting time. You heard the sirens."

"I thought they were looking for me. That's why I hid."

An answer at last. I'd begun to give up hope. "Now, why would they be looking for you?"

"I ran away."

"I know. I ran after you."

"Yeah, I thought that was you at the mission. You don't run so good."

"I know when to stop. My name is Amos Walker. I'm a detective."

"Cop?"

"Private. Missing persons is my specialty. Is any of this starting to make sense?"

"Did Chata hire you?"

"I'm working for your uncle."

"My uncle lives in Mexico. We never met."

"Not an uncle, I guess, the one I'm talking about. Your brother-in-law's father. There may not be a word for it. Him you've met."

"No cops in my family."

We weren't getting anywhere, and I was losing the light. If he slipped me again I didn't stand a chance. "It's getting cold. Let's sit in the car and turn on the heater."

"I'm not getting in any car with you."

"If I were a pervert, your pants would already be down around your ankles."

He jumped, blushed; I'd thought that reaction had died along with wearing your underpants out of sight. But he recovered quickly.

"Working for a cop is the same as being a cop. You'll take me in."

"I won't have to, if you walk a block in any direction from this spot."

He shook his head. I let out air.

"Kids. Why do you argue when you know it won't change anything? Get in the car. I'll let you play the radio. No hip-hop, though. All this stimulating conversation is giving me a headache."

"You going to shoot me if I don't?"

"In the foot. Easy target. What do you take, a size ten at least?"

That made his eyes widen. He was young enough to know I wasn't bluffing. Most of us lose that ability when we get old and sneaky. He reached up to pull a long blade of dead grass from under his collar and started around me in the direction of the Cutlass.

"Just a second." I stopped him with my free hand on his shoulder, lowered the gun to my hip, and patted him down. From chest to crotch he wasn't carrying so much as a billfold. I stopped there. A thorough job would include his legs and ankles, but you need a partner for that. I didn't want to catch one of those clodhoppers in the face.

I didn't think he was carrying. It would have been in his hand when he stood up.

"*Un grande desperado,* hey?" he said when I finished and backed away. Where do teenagers get their perfect timing? I wanted to turn him over my knee, but he looked like a biter.

I did some head-shaking of my own. *"Un niño idiota."*

"I'm not a baby!"

"Okay, I was half wrong. Make with the big feet, Murietta."

"Who's that?"

"A man without a head. You'd get along." I gestured with the artillery.

When we were inside the car I returned the revolver to its clip, started the motor, and switched on the heater. He had leg room to spare; Alderdyce hadn't adjusted it when he got out. The boy scratched the back of the hand with an indigo tarantula spread out on it. It was healing. "Your car smells like cigarettes."

"Can't think why." I reached past him for the fresh pack in the glove compartment, unzipped the cellophane, and offered him one. He stared at it and shook his head.

"You're not supposed to do that," he said. "It's against the law."

"Chata didn't tell me you were funny."

He said nothing. If I didn't dial it down I'd lose him.

"You're shooting each other in school hallways. I don't care if you're smoking." I lit one and cracked the window. I turned on the blower and let it drive the cold and damp out of my leg. "Speaking of shooting."

He jumped again.

"You saw him," I said.

"Who?"

"*El Tigre.* Zorborón. Maybe you saw him get that third eye."

"I don't know who that is."

"Not good. Spend any time in Mexicantown, you know the Tiger, by reputation at least. You lie about that, you lied about the other. You need to work on your answers if you plan to run with *bandidos.*"

"Yeah, I saw him. I went there to ask him for a job. He was dead when I opened the door." His voice shook a little.

I got mad for no reason, except a really first-class murderer wouldn't let a youngster walk in on that. They have standards. If he thought he was the one I was mad at, that was okay. I wanted him scareder of me than who he was hiding from.

"They just keep coming," I said.

"What?"

"The lies, *muchacho.* Not even good ones; a good one I can at least appreciate for the effort. You're a carpenter, not a mechanic. And the last person Zorborón would hire is someone wearing that tattoo. What was it really, some kind of initiation?"

He said nothing. It was a shot in the dark — literally; the sun had gone and all I saw were the lights from the dash reflecting off his forehead and cheekbones — but it had struck home.

"Anyone can visit an ink parlor," I said. "They can lose their license when it's a minor without the permission of a guardian, but they're not supposed to use dirty needles either: All those cases of hepatitis started with a toilet seat. Once you get a tat, you have to prove you deserve it. Your uncle John thinks you may have capped Zorborón with that in mind."

"Don't call him that."

I inhaled deep and let it stagger back out. "I have to wonder why you'd be more upset about that than about a cop thinking you killed someone."

"I'm not worried about that. I didn't kill anybody."

"What were you supposed to do, walk in and smack him on the shoulder, then run out? Ever see a western?"

He shook his head after a second. I was confusing him with questions that didn't mean anything. You won't find that in the manual under interrogations, but every cop knows about it.

"Indians used to do that," I said, "count coup. In the movies, anyway. Places like Wyoming and Arizona. I don't know about Mexico. Maybe they were too busy building pyramids. One of a hundred ways to show off your *cojones*."

"It was something like that."

I needed time to process the answer. It was just idiotic enough to be true, if I hadn't given it to him. I shifted gears. "What were you doing in the rooster house? Don't waste breath denying it. You called your sister from that phone over there, and who'd think of looking for a runaway Hispanic hiding behind a bunch of fighting cocks? It's like tracking a stolen cantaloupe to the farmers' market. That's how a kid would think, anyway. Cops look everywhere."

"You know that already, why'd you ask?"

"I was breaking the ice. What did you see before you ducked out?"

He said nothing.

"Anyone see you duck out?"

He repeated himself.

"You didn't come out the front, so you waited until the fire door was unlocked and went out that way. Hid in the alley and circled around while I was inside looking at Django and Berdoo, what was left of them. Then the cops came and you had no place to run, so you dropped to the ground. How much did you see or hear before you left?"

Nothing. He'd gone inside himself, which was a better place to lie low than an open lot. I shifted gears again.

"Let's go back to the garage. What did *El Hermano* tell you to do to let Zorborón know you existed?"

He jumped a third time. He was part jackrabbit. "Who's that, another man without a head?"

I nodded. His body language made more

sense than his speech. “Yeah, I thought it was Guerrera. He’s got taste. Seventh Sunday would have told you to chop his head off and bring it back; *no es sutil,* our Domingo. What was it?”

For a moment I thought he’d returned to that place where I couldn’t follow. Then clothing rustled and he leaned forward, taking his features out of the glow from the dials. He was going for his ankles. I reached back and loosened the Smith; I’d been wrong about other things than how far to frisk. Then he sat back and something glittered in his palm. He wasn’t holding it like a gun or a knife.

I took my hand off my gun, reached up, and switched on the dome light. In that noninfrared light, the enameled thunderbird on the lighter was orange and turquoise.

Fourteen

"Where'd you get it? Don't answer," I said when he opened his mouth. I knew what he would say anyway. I pocketed the lighter, turned off the blower, and put the car in gear.

"Where we going, police station?"

"Home."

"Whose?"

"Yours." I turned on the radio. All I got was a bunch of blowhards taking off on the government. I'd been hoping for salsa. I turned it off.

"Why?"

"Because that's where you live."

"I was going to —"

"Ridiculous extremes. Rack and ruin. Hell in a hand-basket. The Hop. Pipe down or I'll swing this car around and put you back where I found you."

He piped down. He hadn't showered in more than twenty-four hours and puberty makes full use of the glands. I opened the window wider for fresh air.

The whoosh of wind and cold discouraged conversation and helped make my mind a blank. I didn't want to hear anything and I didn't want to draw any conclusions from what I'd heard that would make me a witness against him.

I turned on the radio for the traffic report and took the surface roads. The reporters hovering over the expressways were announcing more clogged arteries than Burger King. Everyone was in a hurry to get home and drown the day in beer. I was too busy babysitting and harboring to join them.

On Outer Drive I pulled into a gas station and up to a pay phone opposite the air compressor. A man's voice answered in Beverly Hills.

"Gerald Alderdyce?"

"That's not my name. Who's calling?" His voice was shallower than his father's, but he'd inherited his telephone etiquette.

I'd forgotten he'd changed his name. I told him who was calling. He interrupted before I could say anything more.

"You're fired, pal. I don't care what John says. He gave up the right to make my decisions for me before I was eighteen."

"Talk to him, not me. I've got your

brother-in-law in the car. If you won't take him, the cops will. He's a witness in three murders."

"What the hell are you talking about?"

"Is your wife there?"

"She's sleeping. She didn't get much rest last night. I won't —"

"I didn't ask you to. Give her another ten minutes. We'll be there in twenty." I slung the receiver back on its hook.

"Jerry's a fucking pain in the ass," Nesto said as we slid back into traffic.

"He's your brother-in-law. It's in the code."

"He thinks I'm going through a phase. Fuck's that mean?"

"It means when you can't get through a sentence without sticking 'fuck' in it."

His sister was standing on the little front porch when we turned into the driveway. She wore a gray Aéropostale sweatshirt with the hood folded back, red shirt, jeans, loafers. She'd pulled her shimmering black hair into a ponytail. When I braked, crunching limestone, the door behind her opened and a big man came out and rested a hand on her shoulder. He was as tall as his father, not as bulky, but every bit as dark as when I'd first known John, like burnished cast iron. His shoulders were broad under a dress shirt open at the collar with the cuffs turned back, tucked into pinstripe slacks; he'd left the office in the place where he hung up his coat and tie and changed into slippers. Something liquid caught the porch light in a glass in his other hand.

Nesto was out of the car before I could get my door open. He trotted up the steps and brushed past his sister just as she stepped forward with her arms open. Jerry turned, opening an angry mouth, but with one hand on his wife's shoulder and the other holding his drink all he could do was say, "Hey!" He was just as articulate as the old man.

"What —" she said, as I reached the porch, and put a hand to her throat, choking herself off. She had circles under her eyes, frown lines bracketing her nostrils all the way to the corners of her mouth. She was still pretty and plump, but she'd aged five years since I'd seen her last.

An interior door closed with a bang.

Jerry said, "I warned him I'd take that door off the hinges next time."

"He's home," she said. "Let's not drive him away again."

I jerked my chin toward the living room. Jerry held his ground for an instant, but his wife's hand on his arm made him step far enough aside for me to squeeze through the door. They were a couple that communicated with touches and gestures.

"So you're Walker." He stood with his back to Jesus, moving the liquid around inside his glass. It was clear, with a couple of tired ice cubes floating on top, rounded at the edges like soap. I smelled pure grain alcohol. They say vodka has no smell, but why should they be right about anything? "I thought you'd have a cauliflower ear at least."

"Don't be rude, Jerry. Can we offer you a drink?"

"Maybe later." I sat down and waved toward the other seats. "Make yourselves at home."

He opened his mouth again, but sat without having his leash tugged. Chata took a place next to him on the sofa, not close enough to lean against him, and rubbed her upper left arm with her right hand, just to be doing something. I doubted she knew she was doing even that. She stopped when I told her all that had happened, repeating some things she already knew, and what I'd gotten from her brother. The muscles in Jerry's jaws stood out like dumbbells. He looked down into his glass, then took a deep swallow.

I took the lighter out of my pocket and stood it on the coffee table. "That's evidence. The lawyer's going to want it."

"Lawyer?" she said.

"Ernesto needs to talk to someone who can't be made to report what he said to the police. I stopped questioning him because I can be made to, theoretically; private investigators can't claim client privilege under the law."

Her eyebrows went up; she'd heard the *theoretically.* "And realistically?"

"Realistically, the cops have tried before and I've been a disappointment to them, but that means jail time. I'm no good to anybody inside. With an attorney in the picture I can refer them to him, and that lets me off the hook."

"Theoretically," Jerry said.

"Theoretically. Math is the only exact science."

"Does disappointing the police mean disappointing my father as well?"

"That's the tough part. He's the client."

Chata said, "But if you tell him what you won't tell the police, and he *is* the police — what?"

"I'll have to dance on the head of that pin when I come to it. Meanwhile, the lawyer will probably insist that Ernesto turn himself in."

"To jail?" Horror clouded her eyes. They were identical to her brother's.

"It's not like prison. Michigan law says jail inmates get a cell of their own, and he'll be booked as a material witness. That means he won't be treated as a common criminal and he'll have protection twenty-four-seven."

"Is he in danger?" she asked.

"He won't see seventeen if he spends one more day on the street."

"So you say." Jerry drained his glass. Ice crunched between his powerful jaws.

"We can always take the chance I'm wrong." I was fed up with him. He came from mulish stock, but his father knew reason when he heard it, even if he didn't follow up. I was ready to take sides in their fight.

She rose. She looked taller now. Some people call that character. There is probably a better word for it in Spanish. "I'll talk to him."

"To his door, probably. Do just as good as if he wasn't on the other side." Jerry swallowed ice.

She went upstairs. He got up. "Let's have that drink."

I stood and followed him into a small clean kitchen with a butcher-block island holding up a bottle of Smirnoff and a bowl of ice. Vodka's not my favorite by a long shot, but I helped myself to a glass and filled it with cubes and splashed clear liquid over it.

He did the same. The ice was still cracking from the shock when he took a gulp, then replaced what he'd drunk. "I didn't sign on for this," he said. "I expected kids — our kids — the terrible twos, teenage rebellion. I figured I could condition myself as I went along. I wasn't ready to deal with all the worst all at once."

I drank. The stuff made my tongue tingle.

He said, "I know what you're thinking."

"Bet you don't."

"It was different between John and me. He tried that tough-love crap right off the bat. That's a last resort. At least I made an effort to understand Nesto. I even thought I was making progress, but kids are good at pretending to know what you're talking about."

"Actually, I was thinking that whoever invented vodka didn't like drinking and didn't want anyone else to like it either. But I think you're right about kids. Lunatics are the same way. They can imitate sane behavior and fool a trained psychiatrist."

"I wouldn't go that far. He isn't a lunatic."

"I'm wrong, probably. I never had a kid."

Chata came back downstairs and found us standing there. "He wants a Mexican lawyer."

"My God." Jerry drank.

She stiffened. "What's that mean?"

I intervened; a mistake, of course. "I know some lawyers who can probably recommend one. Good ones come in all packages."

He barreled on, right over me. "I didn't mean anything. It's just that when you think of hiring a lawyer, 'Mexican' isn't the first adjective that comes to mind."

"As opposed to hiring a bricklayer."

"I'll use your phone if it's okay," I said. "My cell's dead."

I don't know if they heard me. I took myself out of the crossfire and picked up the telephone in the living room. While I was waiting for someone to answer, Jesus smiled sympathetically at me from above the gas fireplace. He had blood in His eyes from His thorn hat.

The lawyer's name was Rafael Buho. *Búho* in English is owl. Poets say owls are wise; ornithologists say they're swift and ruthless predators. The two things aren't mutually exclusive. I figure the family had been founded by a lawyer.

He was a small, soft, alert man with caramel-colored skin, fine graying hair smoothed back from his small face, and eyes that showed white around the irises under brows raised perpetually, so that he seemed surprised by everything he heard. That made him bulletproof in a courtroom; a poker face doesn't mean one that has no expression, just an expression that never changes. You could tell him you'd cut up your sister and mailed her to every zip code or that you'd forgotten to separate your darks from your whites at the laundromat and he'd look just as shocked by the one as by the other. He wore a tiny black moustache shaped like a carpenter's square set at an angle and a powder-blue suit that would photograph white under a strong light. His red-and-white polka-dot bow tie looked like a clip-on, but when you studied it closely you saw it was perfectly tied, all the edges even. An attorney who pays that much attention to the only purely ornamental man's garment is a comfort to his clients.

He could pass for the concierge in a one-star hotel in San Diego, but his hands were a dead giveaway: soft, paraffin-treated, with nails pared round and as white as cane sugar. I wouldn't trust him at blackjack. But the law is a different game. My source, a former federal judge, now a consultant to one of the biggest firms in Detroit — a lawyer who represented lawyers — had told me that Buho could reduce a thirty-year sergeant in Major Crimes to a blubbering penitent on the stand. I disliked him on sight, and as a rule I was prepared to like Mexicans. He was too studiedly humble, which is colossal arrogance of a kind. But I wouldn't place my life in the hands of a lawyer I liked.

He bowed to Chata in the living room, gripping a moleskin briefcase in both hands at his chest like a shield, and asked if there was a place where he could speak with the boy in private.

"I'm his guardian. Anything you have to say to him you can say to me."

"No, *Señora.* I have my oath." His tone was firmer than his actions.

"It's true," I said, when she looked at me. "Unless Nesto says you can sit in."

"He's asked me not to. I thought perhaps his lawyer —"

"Your pardon, *Señora.* Mr. Walker is my client."

"That's so he can tell me what Nesto tells him. It lets me claim privilege. *Señor* Buho confirmed it when I talked to him on the phone."

"Then you can insist I take part," she said.

"You think he'll say in front of you what he'd say to his mouthpiece?"

"I do not like this term." Buho looked bemused. He might have been calling me all kinds of a *puerco* inside.

"Then you can tell me afterwards," she said.

"I can. I probably won't."

"But you'll tell John!"

"I don't know that yet. I already said that."

"Give it up, honey. He's as much a brick wall as my old man." It was the first thing Jerry had said since the lawyer had arrived. He sat on the sofa with his knees spread and his glass cradled in both hands between his thighs. His eyes were out of focus and he missed half his consonants.

"He's my brother! You talk as if I haven't any rights."

Buho bowed again. "You grasp the situation very well, madam." He seemed to be able to turn the Antonio Banderas accent off and on. A smart lawyer has more skins than an onion.

She called off the assault. "His room's the first door on the left, top of the stairs." She sounded as tired as she looked.

"Thank you. I should like to speak with Mr. Walker first, in private also."

She didn't even react to that except with a tiny nod that might have been her chin quivering. Buho and I went into the kitchen. No door separated it from the living room, so we kept our voices low. I told him everything I'd learned, went over with him the questions I wanted answered, and let him examine the lighter. He hefted it on his palm, turned it upside down to read ZIPPO engraved on the bottom, ran his thumb over the raised enamel design on the side. For good measure he flipped it open and spun the wheel, getting a spark but no flame, snapped it shut.

"The fluid, it evaporates even when you don't use it. You think it is the same lighter from the video?"

"That's one of the questions I want you to ask Nesto."

"Is a complicated affair, no?"

"Is a complicated affair, yes. And stop talking like the Cisco Kid. You were born in Santa Fe, so was your father and grandfather, and you went to Harvard. I like to know all about a man before I do business with him."

He smiled, showing a row of teeth so white and even you couldn't see the divisions between at first. I didn't count this as a genuine expression any more than the eternal surprise. "Okay, fella," he said. "I'll go up and see the kid."

FIFTEEN

He was alone with Nesto forty-five minutes. It would work out to ten minutes of solid questions and answers and a half-hour of art. That left five minutes of silence; but silence is an art also.

I spent the time watching television with Jerry and Chata. The program happened to be a National Geographic special about interesting aquatic fauna. I doubt when it wrapped up that any of us could repeat anything we'd learned about life at the bottom of the wine-dark sea, except that it bore a disturbing resemblance to Mexicantown. Jerry had finished drinking and sat glassy-eyed and silent. I pegged him as an amateur with beginner's luck; a dedicated alcoholic would have slid under the coffee table ten minutes into the androgynous world of the sea horse. I nursed my second vodka, the fastest-acting and sneakiest of distilled poisons. It made hail-fellows-well-met of axe murderers and horny Vikings of Baptist lay readers.

Buho and I reconvened, alone with our hosts' permission, at a glass-topped table on a poker chip–size deck in the backyard. A pair of coach lamps mounted on either side of the glass doorwall coaxed a number of tough tiny moths into self-immolation. They were doomed anyway, because outside those auras of intense heat, sitting there was like picnicking on the Aleutians. I turned up my collar against the frigid breezes that whipped around the corners of the house, but Buho was plainly suffering in the cold. His nose was cherry-colored and he shivered visibly, without a word of complaint.

"That's one scared *muchacho,*" he opened. "He's all right, I think."

"In general, or in sworn testimony?"

"In general. He's no killer. He's a pretty good liar, but aren't they all at that age."

"Youth isn't for wimps. So much for philosophy. Give me something I can use."

He opened a cigarette case made of black silk stretched over a frame, aluminum or bamboo, and offered me something brown with a gold tip. I don't know where they get them; probably through the mail from some reservation so they don't have to pay state taxes. I shook my head and stuck a Winston between my lips. "I like my poison slow."

He shrugged — an elegant gesture in his culture, insolence personified in mine — and lit us both up off a butane lighter that shot a blue flame two inches high, endangering his toy moustache. His brand smelled like autumn — downwind of a city incinerator. "He's telling the truth about Zorborõn. Luis Guerrara put him up to returning that lighter. It belonged to *El Tigre* originally, according to The Brother. Lighters, they are always being misplaced, yes?"

"*Sí.* You're forgetting our conversation. Save the pidgin English for the tourists."

"I underestimate gringos. It's a failing." He blew smoke at the wind, which took it and tore it to shreds. "It was a warning of some kind: If we can lift your lighter from under your nose and use it to destroy your business, we can destroy you as easily. This convinces me the Maldados were not involved in his murder. Why warn a dead man?"

"He ignored the warning."

"The timeline was too tight. If they are in protection, they know these things need to sink in."

"A rogue gang member, maybe. A lot of Mexicans are part Indian. The tribes elected their chiefs. They didn't coronate them.

They went their own way when they didn't trust their counsel."

"I think you've been reading Mari Sandoz too much. Most *mestizos* don't know her from Marie Osmond. But you're right in principle. There is no allowing for the actions of the individual. However, I think we can eliminate Guerrara as a prime mover in Zorborón's fate."

"You can. I'm keeping my options open. What happened in the coop?"

"The boy says he sneaked past the two caretakers and went upstairs to wait for sundown before making his way home. He couldn't be sure he wasn't seen near the garage, or what he might have seen when he approached it. He had no idea when he'd find opportunity to leave. When the fire door was opened, he took advantage of the situation and slipped out — unobserved, so he thinks. He took cover behind some trash cans in the alley, and when the time seemed right he ran, straight to the overgrown lot where you found him. The arrival of the police kept him there until the coast cleared. That would be the moment you stumbled on him."

"I stumble a lot." I flicked ash into the wind. "There were no trash cans in that alley."

He smoothed his moustache with a knuckle. "You're certain of this?"

"I looked out into it after I stumbled over Django and Berdoo."

"These, I take it, were the two men you found dead. He said he knew nothing about that. He didn't even hear the shotgun blast. By then he might have been lying in that lot." He frowned. "I wish I'd known about these phantom trash cans before I spoke with him."

"I didn't know he'd say he hid behind them. I deliberately didn't grill him until I had the rule of law to stand in front of me."

He smiled, showing that row of teeth like poured concrete around a reservoir. "You've an impressive knowledge of legal terminology for a layman."

"I've got cable. Stop oiling me up. What's next?"

"It's early to speak of a defense strategy. Normally in cases such as this I explore the home environment, but I could not draw him out on that subject."

"It's lousy, just like everyone else's."

"Please do not presume to speak for me. I was the only surviving child in a devout Catholic household, and doted upon shamelessly. I had to learn humility the way a high school dropout acquires his GED."

I figured he'd cheated on the final. Aloud I said, "The sister's indulgent and the brother-in-law —"

"Yes. I observed the brother-in-law."

"I was going to say 'doesn't have a clue.' Drinking's not his problem, apart from not knowing how to do it. His father took the other tack. That worked out about as well as you can imagine, so he's just sitting out the kid's puberty and waiting for Mr. Miyagi to come along and put him right."

"He's a family friend, this *Señor* Miyagi?"

I couldn't tell when he was monkeying around, so I let that one swing. "What you do in court's your headache. I meant what do we do with Nesto? That father I mentioned is my client. He's also a cop. Guess which one kicks in when he finds out I found the boy and he was on the scene of a double homicide he happens to be investigating?"

"I should think it would be unpleasant." He shook his head. "In matters such as these, a man who prides himself upon his professionalism would be inclined to treat the boy as he would any other subject. This in my opinion would be a mistake. He wouldn't last an hour in County."

"He wouldn't last an hour in Beverly Hills once word gets out."

"I can get him a room in the Boys Training School in Whitmore Lake. The young men there are more interested in getting out and getting back to their misdemeanors than shivving a fresh fish."

"I told his sister and brother-in-law he'd be safe in County."

"I wouldn't take the chance. Based on what you just told me, he knows more than he lets on, and it stands to reason someone out there knows it as well. The word, as you put it, is out already, or I do not know my neighborhood. What is one more jail house tragedy in our sad community?" He sighed smoke, crushed out his butt fastidiously on the glass table, and lit another off his pocket blowtorch. The tobacco, or whatever it was, burned as fast as dry straw. "You must not take this as legal advice. If you repeat it, I shall of course deny it. I have a license to preserve."

"Me, too. People forget that. The advice, *Señor* Buho. I'm not paying you out of pocket to flap your arms."

"This is a saying, yes?"

When I gave him the blank wall, he flushed under the brown and lapsed back into American. "Your client's a policeman. You'd be within bounds if you laid all this before him; let him make the decision."

"That's a hell of a load to dump on a friend."

"I wasn't aware you were friends."

"It's complicated. What else you got?"

"Again, this isn't professional counsel. Do nothing."

"I could come up with that myself for free."

"I see I must be specific, at the risk of my livelihood." The taste of what he was smoking had gotten to him. He pressed out the fresh one next to the old butt and committed his last drag to the wind. "You've fulfilled your mission, which was to return this boy to his guardians and convince him as to the toxic nature of gang activity. Recent events have seen to the last, or I'm no judge of human behavior. Your job is done. Walk away from it."

I shook my head.

"I will not argue the point. I owe the success of my modest practice to human nature, after all."

"I know your rates. What do you call substantial?"

"As I said, a difficult language." He got up and tucked his briefcase under his arm. "I called the police."

"I don't think I like that."

"As an officer of the court I had no

choice. I told them the boy knows nothing, but that he will be there bright and early tomorrow morning with me by his side."

"I'd love to have been in on that call."

"I've had unpleasant conversations before, and the boy needs rest. I said if they insisted on seeing him immediately, all they'd get would be silence on the advice of counsel. He is a minor, and entitled to certain protections under the law. I added that I've represented the ACLU and the Hispanic League, and that I have brought action before on behalf of my people. The police know me as a man of my word."

"I bet that's just how they put it." Nesto had good instincts, whatever other reasons he had for insisting on being defended by one of his own. The race card carried so much weight in Detroit it ought to be registered along with firearms and explosives. "Okay if I talk to him?"

"You don't need my permission. I'm not his attorney, although naturally I let the officer I spoke to assume what he wanted to. As yours, I'd advise against it. Anything you learn from the young man would not be protected. Wasn't that the reason you retained me in the first place?"

"I wanted a lawyer in the picture, not around my neck. I need to know what the boy knows or I can't go ahead."

He grinned again, then returned to his look of innocence personified. "Here is my card. I think you have more need for me than he."

I looked at it: They were printing them vertically now, to make room for landlines, cell phones, e-mail, and Web sites. Amazing how much information you can get onto a scrap of pasteboard without including anything you could use.

Sixteen

After Buho bowed and left, I said I wanted a few minutes with Nesto. His sister crossed her arms. "He's exhausted and filthy. Come back tomorrow when he's rested."

I wanted him too tired to tell any more lies, but I came up with a reason that wouldn't get me thrown out of the house. "It's in his best interest to talk to me before he talks to the police. They won't care if his face is washed."

"Isn't that why you got a lawyer?"

"Five minutes."

She glanced at Jerry, who was sitting in that same splayed position on the sofa with his chin on his chest. No help there. "Five minutes. I'll fill the tub."

He wouldn't be a teenager without a sign tacked to his door. This one was diamond-shaped yellow cardboard reading CUIDADO in black block letters. I knocked.

"Who is it?"

"Walker."

"Go away."

"Not an option."

"Go away!"

I tried the knob. It was locked. "If we talk here, you won't have to tell the cops the same lies you told the lawyer. Ever try lying to a cop? I don't recommend it."

After a long silence, bedsprings shifted. The lock clicked. He was sitting on the edge of the bed by the time I let myself in, wearing the black T-shirt he'd had on under the flannel shirt, dirty socks on his feet. He'd washed his face, but his eyes were red-rimmed and his mouth was sullen. The room was just big enough for the bed, a nightstand, and a student desk and chair. A lean, muscular Brazilian was kicking the stuffing out of a soccer ball on a poster taped to a wall. The look on his face said it was stuffed with rocks.

"Your sister only gave me five minutes," I said. "I don't want to waste any of them listening to the same horseshit you fed Buho. You want to make up stories? Save them for your dentist. You can always buy false teeth."

"I didn't lie."

"He'd have gotten the truth out of you if he knew there weren't any trash cans for you to hide behind in that alley."

He started. His face turned as red as his eyes. I wish all the liars I had to pry open had the decency to blush when they were caught out.

He looked away. "It might not have been trash cans. I didn't take notes."

"Maybe it was that stack of boxes."

"Yeah. Come to think of it."

"You stink at this, you know it? And I'm playing on your team. Think what a tired sergeant with a heavy caseload could do with what you gave him. There were no boxes either. No trees, no window drapes, no Chinese screen, no cloak of invisibility. If you ducked behind anything, it was the truck they were loading with rooster cages."

He jumped at that, too, but his lips formed the start of another lie. I cut him off. "Cops are simple organisms. If you don't give them the bird in the bush, they'll close their fists on the one in hand, that bird being you. Too metaphorical? How's 'tried as an adult' sound?"

He bit his lip. He was acting now, but he knew I knew. A puff of air would blow him over.

I puffed. "You couldn't miss it. It had to be a big truck."

"I saw a truck," he said. "A big one."

"Spoiler on the cab? Mud flaps with naked women on them?"

"I don't remember anything like that."

I nodded. I was prepared to believe him now. A desperate liar will jump at almost any bait.

"The old guy in the building took the chain off the door. I came down from upstairs, he didn't see me pressed up against the end of one of the metal shelves. The other one, the Mexican, was watching the front. The old guy went out the alley door and I went out right behind him. He didn't turn around or he'd've seen me. The truck was just stopping. I don't think whoever was in the front looked in his mirrors. I don't know for sure, but when I slipped around behind the back and ran out of the alley, nobody yelled at me. I stood in a doorway for a while, but then I heard somebody unlocking it on the other side and I took off for the grass lot.

"It was too open. I didn't know who might see me, a cop or somebody, maybe one of the guys from the rooster place or the truck, so I hit the dirt. I thought I'd wait for dark, but it was a long time coming. I don't know how long I was there before I made up my mind to jump up and take my chances. I'm pretty good on my feet; I tried out for track, made the scrub team. But then I heard sirens and I figured somebody had spotted me and they were coming for me, so I stayed put, until —"

"I was there for the rest," I said. "What else did you hear besides sirens?"

"I don't know, city noises. I didn't hear a gunshot, if that's what you're getting at. I didn't know about what happened in that place till you told me."

I didn't know if I believed him, but our time was almost up. "What do you remember about the truck? I'm not asking about spoilers and mud flaps."

"It was a truck. Big and square. Not a semi; the cab and the box were in one piece. It was old. There was rust on the fenders. I can't tell you what kind it was, the year it was made. I don't know much about cars and like that."

"Any markings?"

"No. I mean, no words. Some scraps of paint still on the box. Some kind of picture. Balloons? Red and blue and yellow."

"Sounds like a lot of truck just for balloons."

"I'm telling you what I saw."

"How many in the cab?"

"I don't know. I couldn't see on account of the angle."

Someone knocked on the door. "You have to go, Mr. Walker." It was Chata's voice. "He needs to clean up and rest. Mr. Buho's coming for him at seven A.M."

I leaned in close and dropped my voice. "Tell it to the police the same way you told it to me. Don't embellish. If they think you lied about one thing they'll assume you lied about everything else. You may think you're pretty good about keeping things from your sister and your brother-in-law, but they want to believe you. Don't count on that with Jerry's father. Cops aren't related to anyone when they're on the job. They expect lies and they go after them like rat terriers."

"Mr. Walker," Chata said.

Nesto said nothing. He was staring at his sweaty athletic shoes on the floor. One of them lay on its side.

I said, "I need to hear an okay."

"Okay."

"Okay."

Out in the hall I told Chata, "He's all yours. Let him leave a light on tonight if he wants."

"I've never known him to complain about nightmares."

"You'd better hope he has them tonight. If he sleeps like a baby after today, you've got a young psychopath on your hands."

■ ■ ■ ■

I waited until I got home before I called John Alderdyce. He was still in his office in the old precinct house where Homicide had moved to escape the political and physical corruption at 1300.

"I've been calling you all night," he said. "The only place I didn't get voice mail was at your house. There it just kept ringing."

"My cell turned into a pumpkin." I told him what Nesto had told me.

"Why'd he leave the truck out the first time?"

"I didn't ask. In his place, not knowing any more than he did, I'd think twice before I ratted out anyone who had access to those roosters."

"That's more than I got from Buho. I don't get mad at lawyers anymore. It's like yelling at orange barrels on the highway. But if the boy isn't here when we open up, I'm calling out the cavalry. I can't cut him slack the way I could someone else."

I'd never heard him explain himself before. "He'll be there. He didn't kill anyone. He blushed when I caught him in a lie."

"I've seen plenty of killers blush. One of 'em embarrassed himself into two consecutive life sentences. What about the fire?"

"He says he never saw the lighter until Guerrera gave it to him to wave under Zorborón's nose. I couldn't get any color out of him on that. It's a misdemeanor, if you want to make anything of it. I don't see how you could jack it all the way up to felony arson. It was a prank."

"Soaping windows is a prank. No one ever got burned beyond recognition from a prank."

"I didn't say it was smart. But any p.d. could plead it down to a hundred hours of community service."

"I'll make sure he doesn't know that if he wants to dick around. That balloon story sucks."

"Could've been something else. He says scraps of paint were all that was left."

"I want the truck. I don't give a damn about the roosters, but whoever took 'em made sure Berdoo and Django didn't tell anyone where it went or who sent it."

"Whoever it was wasn't covering up a cockfighting ring. It's connected with the Zorborón kill."

"The chief wants this one over. Last thing we need is a zoot suit riot."

"He said that?"

"He's a student of criminal history. That's

who's running things now. Job's too cerebral for a cop."

The conversation was losing steam. We ended it.

I went on sitting in the armchair until my leg began to seize up. It was trying to pass a baseball through the big artery. A drink would help, but I needed to put something in my stomach for it to sit on. In the little kitchen I found a slice of cheese and half a loaf of bread. I never got the twist tie off. I was going for the phone when it rang. It was Alderdyce, who'd figured out the same thing I had, and without the visual aid.

It's a big old wreck of a building now, in a city overcrowded with derelict structures, but for decades it had provided most of the bread for America's breakfast toast and peanut butter sandwiches. "Helps build strong bodies twelve ways," the slogan said; it's hardwired into every baby boomer's memory, along with the Lord's Prayer and the theme from *Gilligan's Island.* It was all white bread then, the dough whipped and pureed to eliminate all those unsightly holes and turn it into library paste between your molars. The steel stencil sign that had greeted visitors driving down the John Lodge Expressway — greeted them backward, because when it was placed there, most of the motorists entered the city through surface streets running in the opposite direction — had been taken down when the Motor City Casino moved in, but now that that enterprise had decamped for a building of its own construction, even the neon replacement had vanished. The signs had contributed most of its charm.

There was no sane reason for me to visit the factory. I don't believe in psychic aura. But I thought rearranging my regular route to the office in order to drive past it might bring inspiration.

It didn't. The fleet of trucks Wonder Bread had employed to deliver its goods was gone, sold for scrap or to community libraries for bargain prices or donated outright to them for conversion into bookmobiles. The big square boxes, with no partitions separating them from the drivers, lent themselves to shelving half a mile of books for borrowing by rural and small-town residents who had no libraries within easy traveling distance.

But bookmobiles have gone the way of the Detroit bread factory. Expressways have made driving more convenient, and the district library system has made it possible for most communities to designate brick-and-mortar venues for the books to circulate on a rotating basis. There are more places to buy books, too, and Americans prefer to own things rather than bother themselves with returning them. So most of the big diesel dinosaurs have wound up in junkyards and small kitchen appliances and their garage space gone to DVDs and video games.

Wonder Bread. Helps build strong bodies twelve ways during the formative years. Look for the one with the balloons on the package.

"Gives us something to look for," Alderdyce had said the night before when he'd called. "There aren't many of those old stink-pots left on the road, and the Secretary of State's office can trace the registrations of those that are. This isn't for publication," he added. "The minute the bastards know we're looking for it, they'll drive it straight into Lake St. Clair and jump to Canada."

"Not before they stow the cargo. Those roosters are a big investment. One champion's worth five of those trucks. They need a place big enough to hold them, and it's got to be a place where the clucking and squawking won't be heard, or at least make anyone curious. Where they were, nobody much cared. But that was before double murder was involved."

"Yeah. Good thing there aren't many chicken farms in the state of Michigan. We can finish the barn tour before the next census."

"Which makes the bread truck that much more important."

"Nesto, too. We better hope he's right and nobody saw him in that alley."

Every case — if it doesn't resolve itself in an hour or a day — is like a newspaper maze. You drag your pencil between a pair of promising lines only to run into a dead end and have to start over between a different pair of lines. I'd run out of them. I sat in the office, but I didn't go back to reorganizing the files. Turning over dead leaves seemed redundant. I waited for something to happen, a bulb to light up above my head or the telephone to ring with a bombshell clue or the captain of a tramp steamer to stagger across the threshold and fall over dead and dump the key to the whole thing on the floor. While I was waiting I called Chata. Ernesto, she said, had left with Buho an hour ago and was still with the police. She'd wanted to accompany them, but the lawyer had said it wasn't necessary, that she was of more use to herself doing whatever she did at home than stagnating in a waiting room, because there was no way she would be allowed to sit in on the interview, either by the police or by him. Animals in zoos behave differently from animals in the wild and people give different answers when family is present.

After we finished talking I checked voice mail, but there were no brainstorms there, not even an attempt to sell me a time share in a condo in Florida. I smoked a cigarette, staring at the door and willing it to open. I made sure the buzzer was working. When I got tired of all that I called Alderdyce's office to find out if the interview was over.

"We're holding him for now." He sounded tired. It wasn't unusual for him to stay up all night on an investigation that *didn't* involve him personally. "Material witness, for his own protection. I think he's told us everything he knows, but they don't; whoever *they* are. You just caught me on my way out. If you want to make yourself useful, meet me across from Holy Redeemer."

That stumped me until I remembered what had brought me there last. "Sister Delia's?"

"Yeah. Look for the place with fire engines in front of it."

Seventeen

The blaze was far enough along that the fighters were letting it burn. They'd done as much damage as they could with their axes and gushers and shifted their attention to the nearby buildings, spraying the walls and roofs with hoses to prevent them from catching fire. Holy Redeemer, up the street from the scene and across from it, avoided their notice. It might have been standing in a time warp for all it belonged to that fragile neighborhood.

The storefront hadn't that advantage, although it was nearly as old. Nothing remained but the iron façade, which was glowing in spots, and whatever was inside that was still feeding the flames. They stretched twenty feet above the caved-in roof, a twisting yellow-and-orange plume pouring black smoke into the overcast and reflecting off a quarter-acre of shattered glass from the plate windows. The engine crews bustled about in gas masks and glow-in-the-dark slickers, boots crunching the broken glass — they sounded like miniature icebreakers — no movements wasted; when a piece of burning goo landed on a coat sleeve and started licking at the resistant material, a firefighter passing by with an extinguisher paused long enough to blow it out like a birthday candle, then moved on. The man wearing the coat flicked two gloved fingers at the visor of his helmet and went in the opposite direction, trailing smoke from the sleeve.

Alderdyce was in conference with a pair of uniforms and a plainclothesman I didn't know in a leather trench coat and snap-brim hat, so I strode around the gawkers and approached the acid-green EMS unit parked against the curb. The attendants were trying to talk Sister Delia into letting them load her aboard. She was strapped to a gurney, in no position to make a fight of it, but they couldn't by law take her anywhere without consent. Her short-haired head, not constrained, shook from side to side.

"Do I look like I need treatment?" She sounded calmer than she appeared; her eyes were white around the irises in a drawn face with smudges of soot on cheeks and chin. "Get me out of this thing."

"You need those burns looked at." The woman in an attendant's uniform spoke in a peeved, singsong tone; she'd had this argument before.

I saw then Delia's hands were bandaged as far as the wrists.

"They're second-degree," she said.

"Third."

"You want to try for first? We're not haggling over a used car. I've had nurse training. I'll put Unguentine on them and it won't cost me twenty-five bucks a smear."

"You're in shock."

"You think? It happened somewhere between the time someone lobbed a Molotov cocktail through the window and my clothes caught on fire."

The other uniform, a male younger than his partner, said, "A lot of people at the scene of an accident think they're just fine. Then they collapse after we leave."

"Accident? What part of 'Molotov cocktail' didn't you understand? Look, give me a release and I'll sign it. Just get me out of this Soap Box racer."

Alderdyce came over while they were unbuckling the straps. He'd overheard some of the conversation. "You can take the nun out of the Church, but —" He grinned; in his case it was just facial hydraulics.

"She's not a nun," I said. "She's St. Joan at the head of the hundred-and-first airborne. What's the story?"

"First responder got everything out of her before EMS showed up. She was working, she says, didn't hear or see anything before the bottle came through the window, and after that she was busy putting herself out. What was that you said about the Maldados taking on the leaders of the community?"

"I was spitballing. A crackpot theory's better than none. Someone keyed the sister's car, someone set a match to *El Tigre*'s garage. Draw a triangle anywhere on the city map, you'll find two of the same or worse."

"It's worse. Arson squad's got witnesses — to the fire, not how it started. Nobody saw anybody, but based on how fast the place went up, some new kind of accelerant was used, three–four times more volatile than high octane. I can't pronounce it, but according to them if she'd been sitting in her usual place, she'd be giving God an earful instead of those attendants." He turned Delia's way. She was free now, sitting on the edge of the gurney rubbing circulation back into her arms. The bandages looked worse than the injury. The pain of severe burns would be settling in and she wouldn't be so concerned with where her blood was in her body.

I put a hand on the inspector's arm. "Give me first crack. She didn't leave the Church because she's a fan of authority."

"That'd be like preaching to the converted. Have at her. She already thinks King Herod was the chief of the Jerusalem Police." He left to greet the fire marshal, who was just unfolding his six-feet-four from the front seat of the snazzy red station wagon he rode in during parades.

"I thought the lake of fire was for nonbelievers," I told Sister Delia.

She looked up at me, shielding her eyes against the sun with a bandaged hand. "The wanderer in the wilderness," she said. "Chasing fire engines now?"

"Just wandering. Town's running out of landmarks."

"I don't care so much about the building. This place is full of empty storefronts; if we could figure out how to export them, we'd be back on our feet in a year. I can't reconstruct those files. There are people who need help and people in a position to help them, and their names went up with the internal and external hard drives and the papers. I had them all in one place. Talk about blind faith."

The female attendant cleared her throat. "You need to take this conference someplace else. The gurney's for patients."

I offered Delia the crook of my arm. She grabbed for it automatically with a hand, drew her breath in sharply between her teeth, and hooked her arm in it instead. I exerted very little pressure and she was on her feet. She's nearly as tall as I am, and strung with steel wire.

We crossed the street away from the emergency traffic and sat on the steps of Holy Redeemer. She looked at her hands. "I've never been vain about my nails, that kind of thing. I took it all for granted. I hope there's no scarring."

I took one hand gently, peeled back adhesive tape and folded back gauze. "Blisters is all. Your mother was right: Put butter on them and leave 'em alone."

"My mother was a Holy Roller; she only pretended to convert. She threatened to disinherit me when I got my hair cut."

"You're running out of churches to drop out of. What happened in there?" I tilted my head toward the burning building.

"I didn't see it. I was writing genteel blackmail letters to prospective donors and got up to get some envelopes from the supply closet. They tell me if I hadn't done that" — she shrugged — "anyway, the front window crashed and the place was in flames. I tried to get to the desk to salvage what I could. That's when my blouse caught on fire." She plucked at a sleeve where the material had been cut away by the paramedics. "It fused to the flesh. Natural fabrics for me from now on."

"How many people know when you're in the office?"

"Only everybody in the neighborhood. But I'm not important enough to murder."

"What's important varies from person to person. They didn't need a state-of-the-art accelerant to take down a vacant building."

"Amos, I didn't know anything could catch fire that fast, I mean the whole place in an instant. I'd swear it was napalm."

"Pretty sophisticated for someone who started out by keying your car."

"Do you think they're connected?"

"Maybe. They went from a little scrap fire at Zorborón's to first-degree murder."

"I heard about that. I won't be attending his memorial service, but I wouldn't wish that on anyone, including my worst enemy. Which he was."

"He didn't have any more control over what's been going on here than you did. This new breed is too close to what's happening down on the border. Zorborón was just a symbol. They tipped him over to make their point: This isn't your father's Mexicantown."

She shivered a little. She wasn't dressed for a Detroit street in late winter. I left her for a moment to beg a blanket off the EMS team, came back and draped it around her shoulders. She smiled thanks and drew it together at her throat. She was acclimating herself to the pain in her hands.

"Was that on the level about the gangs selling protection?" I asked.

"Street talk. No one approached me."

"They wouldn't, if all they were interested in was taking you out of the picture. The Tiger didn't say anything about it, so I'm assuming they didn't try to sell him either. Why waste your pitch on a carcass? Who's running the Zapatistas these days?"

"What makes it them and not the Maldados?"

"I talked to *El Hermano.* I'll talk to him again. I was asking you about the Zaps."

"They take turns."

I looked at her.

"I'm serious," she said. "Whoever's in charge depends on whether the rank-and-file are satisfied with the job he's doing. They model themselves after the Old Country Zaps: True Marxists don't believe in centralizing leadership. They take a vote on everything, and if someone dissents, he goes his own way, no consequences. Trying to talk to them is like taking a swing at Jell-O."

"That Indian thing again. Marx was a Johnny-come-lately. But what happened here and at the garage weren't committee decisions."

"What about the rooster house?" she asked. "I heard about that this morning."

"I don't know. It feels different somehow. Not Maldado, and not Detroit Zaps. I could be wrong."

"A third wheel?"

"I could be wrong," I said again. "My leg says different."

"I see you limping on it sometimes. I've been curious about it."

"An old mistake. These days it only acts up when I live wrong or something doesn't hang together. I always had it, I guess. It's just gone into the bone and curled up there."

"Where I came from we called it divine guidance."

"Kind of like what made you go to that supply closet."

"That was dumb luck. Part of the trick is knowing the difference."

"Got a place to stay?"

"I have a room. I only slept in the store when I worked late. When I've had some rest maybe I'll be able to reconstruct some of those files from memory. When Arson's through maybe they'll let me stir among the ashes."

"They'll have them all sorted out for you. Those boys get plenty of experience every Devil's Night."

"Apart from that I'll start from scratch. Someday I may even find it in my faith to forgive the rotten sons of bitches."

When I left her, a heavyset blonde with big eighties hair was doing a stand-up in front of a TV camera. She managed to crowd "conflagration," "holocaust," and "inferno" into one sentence.

Alderdyce was just finishing up with a reporter from another station. When the lights went out I told him what I'd gotten from Sister Delia. I threw in the third-party speculation at no charge.

"Let's keep that a wild guess," he said. "We got plenty to work with as it is. We kicked Mendoza over to INS this morning. He's their jurisdiction now, theirs and Mexico's over those two dead *rurales* a while back. He didn't do his boss."

"Wild guess?"

"His hands and clothes tested negative for gunpowder residue. He didn't have time to wash up and change and ditch his old clothes and get greasy again between the time Zorborón was shot and you found him."

"Where are you holding Nesto?"

"We're not. Buho sprang him. He plays bridge with a judge. I asked Chata to keep the boy home a few days. It didn't take much persuading. I put a car in front of the house. I doubt this bunch would try anything that far outside the neighborhood, but I've been wrong more often about what *won't* happen than about what will."

"Anything on that bread truck?"

"Not yet. Secretary of State's priorities aren't ours."

"Mind if I look into that end?"

"You play bridge too?"

"Not with Lansing. My source wouldn't pass a civil service background check."

"Too much information. Have fun. Just come to me with what you get."

"Don't I always?"

He inserted a thumb under his necktie and turned the dimple into a blister; dimples offended his sense of order. "Jesus, I'll be glad when this one's finished and I can go back to hating your guts."

EIGHTEEN

Petey Kresge had been holding down a corner booth in the Sextant Bar on Lafayette since before cell phones. In the old days he'd had a line installed so he could take and place calls without leaving the table and the pitcher of beer that was always on it, just like the old-time news hawks whose black-and-white photos decorated the walls in their fedoras with cigars in their kissers; the place was a five-minute walk from both the *News* and *Free Press* buildings — the originals — and from Prohibition until the Joint Operating Agreement reduced both papers to daily shoppers, if you'd hung out there and kept your ears open you'd have known tomorrow's headline and saved yourself a nickel.

That's history; so's Detroit. Today's journalists — the ones who still write for print — drive home straight from the office and their phones don't ring in the middle of the night. That's good for family, but it's taken all the sense of anticipation out of fishing the paper out of the bushes, and even that happens only three times a week now.

Petey claimed relation to the family that founded Kresge's Department Store, later Kmart, but the rest of the family hadn't gone along with the claim, so he made rent forging vehicle registrations in cases where the VIN on the engines didn't match the numbers on the chassis. It paid well in the town that invented carjacking. I was banking on the theory that whoever had arranged a bread truck for a chicken run wouldn't have gone through the Michigan Secretary of State's office and risked leaving a paper trail.

If you didn't know him you'd think him younger than he was by ten years, a slender lad with a long jaw always working at a wad of gum under a Red Wings cap, who didn't need a razor more than every other day. His eyes were blue and clear and he had less than 10 percent body fat. Beer was his only vice, and he could make a glass last all afternoon. Unless you joined him in the morning just after he set up shop, you found the stuff in the pitcher invariably lukewarm. That was if he asked you to join him.

I found him in his usual circumstances,

with a laptop open on the table and his cell, pager, and Etch A Sketch electronic notebook lined up side by side next to it. His glass steeped on a paper coaster, but a puddle of condensation had formed around the base of the pitcher. His fingers were a blur on the keyboard.

"How's the transportation business?" I slid into the seat opposite him.

He answered without looking up. "Shitty. GPS has got all the best boosters too spooked to jump a wire. The cowboys who aren't I won't work with. State cops are promising to have an onboard computer in every prowl car by next year. What's next? I may have to join my brother-in-law in the green card racket. I hate my brother-in-law. Green cards are for saps who want to get butt-fucked by an entirely different class of convict."

"There's always life on the square."

"Don't think I haven't been tempted." He paused in his typing long enough to call out for another glass.

"Not on my account," I said. "I manufacture my own spit."

"Eighty-six the glass," he told the man behind the bar. "Maybe the car-key business, but I'll need case dough. They put microchips in them now, the car won't unlock or start without 'em. Used to be all you needed was a hardware store key-maker and you were good to go."

"Society's tough on free enterprise. Ever do any business in Mexicantown?"

"Best quesadillas this far north."

I wrapped a bill in a paper napkin and slid it across the table. He tapped a few keys more, then unfolded it in his lap. "One of the new ones, huh. More colors than the Polack flag. I know a guy who can beat 'em. All's you need is the right equipment; expensive as hell. They've taken counterfeiting away from the boys with a printing press and a green visor and dropped it in the lap of Al-Qaeda. Took care of the competition."

"You know anybody who *doesn't* have a sheet?"

"My bookie. He works out of the Woodward branch of the U.S. Post Office." He stuck the hundred-dollar bill in the flap pocket of his twill shirt. "I wasn't kidding about the quesadillas. Real lard; what the Greeks called ambrosia."

"I didn't come here for a recommendation. I'm looking for a Wonder Bread truck. Somebody used it to clear out a bunch of fighting cocks."

"I heard about that. Didn't hear anything about a bread truck."

"You weren't supposed to."

"I just know makes and models and whatever VIN they're using now. Nobody tells me what they were used for, and I don't want to know what they're going to be used for. I haven't worked with a Mexican in a couple of years. Ones I see usually have a chop shop going, operating across state lines: Mercedes goes missing from a garage in Chicago at midnight, five o'clock that same morning it's getting a fresh paint job in Southfield. What started out as a local beef is now federal. These days, you go up against the feds, they tie you to bin Laden and yank all your rights. I'm a crook, not a terrorist."

"This is probably local, being Wonder Bread. It would be an old truck, plenty of tonnage. It would throw oil like a son of a bitch, because they don't care about the Blue Book. By now it's dropped off its load and is on its way to Alaska, all cut up into transportable parts to shore up the Bridge to Nowhere. Nobody cares about two dead men, but PETA's got a hard-on against abusing domestic fowl. If this bunch knew you shied away from Mexicans, they might have had an Anglo front for them, maybe somebody you know and have done business with in the past. My guess is they wouldn't have had it for long before they put it to use. Why hang on to a hot vehicle that big and obvious unless you need it right away? Possibly as late as yesterday, after Zorborón got popped."

His fingers resumed moving. I got out a cigarette, just to play with; you can't smoke anywhere anymore, not even in a bar where you could make pictures out of the old nicotine stains on the ceiling, like cloud formations. After a little while I felt neglected. I put the cigarette back in the pack. "If I had one of those, we could play *Battleship.*"

He shut the laptop. "You know what I was looking at? South African gorillas. If I saw a piece about gorillas in the paper I'd go to the sports section, because I got no interest in gorillas. But everything on the Net's fascinating. It's not really an addiction. Nobody ever died going offline for a day. Jacking off, that's what it is. I didn't do any truck business yesterday."

"That was speculation. They might have been planning to move anyway. They'd store it inside, maybe in a barn or storage unit, something outside the city. The job might have come in from a county with plenty of rural real estate. If they left a contact number, the area code would belong to one of those. Go back say a month. Go back farther if we have to, but these guys don't take much in the way of chances. They didn't waste any time clearing out the inventory after I told their caretaker the cops would be getting around to them sooner or later; took out the caretaker and his partner while they were at it. Where they come from, what they've been doing, chickens are worth more than humans."

He'd opened the laptop again. He didn't seem to have been aware he had. Now he slapped it shut again and pushed it away as if it were a salad and he'd found a bug in it. His lids were sleepy. He always looked like he could barely keep his eyes open, just before he pulled the emergency cord. "You tipped 'em?"

"I was looking for a kid I figured had gone there to ground. It was friendly advice. I couldn't get a reaction otherwise. If I thought it would lead to double murder, I'd probably have gone about it differently. I'm a sleuth, not a seer."

He played around with that. Inside his head, keys were rattling.

" 'Kay," he said after a minute. "I don't care about rats one way or the other. I just try to keep clear of 'em. Let me get back to you."

That was the brush-off, to give him time to check me out and make sure I hadn't gone over to the other side, whichever side that was; the underworld isn't a two-headed coin so much as a rough-cut diamond, with a new facet every time you turned it in the light. Cops worked with crooks, crooks worked with crooks who worked with cops; you couldn't be choosy, but you liked to know whose team you were playing. It was no wonder he needed a computer to keep it all straight. His whole life was right there in that laptop, with a ducky little feature that would wipe it clean clear back to Eden at the touch of a key. He could stroke his mouse and tell you what he'd had for breakfast five years back from today. But if I put up an argument, he'd just go into sleep mode.

How the criminal classes managed before Silicon Valley was one for the social historians.

I left him one of the new cards with my cell on it. It went into the same pocket with the C-note. He had the laptop back open and the keys rattling by the time I got to the door. The gorillas of South Africa: Sell that one to Dian Fosse. He probably had my whole history flayed out in front of him, as far back as Basic Training.

I had lunch at the Caucus Club, a brisk walk from the Sextant. The Reuben sandwich they served there had nothing on the place I'd left, but I didn't want to look as if I was hovering. I washed it down with a Stroh's — no longer a local product, but it had the virtue of being ice cold — got back into the Cutlass, caught a movie at a cut-rate theater on the way to the house — a superhero flick whose plot I lost track of among the computer-generated special effects — and went home to catch the news on TV.

It was a slow news day, with the Zorborón kill behind the weather report and the murders in the chicken coop down to "the police are asking citizens for help" and the fire across from Holy Redeemer claiming a full minute. It seemed like overkill for a two-alarmer, but no mayors had been caught fondling strippers lately and the cardinal said the Vatican had the pederasty situation well in hand. Alderdyce looked tired on camera, Sister Delia impatient with the interviewer. They could both use a week in Florida. So could I, come to that. None of it looked like anything I had had something to do with. They should run a banner at the bottom saying it was for entertainment purposes only.

I woke up in the dusty light of dawn with a gnawing at my gut I knew well: Somewhere there was a Vicodin with my name on it, and it was working its way down my street peering at addresses. I lumbered into the bathroom, shoving bottles back and forth on shelves, knowing damn well the plastic vial I was looking for had long since gone out empty with the trash. Clawing at my stomach, I lurched out in the direction of the kitchen and the bottle in the cabinet above the sink, when my eye lit on a tiny white oval lying on the floor at the edge of the shag mat.

I plucked it up, knowing it for a pill I'd dropped six weeks before and had been in no shape to track, a beautiful oval with a score line in the middle for those who cared to cut it in half. I'd never used that feature.

I didn't care what sort of microbes had been crawling on it for a month and a half; a shot of Scotch would kill them and break down the pill more quickly than water or chewing.

I spent a minute looking at it. My leg wasn't hurting so badly I needed it for the pain. I needed it for the Vicodin. All I had to do was toss it into my mouth and swallow.

My eye wandered to the mirror, and the

face that didn't belong there, drawn and old and hungry. I shook myself like a dog and brushed the pill off my palm into the sink and pulled on the faucet full blast. Then I went to the kitchen. That little decision cost me the rest of the night and most of the next morning.

I had a bright idea, and when it still hadn't lost its glimmer after a plate of scrambled eggs and two cups of coffee I could have used to re-tar the roof, I called Rafael Buho. He could see me at eleven o'clock in his office.

The trim soft little Mexican practiced above a gift shop on West Vernor, filled with laminated frogs playing guitar and bottles of hot sauce with names like Forty Miles from Hell and Call the Coroner; the stuff was made from caramelized habañeros with Tabasco stirred in to take off the edge. They manufactured it on the premises, with welding masks and steelers' gloves. I had to stop twice on the narrow enclosed staircase to wipe my eyes and blow my nose.

It was a stuffy little office with mustard-colored law books crammed into the shelves at every angle and scurvy-looking leather portfolios scaling the corners to a pressed-tin ceiling left over from the Gilded Age.

Young Abe Lincoln pled the case for the railroad in a steel-point engraving in a frame that had come with it. The desk was made of pebbled iron with a black Formica top, a ring burned into one corner where a bottle of battery acid had stood when it belonged to a garage. Dog-eared file folders stuffed with tattered papers had settled into compost on nearly every other square inch, leaving just enough room for a telephone, a fax machine, and the usual computer equipment, some of it balanced atop a stack of case histories. A window looked directly into the window of an office-supply warehouse next door, a case of spite between rival architects back when soft collars meant the end of civilization. All of it was so true to the template there had to be a decorator involved, with two years of pre-law in his misspent youth. The only things missing were a sampler with the Bill of Rights in Spanish and a marimba band.

Buho looked up at me from behind the detritus in what might have been the same powder-blue suit and perfectly knotted bow tie. He looked as astonished as ever. I might have been his first client.

"Is it the boy?" he opened. "I thought he'd be safer at home. I am frequently wrong."

I said, "Then you shouldn't be giving

advice. He's fine, so far as I know. It's your other clients I came to talk to you about."

"Naturally, I am constrained by the bonds of my profession. Within those bonds, I am at your service."

I moved a stack of torts or whatever they were from a tired desk chair on the customer's side to the floor and dropped the old bones onto vinyl. I was still jumpy from the wrestling match with prescription drugs. "Someone torched Sister Delia's place of business yesterday. You probably heard about it."

"I am as well informed as anyone who owns a television or reads the newspapers. I do not know the lady, but I am aware of her. She refused treatment, I understand. I hope this means she is as well as can be expected."

"That's got to be the most self-contained phrase in the language. It answers its own question."

"You are free to say so. I am not, because I speak it with a foreign accent. No matter that my family has been speaking it since before the War of 1812. But we were discussing Sister Delia."

"She won't be playing the violin any time soon, but I'm more interested in who torched the place. Any arsonists in your

Rolodex?"

"I see." He sat back and set fire to one of his torpedoes. That law was running into more trouble than Prohibition. "All of my clients are innocent until proven guilty. Since it is my job to see that they are not, I can hardly answer that question as framed."

"Not bad. It's no *no hablo inglés,* but I guess we've moved on from that. I'm not asking you to betray any confidences. I can go to the record and find out who you represented in cases of arson, but there's a fee involved. I'm trying to keep the expenses down on this job."

He blew an imperfect smoke ring — I was pretty sure he could blow a perfect one any time he liked — and frowned at the finished product. He was a man who would step out of character if you punched him in the throat. "The person you wish to see is named Miguel Ortiz: Mike the Match, some Anglos call him. He served two years in Marquette for setting fire to a bar in West Bloomfield: Something about an outside partnership that could be made profitable only by an astounding claim on a fire insurance policy. I was not the attorney of record, or it could have been pled down to malicious destruction of private property. Patience costs nothing, but certain of my colleagues behave as if it came at fifty dollars the pound."

I said, "I'm beginning to see their point."

"Then I shall come to mine. I represented *Señor* Ortiz in another matter which is still pending. You understand that I cannot go into detail."

"Why him?"

"It is the only case of arson I have handled. I dislike the crime. The effects are too random. You will find him in a halfway house in Iroquois Heights; he is in the process of parole on the West Bloomfield business. The prosecution is of the opinion that he employed his furlough in a manner not endorsed by the board. Do you suspect him for the fire that put Sister Delia on the street?"

"Not until just now." I got out my notepad and put it on top of the mess on the desk. "The address of the halfway house, please. It's just an interview. He doesn't have to know who gave me directions."

"You may name me or not. The whereabouts of a client are not in this case a question of confidence." He produced a fat green fountain pen from an inside pocket and scribbled on the first blank page he came to. His wide-open eyes scrolled down the notations on the way there. "You have an intriguing shorthand. I doubt an experienced detective could make it out without the key to the code."

"My own invention, coupled with bad handwriting. I can't figure it out myself if I don't transcribe it onto a scratch pad five minutes after I wrote it."

"You're a careful man. Careful enough to obfuscate your caution with a show of — how do you put it in your ingenious language? — improvisation. You've more of a professional frame of mind than you pretend."

"Yeah. You wouldn't know anything about that. *Gracias, Señor* Buho." I took back the pad. "How's Nesto?"

"You tell me. Your Inspector Alderdyce has him under constant surveillance. I myself cannot afford to spend so much time on one charge." He blew a jet of blue-gray smoke past my shoulder, waving a hand at it to deflect it from my nostrils. A polite man, Buho. "You do not like me."

"Must I?"

"It is of no consequence. Recently I addressed a meeting of local attorneys. In search of a light beginning, I sought a quotation about lawyers that was complimentary to the profession. I spent many hours with Bartlett's and on the Internet in this pursuit."

"How'd that work out?"

"I spoke of recent Supreme Court decisions. Mine is a thankless service."

"Lawyers are okay in my book. I get most of my work through them."

"But you wouldn't want your sister to marry one."

"I'm an only child." I stood. "Thank you again, Mr. Buho."

"De nada." He squashed out his butt in an Indian pottery bowl and sat back without offering his hand.

■ ■ ■ ■

Tres:
Law of Flight

■ ■ ■ ■

Nineteen

I was still shaky in the joints when I drove away from Mexicantown. My nerves lay right on the surface. The vibration of the engine stung the soles of my feet on the pedals and the palms of my hands on the wheel. I'd known I wasn't cured, that I couldn't pop a single Vicodin when my head hurt without spilling back down into the deep well I'd spent months climbing out of, but no one had told me it could come back on me right out of the blue, like the stuff Jekyll drank. Maybe someone had; if you paid attention to the disclaimers at the end of the prescription-drug ads, you'd learn to live with your condition instead of taking something that duplicated all the symptoms you'd taken the drug to get rid of in the first place.

Iroquois Heights. It isn't particularly high and they ran out the Indians when knee breeches were still in style. In the Old West they'd have called the place Perdition or Purgatory; the pioneers were candid if not always honest. It was the kind of town the hotshot gunfighter rode into to do the job the locals hadn't the sand for, then had the good sense to ride out of before it fell back into the same bad habits he'd found when he came. Gary Cooper didn't go back to Hadleyville, nor Lot to Gomorrah, but it was my fate to cross the Iroquois Heights city limits ever and again until I found my salvation.

I serpentined my way through the new downtown, with curbs laid out as jaggedly as a drift fence and clever tree plantings that when the leaves filled out would cover the speed limit signs — 15 mph, ten lower than the average, to snag the unwary — and up the gentle elevation toward the old industrial district. Earth movers were spreading soil like spackle over a hundred years of lead and cyanide leeched from the foundries and coke ovens where a sign advertised the future site of Ottawa Lodge Estates: IF YOU LIVED HERE, YOU'D BE HOME.

Miguel Ortiz sounded like a made-up name. Mike the Match was straight out of *Dick Tracy.* I had no reason to distrust Buho more than any other lawyer, but first-class arsonists didn't leave evidence behind that would put them in need of good legal help; the very evidence required to identify and convict them went up in the act of their crime. Either this one was careless enough to do something rash when I braced him or he was incompetent enough to make the kind of mistake that got me killed.

The halfway house, on West Tecumseh, was a venerable building with no charm built into it, and age hadn't corrected the oversight. It had "transient hotel" scribbled all over it. It was four stories built Lego fashion, block on cement block, sided with tiles that had been white once but now looked like neglected teeth. The city would have scooped it up for back taxes, hoping to sell it to a casino chain or for the detective squad to interview prisoners it didn't want to be photographed entering the police station on account of what they looked like in photographs coming back out. But casino owners shop around for sweetheart deals, not graft, and a reform movement had put the police department on its good behavior until the movement lost steam and the same old city officials were shuffled around into different positions like a repertory company. But bad actors are just as bad in fresh roles.

After that the place would have stood empty for a few years, attracting the homeless and traffic in controlled substances and contributing to sexually transmitted disease, until the governor decided to cut costs by emptying out the prisons. That meant shuttling the more serious felons into cooling towers, and state funds directed to communities willing to board them during the transition to responsible citizenship; in other times a place like the Heights would have distributed the money among its various pockets, then piled the wards of the state into the wagon on release and dumped them out on some rural road across the county line. But for the moment at least the world was watching.

The front door wasn't locked, but I passed through a metal detector on the way through, without tripping it; I'd had the foresight to lock the Chief's Special in the car. The old institutional smell of must and disinfectant greeted me on the other side, also an alert-looking woman sitting on a tall stool behind the former registration desk. She had red hair harvested close to the scalp and the build of Rosy the Riveter. Her blouse was plain, but a prison matron doesn't need the uniform to tell you who she is. She frowned as if I'd put something past the detector and asked what I wanted.

"Miguel Ortiz." I showed her my ID, folding back the half of the wallet with the star pinned to it so it was out of sight. It wouldn't have impressed her other than unfavorably.

As a matter of fact it didn't impress her at all. "I've got one of those, too," she said. "Can't swing the country club on what I make here. Who's the bankroll?"

"Actually, I'm the client. Rafael Buho, Attorney-at-Law. He represents Ortiz, too. That makes us brothers."

"I doubt it." Nuance was lost on this woman with freckled muscular forearms and no jewelry of any kind. "What's the interest?"

"I want to ask him a couple of questions about an arson."

"When?"

"Right now, if it's convenient."

"I meant when was the arson."

"Yesterday afternoon."

The desk was in a cubicle partitioned off from the rest of the old lobby by heavy pine, with only a door at the side and the opening through which we were communicating providing access to the rest of the building. She took a clipboard off a nail on the wall at one end of the desk and paged back through it, drew a spatulated finger down a column until she found what she wanted.

"Uh-uh."

" 'Uh-uh' means what?" I thought she was turning me away.

"He checked out two hours yesterday morning to attend Mass — we have to let them do that — but was back here by noon. No one checked him out after that."

"Anybody go with him?"

"An attendant. They're to stay with them the whole time they're out."

"Must've been crowded in the confession booth."

"Can't do that, but last time I looked, St. Ambrose hadn't installed any trap doors."

"All the same I want to talk to him."

"Buho, you said?" When I confirmed it she consulted another sheet, and with her finger planted on it she lifted a gray telephone receiver and dialed a number. She spoke with Buho briefly, then hung up and paged Ortiz over a prewar PA mike. "Have a seat."

"Had one already, thanks."

She didn't care for that, but then she picked up a puzzle book folded to a page near the middle, retrieved a sharpened pencil from behind her right ear, and after that I didn't exist. I'd barely been there to begin with.

I'm an expert on waiting rooms. At the

high end there is the showy front, with tufted leather chairs like in a cigar bar, swanky magazines on smoked-glass tables, black-and-white blowup photos of watchworks and steel girders in sleek frames on the walls, and a carpet you wade across to a curvy desk with a curvy receptionist behind it who is as expensive to maintain as an Italian convertible. There might be a lot of gaudy fish swimming inside a glass tank the size of an elevator car. A decorating team was involved in the creation, and odds were the room where the clients' assistants originally waited to meet the team was the model. In the broad middle is the charmless chamber with airport seating, coffee rendering in a maker next to a stack of Styrofoam cups, thumb-smeared copies of *People* and *Time* long past their expiration dates, and a talking head on a flat-screen TV for company. At the low end lurks a grubby way station with nothing to read because most of the clientele doesn't know *Moby Dick* from Moby, metal folding chairs that put your fanny to sleep after ten minutes, and a smell of boiling cabbage solid enough to bark a shin against. In the old days it came equipped with tarnished spittoons and smoking stands rounded over with White Owl stubs and unfiltered Camels and smelled like a building that had burned to the ground. This one still smelled a little like that.

The first example stands outside places where bankers do business with bankers, cosmetic surgeons sit behind black volcanic glass talking about staples and rhinoplasty, and architects plan shopping malls. The second is where every automobile owner in America waits to hear if his problem is a faulty CHECK ENGINE light or a two-thousand-dollar overhaul, where visitors talk in low voices and hope Mom's trip to the ER came with a return ticket, and where customers sit with accounting books and boxes of crumpled receipts on their laps wishing they hadn't claimed their French poodle as a dependent, because unless the examiner is flexible, the next waiting room they use will be the third one, at the bottom: a desperate place populated with parolees, patients claiming slipped disks and sciatica but who are really there for the muscle relaxants, and people who have worn out their credit with every loan officer who doesn't double all his negatives and use a blackjack for a paperweight. That one is hell's waiting room and the time there is measured by the passage of the constellations.

The room I walked around, looking at the necessary licenses framed on the painted-partition walls, hovered somewhere between the middle and the low end. The folding chairs were metal, but there were some *Reader's Digests* curling at the corners in a heap on a low round yellow table that might have been where kids played with toys in a dentist's office and the smell was mostly secondhand instant coffee and old cigarettes. I tapped on the glass of an ant farm — some former penal director's idea of entertainment for the visitors — trying to raise the ants from the dead, and added the room to my collection.

"Here he is." The gargoyle behind the desk was looking up at something mounted inside the frame that enclosed her station; a monitor, probably. "Do not pass anything to the resident. Do not shake hands with the resident or make any other physical contact. Make sure both you and the resident remain in my field of vision at all times. Do not at any time block my view of the resident. Understand all that?"

"I've been to halfway houses before."

"Lovely. Do you understand?"

"Yeah."

She reached under the desk. Something buzzed and the inside door opened.

I don't know what I expected, but it wasn't what I got. Miguel Ortiz looked like a Spaniard on both sides of his family, with black eyes straddling a strong, straight nose, a long upper lip, and a face that seemed even longer than it was with his hair receding toward the crown. He reminded me of a picture I'd seen of Picasso in middle age, fierce and aware and better than the place he was in. He was a solid six feet and two hundred pounds in a Polynesian print shirt exposing powerful forearms with the square tail hanging outside beige flannel slacks; no County jumpsuits on the way back into the general population, only on the way out. His shoes were Hush Puppies, easy on the feet after the stiff institutional jobs they made in the prison shop.

I told him my name and invited him to sit.

He didn't stir, standing there with his hands crossed at his waist. "All I do all day is sit."

His accent was Castilian. That together with what I'd seen of him so far sent my plan of approach out the window. You can browbeat a *mestizo,* but a purebred Iberian will just stare you down. For sure his wasn't the faceless figure in the video behind Zorborón's garage.

But a man's work inevitably leaves its mark. In his case, it was literal: an angry puckered red patch shaped like a salamander branding the left side of his face from just below the ear to the corner of his jaw, tightening the flesh and pulling at the corner of his lips on that side. It might have been a strawberry mark, but it wasn't. A man who can make a mistake with the tools of his profession is a man you can get ahead of.

"I'm investigating an arson at Sister Delia's office yesterday," I said.

"You're with the police?"

"Private."

"So I don't have to tell you anything."

"I just cleared you at the desk. I'm here to consult you, not grill you. The cops think a super accelerant was used, faster and hotter than anything on the open market. Any suggestion as to what it was?"

"What's my end?"

"Civic responsibility."

He seemed to smile, but that was just the dead nerves freezing his mouth at one corner.

"You're set to make a fresh start," I said. "Your parole officer would approve. Maybe even enough not to put the screws on you if you miss a bus and wind up on the street after ten o'clock."

"You'd tell him I cooperated?"

"I will, if he doesn't," put in the woman behind the desk. To me: "Ortiz gives me the least trouble of anyone we've got, and the place is full."

That explained the cold shoulder. She'd thought I'd come to harass her favorite resident. I kept telling myself you never knew about people from outside their skins but it never took somehow.

Mike the Match uncrossed his hands and put them in his pockets. "Plain gasoline should be good enough for anyone. What you're talking about is traceable; the customer list is so short the Arson Squad's waiting for you when you get home. Also the first rule is don't set yourself on fire. Even gas is unpredictable." He touched the burned side of his face, an involuntary movement. "That high-test stuff goes up so fast you better be on wheels."

"No one reported any tires squealing."

"How did they make delivery?"

"Molotov cocktail through a window."

He shook his head. "Either they were lucky or they did it another way."

"What other ways are there?"

"Just one. Bottle bomb."

"Sounds like just another name for a Molotov."

"That's just half of it. You fill one bottle with your incendiary material, another with drain cleaner and a wad of aluminum foil. Duct-tape them together and plant them where you want. That gives you time to walk away before the foil and drain cleaner get busy and set off the accelerant."

"Just ordinary foil and drain cleaner?'

"It's a chemical reaction, like Mentos and Coca-Cola. Only much more volatile."

"How long?"

"Depends on how far you fill the second bottle. The more air, the more time the stuff has to expand before it bursts the glass. You can time it like a fuse if you know what you're doing."

"Then it sets off the other?"

"Like a blasting cap."

I turned that around and looked at it from all sides. "Wearing a tether?"

He reached down and tugged up enough of his left pants leg to show the electronic bracelet wrapped around his ankle.

"Okay."

A smooth brown brow got wrinkled. "Okay?"

"*Sí, gracias.* When do you get out?"

"Six weeks, less a day."

"Who's your p.o.?"

He gave me a name I didn't recognize. I said, "I'll see if we can't knock a piece off that. You don't plan to set fire to anything, do you?"

He smiled for the first time, the scar pulling it slightly out of skew. His teeth were slightly crooked but as white as polished porcelain. "Just a good Havana."

Twenty

Petey Kresge called while I was driving away from there. Since I was still in the Iroquois Heights city limits I checked all the windows and mirrors for prowl cars and scanned the skies for copters. The ink wasn't dry on the governor's no-texting-while-driving ban when the city council doubled the fine locally and tacked on cell use at the wheel. Within six weeks the mayor had a more expensive mistress and every official in town had a backyard hot tub. In that zip code, reform meant a more even distribution of grease.

"How close are you to a landline?" Petey asked.

I said I'd call him from the first public phone I came to.

"Club me a dodo while you're at it." He chuckled and rang off.

I wasn't sure what he meant, but the march of time had continued since I went wireless. There followed a comic ten minutes during which a checkout clerk in a Kroger's in a strip mall thought I was asking for directions to the mother ship, two phones mounted outside gas stations gave back silence for my quarters but not the quarters themselves, and even a drugstore, which is where every snitch in every old movie went to his death while on the wire with the cops, had replaced its vintage oaken booth with a video kiosk. Finally I found a bar where a handful of rumpled figures in rumpled clothes sat on stools in perpetual twilight, and gonged two coins into a black-enamel-and-chrome box in the hallway leading to the john. The narrow passage smelled of kitty litter and bleach and all the time I was on the line a toilet ran and a frantic Brit described the action in a televised soccer game to an audience more interested in seeing the clown face at the bottom of the glass.

"I about gave up," Petey said when I identified myself.

"Don't start. What've you got?"

"Your Wonder Bread truck's seen more of the world than me. U.S. Border Patrol seized it two years ago carrying five hundred kilos of cocaine through downtown Bisbee."

"Where the hell is Bisbee?"

"Old mining town pinned to the hills in

Arizona. They film movies there set in Spain and Italy. You could piss on Mexico from there."

"If they confiscated it, how'd it get back to roost in Detroit?"

"You'll love this. It disappeared from the impound lot six months later, right past the guard and a pack of mean fucking dogs and through a chain-link fence twelve feet high with razor wire on top."

"Graft job?"

"Carelessness, D.C. style. A bunch of vehicles were headed out that day for public auction and somebody strolled right in and climbed onto the driver's seat and jumped the wires and rolled out the gate. It wasn't on the auction list because the case hadn't come to trial, but nobody bothered to check it. Who steals trucks? Anyway the guard's now picking up trash in Gitmo with a nail on the end of a stick and the truck's got a new VIN embossed on an aluminum tab riveted over the place where the original was filed off the engine block. A tin job, we call it; it doesn't fool anyone, but on the other hand you can't prove anything. Engines are made of softer stuff than guns. You can't bring back the number once it's gone."

"How do you know that's what happened?"

"My source makes it a point to enter the legitimate number next to the new one on a program that takes more passwords to get into than Janet Reno's pants. Also a digital photo that matches the description you gave me, including what's left of the balloons in the logo."

"Sounds like he's got his retirement party all planned."

"He's counting on his scrapbook to make sure he *lives* long enough to retire."

"Drugs to fighting cocks. That crate's coming up in the world."

"Depends on how you see it. Dope pays better."

"Less risk, though, cockfighting. The only people who really care what happens to chickens never outgrew the T-shirt phase. Who registered the phony papers?"

"A charitable corporation, it says here. Friends of Emiliano. It sounds better in Spanish. They sell chocolate bars for five bucks a pop in supermarket parking lots to shoppers who care about sponsoring Mexican nationals to come to *Los Estados Unidos* and find a better life."

"How do you say sucker in Spanish?"

"El Norteamericano."

"Emiliano was Zorborón's Christian

name. Anything in that?"

"Possibly. It was Zapata's too."

"Zapatistas?"

"Yeah. Only not the watered-down local variety. The registration was filed in El Paso. These are the babies who declared war on the Republic of Mexico. If they're connected to the fighting rooster trade here, it means they've expanded the declaration to include Uncle Sam."

The toilet was still running when I re-hooked the receiver and the game was still on, providing white noise for the drinkers at the bar. They were as communicative as cattle huddled against the wind. The bartender used his rag to rub the grunge out of the contours of a bottle of vermouth that had stood in the same spot since Bush 41; busywork, between refill orders. I figured he'd forgotten how to make a martini years ago.

I wondered how Sister Delia was getting along. A sergeant I sometimes swapped insults with at 1300 gave me the address she'd left with the Arson Squad in case they had questions. It belonged to a house on the edge of Corktown, a square box in a style architects call American Craftsman so they won't have to call it None of the Above, with ROOMS FOR RENT signs in a couple of windows; accommodations are easier to come by than jobs in Detroit. In the days of stickpins and Spanish Influenza, the neighborhood was where the Irish gathered to smoke cigars and elect the governor, but it had gone Mexican generations ago, breaking stride only once a year for St. Patrick's Day and pitchers of green beer served in the Shamrock Bar by a bartender named Julio. On the way I passed old Tiger Stadium, rubble now with yellow bulldozers crawling over it like maggots.

The owner, a black woman built like an ore carrier, leaned on her dust sweeper in the doorway, decided I didn't look like a home invader or a building inspector, and directed me to a room off the second floor landing. The stairs gasped under a comfortably worn runner as I climbed. A pungent mix of old dry wood and Endust surrounded me, a lemony smell laced with deferred decay. A lot of elbow grease was behind that. The woman with the sweeper was part of the rock that kept the city from sliding into the river.

Delia opened the door on the second knock. She wore a hip-length open-weave sweater over a much-washed University of Detroit T-shirt, mottled jeans hugging her narrow hips. Her hands were still bandaged. I asked her about them.

"Hurting today," she said. "I don't have much time. I have to be at the Henry Ford Medical Center in an hour. That's a daily appointment to drain blisters and change dressings until I'm safe from gangrene."

"I won't need more than ten minutes."

She stepped aside and closed the door behind me when I crossed the threshold. It was a corner room with windows on adjacent walls and lace curtains to filter out the view of neglect in two directions. The bed was neatly made, the patterned rug freshly swept or vacuumed, and a padded rocker and a scruffy but cozy-looking armchair faced each other with a coffee table in between. Christ sagged from His cross on the wall above the bed. A freestanding cupboard would hold the rest of her wardrobe. The house predated built-in closets.

We sat, she in the rocker, her bound hands resting on her thighs. I asked her what they'd prescribed for the pain.

"Industrial-strength Tylenol. But I don't use it."

"Practicing for sainthood?"

"Counting my pennies. Pain goes away on its own, unlike debt." She smiled. "If I were a weaker woman I'd sell the pills on the street and triple my investment."

I changed the subject. Temptation didn't bear examination. "I didn't know you went to U of D."

She glanced down at the T-shirt. "There's nothing wrong with your eyes. It's almost as faded as my memory of the place. I majored in science, if you can believe it. After all these years I still think evolution and the Big Bang Theory are evidence of the existence of God; but neither the faithful nor the clinicians want to hear it. I think they like being at each other's throats."

"That was before the Call, I guess."

"Not a Call in my case. I was next to last in a family of ten. Good Catholics, no seed wasted. Four daughters: two to marry, one — the youngest, my kid sister Cathy — to stay home and take care of our parents in their old age, and one to take the vows and get everyone in good with the Lord. There was never any question that it would be anyone but me. 'Our Savior doesn't care if you're comely.' Quoting my father." She was beautiful when she smiled. There wouldn't have been much of that going on in the house where she grew up.

"What made you stick as long as you did?"

"My mother was determined to make it to a hundred. As it was she cleared eighty-seven. I couldn't drop out while she was living. But Cathy got the worst part of that deal. Mom wasn't the kind of invalid that suffers in silence."

"You've kept on doing pretty much the same thing you did as a nun."

"But on my ticket, not the Vatican's." She scratched the back of her right hand with her left; healing is an itchy process. "Are you here to write my biography?"

"I was breaking the ice." I told her about my conversation with Miguel Ortiz, leaving out the part about bottle bombs. That was just speculation.

"You're sure he didn't go out a window and shinny down the drainpipe?"

"The gorgon at the gate's too sharp for that. Also he's wearing a tether. Anyway, arsonists are in steep supply in this town. Right now I'm less interested in who torched your place than in the accelerant that was used. 'High-test,' Mike the Match called it. I'm going to ask Arson what *they* call it. It sounds sophisticated for someone who just smudged up the back of Zorborón's garage and keyed your car."

"*Keyed* is a generic term. Do you want to see pictures?"

"There are pictures?"

"I took them for the insurance. Hang on."

She got up, opened the drawer in the nightstand beside the bed, sat back down in the rocker thumbing the keys of a cell phone, squinting at the screen. After a moment she leaned forward and handed it to me. "Just push the little camera icon when you want to see the next photo."

They're making those cameras better and better. I got a good look from several angles at a Plymouth Duster with a right front fender that didn't match the color, a replacement from some junkyard. The damage had included the fender and the rest of that side of the car ending just ahead of the taillight. Something a lot sharper than a key had made those thin jagged angry scratches. I thought of Roscoe Berdoo's pocket slicer, ground down to a needle; but he'd struggled with his native tongue and lost. A box cutter would have done just as well. It was a message in Spanish. "*Irse* I know," I said. "It means get out."

"Go away. The other word's harder to look up. One of the advantages of living in a Mexican neighborhood as long as I have is you pick up words you won't find in an English-Spanish dictionary. That one refers to a part of the female anatomy, but you won't find it in a Spanish medical book either. You have to look for it on a board fence."

"That explains the penis."

"Not a bad reproduction, no pun intended. I wonder if it's a self-portrait."

"Where's the car now?"

"At the body shop, waiting in line for spray painting. This only happened two weeks ago."

"Did you report it to the police?"

"And give them an excuse to roust the neighborhood like they did last time someone filed a complaint?"

I flicked a hand at the screen on the cell. "This is a warning. So was that business behind Zorborón's garage. In your case it was probably rape, but they changed their minds. The accelerant that was used on your place can't be easy to come by."

"Meaning it's too sophisticated for either the Maldados or the homegrown Zapatistas," she said.

"There's a rumor going around that the Old Country Zaps are moving in on Detroit. They're part of the drug cartel back home. That would be their style."

"What makes me such a threat?"

"What made Zorborón? They start by declaring war on the most visible opposition. That's how they handle the border patrol; no reason to change their MO just because the climate's different."

"I thought the Tiger was a Zap."

"He was when they were revolutionaries. He bailed out of the drug business years ago. If he'd thought someone else would bail in, he'd put up a squawk. That's a maybe, but these *muchachos* didn't attract the attention of Home Security relying on wishful thinking."

"Well, they've put me out of business for the time being. I have to start my donor list all over from scratch. I can remember most of the names, but my records were full of notes about how much was actually donated against what was pledged, who was a soft touch, who I could guilt and who I could level with, stuff like that."

"That's the kind of language I expect from a con artist."

"Sometimes it flies close to extortion. The charity game isn't for wimps."

"A wimp would have given up the minute that cocktail came through the window."

"Windows break. Things burn. It's why God invented glaziers and fire insurance. State Farm agents have faith, why shouldn't the rest of us? Especially in the charity game."

"You're sure you didn't see anything? The

cops are tapped out for witnesses. Maybe someone slowed down on his way past the first time, glanced in to make sure you were where you needed to be when the curtain went up."

"If someone did, I had my head down trying to make out my own handwriting. You might have noticed the view out the window wasn't the Bay of Naples. I didn't while away hours mooning over the beautiful sight."

"They might come back to finish the job."

"Why? I'm back at square one. Anyway, they made their point, so I'm not exactly top priority anymore. If I were you, I'd concentrate on the natives. With Zorborón on a slab and me parked on a siding, the Zaps are free to squeeze case dough out of the protection racket and use it to flood the streets with dope. In six months, maybe less, they'll be able to buy everything in town right up to City Hall, the way they did in Tijuana and Juarez and a dozen other border towns."

I ran my palms over the threadbare arms of my chair. "That's a tall order."

"Just knee-high. Other places, prosperous places, they'd have to bombard it before they made a frontal assault. Destroy all hope, soften it up. Detroit ran out of hope twenty years ago. The residents expect their cops and politicians to run crooked. They prefer them that way. When they're caught, the suckers pony up to pay their court costs. It's a wonder the barbarians didn't drag the border up here ten years ago." She smiled again, less beautifully: one of those smiles that sharpened the creases in her face and added years to it. She wasn't that old. People age at a different rate in Mexicantown. "Am I bitter?"

"You had a shock."

"Just get the bastards, okay? I'll light a candle for you at Holy Redeemer every day until you do."

TWENTY-ONE

John Alderdyce wasn't at his desk and wasn't answering his cell phone. I left a message both places, fired up the 455 and started drifting downtown on the off chance he'd show up, but I didn't get three blocks before he called me.

"Nesto's off the hook, sort of," he opened; "dangling loose, anyway, one foot in the air. We got the results from his lie detector test."

"I didn't know you gave him one."

"We keep the cap on long as we can. The press doesn't really understand technology. They report all kinds of things based on the slightest variance. We had his sister's permission. He didn't do Zorborón, and the stylus said that story about marching in and waving that lighter under his nose wasn't cock-and-bull after all."

"What about the garage fire?"

"That whole section of the questioning was inconclusive, and the expert circled back twice. My guess? Him. But with no injuries and little damage and without *El Tigre* around to press charges, the economy's too tender to bother. The boy got in with bad company; but that was the whole point of this exercise."

"I think he's salvageable. So is the job over?"

Air stirred. "Why do I think you want me to say no?"

"I'd like to play with it a little. Off the clock, expenses-wise."

"You're still on it if you turn anything."

I asked who was investigating the arson at Sister Delia's.

"Ray Charla: commander who works like a beat cop. Goes through the ashes with a flour sifter. What do you want from him?"

"I'm curious what accelerant was used. I'm working on the theory it was out of the reach of the local gangs."

"So are we. We duplicating efforts?"

"No charge if we are. I'll eat the gasoline."

"Just don't get in his way. He works alone."

"Where can I get in touch with him, Thirteen hundred?"

"What good'd he do there? Go to Sister Delia's and look for the guy with black under his nails as far as his hairline."

■ ■ ■ ■

At first glance the charity shop — it had never been christened, so the locals had just called it Sister Delia's — looked intact. The flames had managed only to blacken the McKinley-era iron front, so that looking at it directly from the street the building looked sound, until you noticed that the panes were missing from the windows and when you saw that you noticed that there was no inside wall opposite. You were looking directly across the street that ran behind the building all the way to the apartment complex on the other side. It resembled a false front on a western movie set, constructed of plywood with a clever paint job, entirely supported by two-by-four braces. But long before you saw that you smelled the piles of ash made sodden by high-pressure hoses and the dirty smoke from flare-ups among the embers. They spurted like orange crocuses, extinguishing themselves when they encountered dead char.

In the middle of all this, visible through the front door that no longer existed, a tall narrow figure with stooped shoulders tramped about in knee-length galoshes, a black fire-retardant Macintosh girded with broad reflectant acid-green horizontal stripes, and a fiberglass firefighter's helmet, distinguishable from the DFD only by a gold Detroit Police Department cap insignia screwed to the frontplate. His face was cherry-red; but that might have been from the heat. Standing three feet in front of the vacant doorway I could feel it leeching all the moisture from my body.

"Commander Charla?"

He glanced up, startled, and leaned on his instrument: not a flour sifter, but the next best thing, a long-handled rake with two sets of teeth, one coarse, one fine. An orange bucket hung at his hip from a shoulder strap, half-filled with unidentifiable smoking debris. "No comment." A respirator like a painter's dust mask muffled his voice. Together with close-fitting goggles and his long thin build, it made him look like a giant praying mantis.

"I'm not a reporter." I showed him my ID. "I'm working with Inspector Alderdyce. You can call him and confirm."

"If you say you're working with Alderdyce and it turns out you're not, you're too dumb to do much damage with anything I tell you. There it is!" He lifted his rake and plucked something curved and blackened from between the teeth with a gloved hand. For one brief moment he sounded like a boy finding an Easter egg.

"Glass?"

"A little more than half of a bottle. Just enough more it doesn't belong to the one I found ten minutes ago." He indicated the bucket on his hip with his elbow.

"So he did use a bottle bomb."

He carefully placed the fragment in the bucket, tugged down his goggles, and looked at me from inside a strip of sunburned-looking flesh that was bare of the soot that covered the rest of his face, a reverse-raccoon effect. "Who said he might've? And who's *he?*"

"Miguel Ortiz. The first who. He's not the second. The Michigan prison system's his alibi."

"Mike the Match. I admire his work, know why?"

"He's made a science of it."

"Not that, though he has. I admire his work because he makes double sure no one's in residence before he torches a place. That's how I know he wasn't in on this."

"He told me he'd never use a super-accelerant in a Molotov without taping a bottle bomb to it so he could be drinking a bottle of Moosehead in Windsor while it was blowing up in Madison Heights. Words to that effect."

He nodded and put the goggles back on. "You're working with Alderdyce okay. That speculation about the accelerant is strictly off-limits outside the department. Cyclostyrene. Combination of styrene and cyclohexane. Not new, either one. Together in sufficient quantity they could blow the moustache off Teddy Roosevelt on Mount Rushmore."

"Hard to come by, I suppose."

"Nope. Cyclohexane's a common saturated hydrocarbon derived from common benzene, a coal-tar byproduct. Any home improvement store that deals in roofing materials has it in stock. Styrene's the base in several glues sold in hardware departments and art-supply shops. The trick's in mixing them without turning yourself into a human Olympic torch."

"So obtaining the materials wouldn't require a sophisticated organization."

"You mean like Al-Qaeda or the Mafia?"

"Or like the Mexican Zapatistas."

"Materials, no. Guts, yeah. I wouldn't put those two agents in the same room without an advanced degree in chemistry, and then I'd use forty-foot tongs and someone working them who is not me."

"How do you know what chemicals were used?"

"I've been on this job since they invented Devil's Night. Every hydrocarbon leaves fingerprints. I know a cyclostyrene burn pattern on first sight; the stuff flashes out in every direction, obliterating on contact everything inflammable within its range and putting not more than a virgin's blush on brick and iron and concrete. The sergeant with the first-response crew saw right away this wasn't a run-of-the-mill burn, and that's why I'm here."

" 'Have rake, will travel?' "

"Damn straight. If I put a notch on this handle for every defense lawyer I made mush of in cross-examination, it wouldn't hold a strand of straw."

I watched him working with the rake. "How long you been on this job?"

"Forty years, man and boy. Just like Captain Ahab."

"I meant today."

"I was here at dawn, but I had to wait a couple of hours for it to cool down enough to go in. I only get three pairs of these a year before I have to start paying for replacements." He lifted a smoking galosh.

"Not much of a harvest for a full day's work."

"Oh, I've refilled the bucket a dozen times. There's the plunder." He pointed the rake handle — no notches, I saw — at a cleared corner where foundation blocks met at a 90-degree angle, now occupied by a heap of sooty evidence that looked more orderly than the rest.

"Mind if I take a look?"

"It's your suit. Just don't put anything in your pocket."

I took off my coat and tie, stashed them on the Cutlass's front seat, rolled up my sleeves and the cuffs of my pants, and waded into the ashes. If Alderdyce put up a beef about a shoeshine and a new pair of socks on the expense sheet, I could always refer him to Ray Charla.

I didn't expect to find anything, or to know what I'd found if I found it; but that's the job description. I turned over charred pieces of hardwood — remnants of Sister Delia's desk — a surprisingly intact patch of leaf-patterned upholstery the size of a long-playing record — part of the armchair I'd sat on during my first visit (God knows what made that evidence) — some bent and twisted pieces of unidentified metal that must have been near the epicenter of the firestorm, and odd black-fringed sheaves of paper that Delia should be glad to see, because they might help her reconstruct some of her lost files. Soon my hands were as black as what I was sifting through, my body oiled with sweat from the heat from the hotspots still smoldering under the ash, and all I knew about the bombing was that fire is a random destroyer, obliterating seemingly indestructible substances while sparing some of the most fragile.

I used a charred piece of wooden molding to probe the pile to the bottom, came across something solid, and teased it out the side until I could pick it up with my hand. It was still warm. I was holding a pointed length of steel half as long as a knitting needle, anchored to a cast-iron base. Apart from being relatively impervious to flame, it looked as if it hadn't been touched. Probably a piece of debris had fallen on top of it, shielding it from the worst of the heat. I wiped off enough smut from the base to examine the embossed design, a crucifix on a hill with rays of light radiating out from it. I got Charla's attention and held it up.

"Bill spindle," he said. "You know; you pay a bill, skewer the stub on the point like kebab and forget about it. You find them in antique stores with the ice picks. These days everybody pays their bills online and trusts the record to the hard drive."

"Everybody but me and Sister Delia. What makes it evidence?"

"Not a damn thing except it's still here. Anything that passed through unharmed is worth a look."

I had an idea that was unworthy of me. "Would you have it tested and let me know what you find? Alderdyce will tell you how to get in touch."

"Well, can you narrow it down? Chemical analysis, microscopic, what?"

"Both, I think. Just the pointed end. I don't care about the base."

"What are we looking for?"

"Tell you when you find it. Or when you don't."

"That doesn't move you any closer to the top of the list."

"Alderdyce will tell you where I belong on it."

"Whatever. I retire next year, unless I get lucky and nobody notices the age requirement. Either way, who gives a rat's ass?"

"You like this job."

"Love it. Ask anyone who works with fire or on the water. Ash and salt, they get in your blood."

"What if they force you out?"

"Then I'll take up smoking and purify my lungs." He went on raking slowly. Ray

Charla; I never got a good look at him, but he'd made an impression.

I used my handkerchief and one of the emergency bottles of water in the car to rinse the top layer of soot from my hands, knocked off what I could from my shoes against the curb, and threw away the handkerchief. At the first service station I came to I went into the men's room and got rid of the rest with liquid soap and half a dispenser of stiff brown paper towels. I went into the convenience-store part of the establishment and bought a package of black crews, then returned to the bathroom, hobo-washed my feet, changed socks, and ditched the ruined pair. On the way out I told the attendant the dispenser was out of towels.

So I was presentable, but inside the car I smelled like burned-over rainforest. That wasn't a bounceable offense where I was headed.

It was Judas weather, one of those deceptively hot days we sometimes get in early spring that tempts us to put away the snow shovel and throw a fresh log on the air conditioner. Then the next day the furnace kicks in. With the bank thermometers teasing eighty and the sun turning the window ledge on the car into a branding iron, the former mission looked more than ever like the Addams Family house it was modeled after, complete with its own pool of gloom and clouds of tiny flying biting insects swarming just above the seedy tops of the dead weeds in the front yard.

There was no sign of the black Lolita who matched her nails to her chewing gum; but it was a school day. The bronze bell knob brought nothing — it had stayed broken after my valedictory pull the other day — so I banged on the door with the meaty part of my fist. If Luís *"El Hermano"* Guerrera wasn't babysitting Domingo *"Seventh Sunday"* Siete, I'd never raise the junky tapping delicately with my knuckles.

I didn't raise him anyway. Before I could, the door snicked, a demure intake of breath, and drifted away from my fist. Whoever had closed it last hadn't made sure the latch sprang all the way back into place.

It hadn't been locked the last time, but this was one more step away from common caution. In cities across the U.S. in our time, criminals are almost the only people left who don't shut a place up tight whether they're at home or not. At this rate, the next time I'd find the door wide open. I checked the load in the Chief's Special and once again had it in my hand as I let myself in.

Same old pungent mix of dry rot and pot; same old finery slumbering under a century and a half of tarnish and grime and general apathy. The staircase griped as I climbed it, same as before, the same bees made honey inside the wall, humming as they worked, and I found Siete, Lord of the Maldados, sprawled on his back on the same mildewed mattress catching flies in his mouth in the same room, not quite as dim as before because no one had bothered to tape the newspapers back up over the windows. The snoring was missing, but whatever blue ruin had him by the throat this time might have taken him to a depth his adenoids couldn't reach.

In fact the only new thing in that fetid room was a pair of ordinary brown beer bottles standing on the floor at the foot of the bed, neatly bound together with silver duct tape.

I went into a dive, hitting the floor on my left shoulder, and in the same motion scooped up the bottles with one hand and lobbed them toward the window. It should have been overhand, but the logistics were awkward. There was an even chance the bottles would strike the frame and bounce back into the room, jostling the contents and bringing about just the thing I was hoping to avoid. As it was, sloshing the stuff around probably did speed up the timetable.

Whatever. The pane gave way and then there was a flash and a *crump* that shook the floor and stained the air bright orange. But I didn't get an opportunity to appreciate the fireworks because the wall hit me in the face and I went to sleep.

Twenty-Two

I woke up burning.

I couldn't have been out more than a few seconds. My coat sleeve was on fire — some of the flaming liquid must have slopped in through the broken window — but it hadn't burned through. I slapped at it energetically and rolled to my feet with smoke pouring from the ruined material. I'd had the suit almost a year, a record.

Through the window I looked down at the burning weedy lawn and flecks of yellow and orange trying to gain a purchase on the house's siding. When the bottle bomb had exploded, it had launched the accelerant toward the street, where the fire was already dying, having consumed the fuel and found nothing underneath but concrete and asphalt. I didn't see any burning pedestrians, so the timing had been lucky.

No sirens yet, but a crowd was getting a toehold on the sidewalk. I turned to rouse

Domingo Siete. He'd slept right through the blast, but that was nothing unusual for a deep-sea doper like him.

He lay on his back, his favorite position, on the filthy mattress. He had on the same green army undershirt and boxer briefs, a few days dirtier and more pungent than when I'd seen them last, and you could scrape your boots on his chin. His face was bloated and plum-colored under the eyes. I reached down and shook him by the shoulder. I took my hand away fast. His skin was cool to the touch.

I looked him over. No wounds or blood showing, but I wasn't about to turn him over for a thorough check without surgical gloves; when a body's had time to cool the microscopic horrors come out to play. I walked around the bed. Something crunched under my shoe; I thought at first it was a cockroach, but when I lifted my foot I saw the plastic syringe and, poking out from under the bed, the curled end of the latex rubber hose he'd used to pop the vein. He hadn't even had time to put the syringe on the nightstand.

Black tar heroin. A Mexican export, many times more potent than the Old World variety, and a bargain at only ten dollars a bag. If you weren't familiar with it and measured it the same way as always, it tore through your circulatory system like fifty thousand volts of electricity and stopped your heart in seconds, if you were lucky. I'd heard tales of nightmares Poe couldn't dream up on his worst day, and I was superstitious enough to think they carried through to the next life.

Eighteen years old. A hell of a waste of youth. A tragedy, if you believed in accidents.

"Who won the scrimmage?" Alderdyce asked.

The firefighters had come and gone. It had taken only a few short blasts from an extinguisher to put out the flames, but getting rid of the spectators was taking longer. DPD uniforms were sticking up barricades and unspooling yellow tape to keep them out of the hair of the Arson Squad combing the charred grass for glass fragments and the investigating team working in Seventh Sunday's bedroom. No sign of Ray Charla yet. He was probably still raking up Sister Delia's life and depositing the results in neat piles.

I glanced down at the syringe I'd crushed underfoot and moved a shoulder. "I was a little rattled. It's been weeks since the last time I was on fire."

He pointed at the rubber tube on the floor for the benefit of a CSI man, a tub with gold rings in both ears who said, "Thanks, Inspector. What should I look for on it?"

"Fuck you." To me: "We've been tracking black tar for a couple of years. I thought we might have a little more time. It was in Toledo last month, but Detroit's a depressed market; a dime bag of pot is primo stuff here, so why waste dynamite? In Chicago the junkies are dropping like turds. Who do you like for it?"

I said, "Who's to like? There's the paraphernalia, all inside his reach."

"Go ahead, play dumb. Waste my time."

I put a cigarette in my mouth, then peeled it off my dry lip and stuck it back in the pack. I couldn't seem to work up a mouthful of saliva. "Okay. The fire makes it not accidental. Whoever shot him up planted the bomb to cheat the coroner out of his autopsy fee and make it look like Siete miscalculated his own Roman candle. That would get the firebug off the hook for Sister Delia. Lucky I came along, huh?"

"You're going to charge me for that suit, aren't you?"

"I haven't decided. I go through them like Kleenex."

"Just what brought you here?"

"I was hoping for Luís Guerrera. If it was old-school Zaps who torched Delia's, he might've had a line on them, if only to keep his gang from another police sweep."

Alderdyce peeled a braid of cobweb clinging to the lapel of his gray worsted and flicked it to the floor. The maid hadn't been around for a couple of decades. "I like Guerrera. I like him a lot. With Domingo out of the picture, the Maldados are all his."

"They were his anyway. The piece of meat on the bed lost interest when he found dope. If anything, *El Hermano* preferred to drive from the passenger's side and let Siete take the heat. As it were."

"He wasn't fooling us."

"These boys aren't afraid of cops. They just don't like interruptions."

"I think I'll let the APB on him ride just the same. If it's okay with you."

"Okay, grouch."

"I'm a little out of sorts. The chief wants Mexicantown out of the headlines, and I'm spending more time here than the locals. I don't even like burritos. What'd you get from Charla?"

"Turns out anyone with a semester in chemistry can mix up the kind of accelerant that's been going around. That narrows down the suspects to every high school and college yearbook in three counties."

"Why stop at three? Gimme one of those plant spikes you smoke."

I found a fresh one and lit him up.

"Inspector, you mind? I'd like the use of my lungs another forty years." The CSI scowled up at him from his tackle box.

Alderdyce blew a bitter stream at the missing window and led the way out. On the front porch he said, "Jesus, I hate those twits and their 'tude. When are they going to cancel those TV shows?"

I dragged in secondhand smoke from his cigarette and coughed. My throat was as dry as my lips, with tremors in my hands to boot. Near-death experiences are always worse after the thrill is over. "I'm hoping they bring one to Detroit so I can play a cadaver."

"You almost got your wish. Those bottle bombs aren't kid stuff. Nothing like making demolition easy for anyone with a Kroger card."

"They take a lot of the grunt work out of Molotov cocktails. You don't even have to throw them, or be around when they go off."

Right away I regretted saying it; but he wasn't paying attention, watching crowd control and looking for something else to criticize. The unworthy thought was still in my head, and I wasn't going to get rid of it until I did something about it all by myself.

That could wait. I couldn't remember when I'd eaten last, but my stomach was keeping track of the time.

My car was hemmed in by police cruisers and lab vans, so I walked to *La Riata.* I took off my coat, inspected my shirtsleeve for burns and didn't find any. I carried the coat and when I got a table I folded and stashed it on the chair opposite to keep the smell of char from interfering with my meal. It was too early for the Anglo crowd in Zorborón's restaurant, but half the tables were occupied by locals, some of them discussing the rumor of Domingo Siete's death in English and Spanish. Nolo Suiz, *El Tigre*'s surly cousin, was nowhere in sight. I remembered Zorborón was being buried that day. A pretty Hispanic waitress with red eyes and nose brought me a sizzling plate of fajitas with a hill of rice and a bottle of Dos Equis. I guessed she was in mourning and that Suiz had been too cheap to give her time off to attend the funeral.

The piped-in music was syrupy with strings and the male vocalist sounded like his heart was breaking. I could take the CD home if I asked the waitress to add it to my bill.

I ate too fast. I was more tired than I was hungry and wanted to be home. I left a fat tip, feeling like a sucker; for all I knew she was crying over the death of a treasured cat. With a full belly and the beginnings of a four-alarm case of heartburn I went back to the car, found it free of obstacles, and drove home, belching into the slipstream. The house smelled musty from being closed up in high humidity and the air was hotter inside than out. I opened windows and set a fan in one to move the atmosphere around.

I drank another beer to tamp down the heat in my chest and watched a news report of the funeral at Holy Redeemer. A monster chain of limos and low-riders followed the casket to the Catholic cemetery, with here and there an unmarked Crown Victoria full of plainclothes police officers taking pictures of the attendees. I couldn't pick out Emiliano Zorborón's daughter among the mourners, but she'd be a woman now with kids in tow, and there were plenty of those present, draped in heavy black veils with diaper bags slung from their shoulders, Dora the Explorer adrift among the weeds. Half the Mexican underworld had turned out to pay respect, but the youngest of them was middle-aged, and the oldest were on oxygen and casting their sad black-olive eyes around for comfortable-looking plots. I could feel the world beginning to turn under their feet; mine too. I looked for Luis Guerrera, not expecting to see him and not disappointed when I didn't. By now he'd know what took place at the old mission and was smart enough to guess the dragnet was out. The reporter the station had sent — one of those pretty quasi-masculine faces Louis Pearman found no use for — had a lot to say about the passing of the old guard.

Back at the station, the first official reports of Siete's death and the fire were just coming in; there was nothing I didn't already know and very little that I did. The funeral reporter was in for overtime. He was in the neighborhood, and even the media was feeling the crunch from Wall Street and the rising price of fuel.

The mood in the newsroom lightened considerably when the meteorologist started monkeying with his maps. An amorphous green cold front was locked in deadly combat with a globular red cold front from Alberta, whatever that meant; the explanation left me more ignorant than I had been at the start, and I had serious problems with the color coding. The official thermometer at Metro Airport had climbed to eighty-one, not quite the record but making it the warmest March in a couple of years.

Next morning it snowed.

Twenty-Three

I remembered something from a long time ago. At first I thought it was a dream, because I was in bed and hadn't been thinking of anything remotely connected when it came hurtling back in vivid detail. But it was too linear. You always have to rearrange the parts of a dream in order to take it in later, like cards in a hand of poker.

It was one of those episodes you knew were important for some reason, but stored away for another time, like a book that needed concentration or a movie you stopped watching halfway through the first scene, not because it was bad but because you weren't in a frame of mind to get everything out of it that went into it.

Anyway I knew I was awake to the point of awareness but not action. The sheet I'd barely tolerated in last night's heat was no cover at all now that the bottom had fallen out of false spring, but I couldn't summon the effort to reach down and pull the cotton blanket over me. So I lay there feeling the chill and thought of something that had happened in Emiliano Zorborón's garage.

At the time he'd happened to be committing a misdemeanor, but it had nothing to do with me and by then I had a free pass anywhere in Mexicantown because of a favor I'd done him in connection with another visit. This trip I was just there for local information.

He nodded at me politely and returned to what he was doing. *"Quántos años?"*

It wasn't my age he was asking. He was examining the rooster on his desk, a cruelly handsome specimen of fighting cock with a comb like a Prussian helmet and the glitter of the undefeated in its eye. It was red and teal and tawny and blue-black, glossy as a showroom Cadillac, and its spurs were as long as switchblades. That last part was breeding, and evidence of possession for illegal purposes. He was holding the bird firmly by the legs.

"Dos, jefe." The obvious owner, a sad-faced *mestizo* with hair sprouting from his ears and the rusty black coat he saved for funerals hanging off his bony shoulders, wore the expression of the born penitent. He wore his hair combed straight down onto his

forehead and the calluses on his red raw hands sizzled against one another as he wrung them at his waist.

"A little more, I think."

"Qué?"

El Tigre smoothed the rooster's feathers; immediately they sprang forward, forming a ruff around its muscular neck. It tried to peck at his hand, but by then he was gripping it by that neck tightly. He glanced up at the owner wearing the look of Lear in the last act. "Such beauty. What a waste."

"Qué?" The owner reversed the positions of his hands and the sizzling resumed.

"Vea." Increasing his grip, holding the bird immobile now, he touched its beak with an elegant forefinger. "This groove, it has been placed there with a thin file. A very faint depression. One must know what to look for to see it."

The *mestizo* asked "what" again. It might have been the only word he knew in any language, but the tone had changed slightly. He was deliberately not understanding now. Anyone could see where Zorborón was pointing.

"As I am sure you are aware, it is standard practice at the beginning of a fight for the owner of each bird to hold its head down to oblige the opposing bird to peck its head, precipitating the aggressiveness required for a satisfactory fight. Roosters are smarter than people and will not harm each other without sound reason."

The other man chuckled uncertainly. The lift in Zorborón's tone and then the pause in conversation seemed to invite something of the kind. I wondered why he insisted on continuing in English.

"I am equally sure you do *not* know, being an honest man and unschooled in the ways of the wicked world, that there are some unscrupulous individuals who will attempt to increase the odds in their favor by introducing a drop of poison into grooves such as this. During the belligerent opening ceremony, that poison enters the opponent's blood stream, causing the bird to drop dead in the course of combat. The effect is delayed, you see; and who after all conducts postmortem on a dumb brute?

"I know you are unaware of this," he continued tonelessly, "and that some *bastardo* has taken advantage of your honorable nature and sold you a tainted bird. *Entiende?*"

"Sí, mí jefe." And I knew then the man had followed every word.

Zorborón sat back, drawing the rooster onto his lap and stroking its feathers as if it were a cherished pet. The bird made a cooing sort of noise and fixed me with a glitter in its eye I could have sworn was intended for me alone. I felt a vague sense of pity.

He smoothed its ruff. "Arrogant, foolish creature; he thinks he brings the dawn with his crowing. There is a word for this, yes?" He looked at me.

"Vainglorious." I was sorry I'd spoken. I didn't want to be drawn in.

"Of course. English is rarely so poetically precise. If I were a rich man," said The Tiger, "I would yield to my charitable instincts and take this damaged creature off your hands for the price you bought it for — not, I need hardly add, the price you are asking — and see to its destruction, that it will never have the opportunity to bring disgrace to the sport we both love. However, I am not so wealthy. Nolo?"

Nolo Suiz, who had been hovering in a corner the way he hung in the shadows of *La Riata* surveying his customers and staff, stepped forward and took the rooster from his cousin's hands. The bird, disturbed from its cozy perch, flapped its wings once before Suiz wrung its neck with one swift motion of his steel-strung fists. The bird made a short, surprised squawk and hung limply in his grasp.

Zorborón shook his head, sad as Job. "Such beautiful promise. Such profanity. I shall dispose of this worthless pound of poultry at my own expense. Take this gift I offer and do not enter my presence again."

The owner of the dead bird withdrew, his hands still at last.

"You could have put him out to stud," I'd said.

The lord of Mexicantown shook his head again and brushed feathers off his lap. We were alone, Suiz having left with the dead rooster dangling by its legs from his fist. "Someone would see it in my possession and leap to an unfortunate conclusion. People are always prepared to think the worst."

"I wouldn't have bet you cared what people think."

"*Pero sí.* My reputation does not belong to me alone. I have responsibilities to my neighbors that require trust. In any case, the bird would serve as a constant reminder of the existence of *puercos* like that fellow who just left. When I was younger, I would have had his neck wrung as well."

He smiled his sad, carefully trimmed smile. "I am not the cynic you might think, who stews in his own bitterness to the point of inaction. My business will not allow it. Now, what can I do for you, my friend?"

"You can tell me that poison-toting chicken won't wind up in the *pollo* pasta in Nolo's restaurant."

Such beautiful promise. Such profanity. It meant something, if only I could raise the aristocratic son of a bitch from his grave and ask him. I fell back to sleep with that thought and woke up with it when the alarm went off. Latins are long on romance and short on exposition.

TWENTY-FOUR

There was just enough coffee left in the can to make a cup, if I dumped it into the filter and used a Dustbuster to collect the rest. I was plucking lint off the surface of the brew when the telephone pulled me into the living room. It was Chata Pasada. I'd almost forgotten about her, about her brother Nesto, and about her husband Gerald, who hadn't spoken to his father the police inspector in years. That soap opera had long since turned into an action melodrama.

"Can you come out?" she asked. "Ernesto has something to tell you."

"I'm guessing it's something he can't say over the phone."

"I'd prefer it that way."

I said I'd be there in a half hour and drained my cup, lint and all.

The drive took a little longer. Snow was falling in big floppy flakes that clung to the windshield like sodden doilies until the wipers slung them aside; they turned the streets to grease and the traffic reports on the radio into breathless commentary on piled-up cars and jackknifed semis. I kept off the expressways, but the plows and salt trucks were out and I poked along behind every last one of them.

Alderdyce's son, Jerry, answered the door. He wore a blue denim shirt and scuffed jeans over his athletic frame. I felt overdressed in my second-best suit; but you never know where the day will take you, into a glass palace in West Bloomfield or a restaurant with a dress code. If your subject ducks out all of a sudden, ditching the rented jacket and tie slows you up that much more. You don't read these things in *The Dangerous Boys' Book of Private Investigation.*

"Working at home?" I asked.

"I'm taking some personal days," he said. "I can't put in eight hours and then come home to this."

We were seated in the bright living room with Jesus on the wall. He was holding a narrow glass with what looked like orange juice in it. When he drank from it I caught a whiff of pure grain alcohol. Whoever invented the screwdriver understood the need for an excuse to drink away the morning.

I said, "Your father says Nesto passed the lie detector test. The murder part."

"I think it's the other part he wants to talk to you about. That Chata wants him to talk to you about. I'm not sure. They don't let me in on everything. These old Spanish families lock up their secrets and don't let any extra keys float around."

"You don't have to be Spanish for that."

He gave me one of his father's looks, up from under the granite outcrop of his brow. "You think I should talk to my father, clear the air, that it?"

"Did I say that? I must not have been listening to myself."

"Maybe he should be the one to make the first move."

"I thought I was here to talk to Nesto."

He didn't hear me. "You don't know what it's like being John Alderdyce's son. There's no one else I can share that experience with."

"No one except your brother."

"Him less than anyone. They always got along. I might've been dumped here from a spaceship for all we have in common. Maybe there's something in that."

"Probably not. What would be the point of a black alien?"

He raised his glass, looked down inside it.

"I'm becoming a lush. You think that'll give us a stronger bond?"

"I've never seen your father drunk."

"You didn't live with him, see how he was after a tough tour. He never abused us, drunk or sober, I didn't mean it was anything like that. In fact, I think he was tougher on me when he wasn't drinking. I just wasn't used to seeing him not in control. Anyway I hear he doesn't hit the stuff hard anymore. Mom said."

"Maybe you should go out and get drunk together."

"That might make it easier."

I got irritated. "I was kidding. Am I wearing a collar? Talk to your wife's priest."

"I'm not Catholic."

"Then find a friendly bartender. On this job alone I've been threatened, pricked with a knife, disarmed twice, and set on fire. I've stubbed my toe on four corpses, and that's not even the record. Every place I go smells like chickens. Maybe I look wise because of all this valuable experience, but I don't feel wise. I know less than I knew when I started."

"Hey, sorr-ee. I never wanted you around to begin with."

"You should have been more forceful about it. What's holding up Nesto?"

When he lifted his brows he looked less like Alderdyce and more like Jerry. He stared at me for a fat second, then got up. "I'll see what's keeping them. Thanks for the ear."

"Don't mention it. I'm just a big old golden retriever you can lay your head on anytime."

In a little while Chata came in with her brother at her side. She was still plump and pretty in a yellow V-neck sweater that showed off the curve of her breasts and ivory-colored slacks with a knife crease. Her toes in her sandals wore clear polish and her blue-black hair was caught with combs at her temples and spilling down her back. Nesto looked fresh and a little pale in a sweatshirt with the sleeves cut off at the shoulders, showing developing biceps, drooping cargo pants, and dirty sneakers. He'd brushed his hair, but curls were starting to work loose like bedsprings.

I started to rise, but the sister motioned for me to stay put on the sofa. She lowered herself into a chair and Nesto flopped down onto the opposite end of the sofa, dragged a pillow in a bright slip from behind his back and plunked it onto his lap, crossing his arms on it and holding it in place like a shield.

"Ernesto," she said.

He nodded, then rearranged himself so that he was sitting cross-legged with the pillow still in his lap. "I set the fire at the garage."

"Uh-huh."

"It was *El Hermano*'s idea; to test my loyalty, he said. Then he told me to go to *El Tigre* and give him the lighter I used. He said a true Maldado had to be prepared to not only take action, but to claim responsibility for it."

"Uh-huh," I said again.

A crease between his eyes drew them close together. "Think I'm lying?"

"I think you're not as stupid as you want everyone to think you are."

"Who says I'm stupid?"

"Not me. That's the point. Did you figure that would be the end of it? Pass the initiation, learn the password and the secret handshake, and tell ghost stories around the candle in the treehouse?"

"Of course not! I —"

"You never thought he sent you into that garage to stand for Zorborón's murder?"

He opened his mouth again, but nothing came out. Progress.

"A crock like delivering that lighter, his own lighter, would fall apart half an hour into a police interrogation. Cops got a lot on their plate and only thirty minutes for lunch. They don't grill a suspect hoping to find an excuse to let him go. Once they get something the prosecutor can work with, they stop looking. You were set up."

"I didn't know. I never —"

"That's why it's called being set up. Guerrera won't bail you out. Even if he wanted to, he'll never get the chance now. He's wanted for killing Domingo Siete and trying to cover it up with the same kind of firebomb that destroyed Sister Delia's storefront. Wherever he lands, the cops will charge in with the heavy artillery. There's hardly ever a best-case scenario in that situation. Once he's on a slab downtown they'll trim the rough edges off the Zorborón case by sweeping you up and tying it in with Guerrera's plot to take out all the obstacles in Mexicantown and set himself up as *El Jefe,* the man to see in the neighborhood when you want a favor and don't mind giving one up to get it."

"They know I didn't kill Zorborón. The lie detector test proved that."

"Not admissible in court. If you think John Alderdyce can help you, you don't know how the department works. The chief will say he's not objective because your sister's married to his son."

Chata said, "They can't do that. We have Rafael Buho."

"Buho doesn't work pro bono. He'll insist you put up your house as collateral, and whatever you can get from everything you own. If this thing drags out — and 'speedy and public trial' can mean anything from three months to five years — you'll never dig out from under, and Nesto will still be in prison. I don't have to tell you what happens there, you've been to the movies, seen cable. He's not important enough to keep away from the general population."

"Are you trying to scare us?" she said.

"I hope to hell I'm doing more than trying."

Nesto tossed the pillow on the floor and unwound his legs. "I'll run."

"You ran before. I've got a generation on you and a game leg, and I caught up to you in one day. Cops have to stay in shape to keep their job. When they drag you in, the prosecutor will use the fact you ran to prove you're guilty. It's a cockfight and you're a capon."

Chata looked down at her hands twisted together in her lap. "What do you suggest?"

"Stay put for now, and keep an eye on Nesto. I don't think I got through to him," I said, looking right through him, through his hot eyes and narrow chest filling and emptying. "It happens I'm working an angle that if it isn't all hooey will blow apart the case the cops have been building. If that happens, your brother will be the least of their worries. He'd just complicate things if they tried to snag him."

" 'If'?"

I nodded. "Whatever 'if' is in Latin, it should be on my coat of arms."

Driving away from there I put on the radio to distract me from my racing thoughts. Warren Zevon was singing "Werewolves of London." Life can be like that. I turned it off in mid-howl.

My cell rang. Alderdyce's cell came up on the screen.

"That Wonder Bread truck was two inches taller than the swamp water they drove it into in Macomb County," he said without so much as a good morning. "Partial print the deputies lifted off the inside of the steering wheel belongs to Antonio Molina. The FBI, Border Patrol, and Mexico City Federales all have a file on him the size of the El Paso phone book. He split with the revolutionary Zapatistas twelve years ago over creative differences. Dope, but cockfighting's his hobby. We think we got him holed up in a duplex on Bagley. Want to go with?"

"You got coffee?"

"I got a Thermos."

"I'm there."

"Don't you want the address?"

"I'll just follow the yellow tape."

The drive back into the city was getting treacherous. The thermometer had slipped ten degrees, polishing the pavement and harvesting fender-benders two or three to the mile. The only really safe way to get around was aboard a Zamboni, but I gunned the Cutlass through the crunchy slush and let the tires find their own way back to the straight and true. A couple of daredevils operating SUVs powered past me as if they were on the way to the beach. I passed one of them in a ditch.

The carnival was in full swing, complete with a midway lined with cops and rubbernecks bustling about inside, preoccupied with their marching orders: a psychological no-man's zone, a pickpocket's paradise. Today's law enforcers, mindful of the public image, chew gum instead of cigars in that situation. If I had the Nicorette concession I'd have cleaned up. It's the new donut.

When the uniforms at the barricades let

me through I found the inspector going over a floor plan spread out on the trunk of a black-and-gold cruiser with an Early Response Team cop sporting gold leaf on his storm-trooper helmet. They were both wearing vests. I said, "Can I get one of those? Is there a deposit?"

"Unless he hauled a Howitzer up two flights of stairs, we're out of range. I'm only wearing it to keep from freezing my nuts off. Where do we live?" Alderdyce blinked a fresh fall of grainy snow off his eyelashes and pointed at a squat square brick building two blocks down the street. The block was cordoned off with more barricades and a steel band of cruisers and armored vans. All the cops had POLICE spelled out on their flak jackets in big reflective letters. The usual TV satellite trucks were parked on the outside perimeter and a helicopter batted the air with its blades, too far up to see anything but the same view you got from the Goodyear blimp above Ford Field. "The talk boy's busy asking him about his dreams and why he has the hots for his mother. He —" A fresh bellow from the negotiation expert's bullhorn interrupted him; the expert had a soothing, Perry Como voice that had fallen into a singsong like a tour guide's spiel, especially when he spoke in

Spanish. "There might be a hostage. Maybe not, but there's a family living on the first floor, so that rules out flash grenades. He opened fire on the first responders from a window when they knocked on the street door."

I asked about the coffee. He reached under his vest and drew out a steel Thermos with a battered chrome top. "Don't burn your tongue. Nothing like steel wool and Kevlar to hold in the heat."

I filled the chrome top and sipped. The stuff was strong enough to stand on its own without the container. "Why not just chuck it through the window?"

"Molina's been questioned in a dozen homicides on the border and did eighteen months in Marion for assault with intent to commit great bodily harm on an agent. His lawyer pleaded it down from attempted homicide. One thing you can afford with dope money is a smart attorney. Close range, long distance, guns, knives, habañero breath, it's all the same to him. If anybody shotgunned Roscoe Berdoo and cut his partner's throat, it was Antonio. So we got first-generation Zapatistas. Makes you nostalgic for the swine flu."

"What's the plan?"

"Commander?"

There were more commanders in on this case than you found at the policemen's ball. This one was a white version of the inspector, carved from the same stratum of granite but with a red handlebar moustache fussily curled at the ends and set with wax. "Wait him out for now. We cut power to the building and the landlord says the stove and refrigerator aren't working anyway, so unless he stocked up with freeze-rations and cans, he has to get hungry sometime. Just to push things along I sent a man for a charcoal grill and steaks and onions. Wind's in our favor. That's how Pat Garrett flushed Billy the Kid out of hiding once."

Most veteran cops are outlaw historians. I said, "What if he's a vegetarian?"

Neither of them made an answer to that.

"There has to be a partner," I tried next. "One man couldn't have loaded all those roosters into the truck in the time I was on stakeout by Michigan Central."

Alderdyce said, "We're running down his known associates. There's plenty, that's the hitch. There's always a big payroll when dope's involved."

The commander crumpled the floor plan and hurled it into a streaming gutter. "This thing's only good for historical reconstruction. When they drew it up, that building was a whorehouse, decked out with brass and plush curtains. I'd sooner go by dead reckoning."

Alderdyce pointed at the sodden crumple drifting toward the storm drain. "The chief'll take that out of your salary. I think it belongs to the Stanford White Collection."

"Out of my pension, you mean. I hoped to make my thirty, but the budget won't hold out that long. Hell with it." He excavated a box of Grenadiers from under the chain mail and set fire to one with a wooden match. The thick smoke looked gray but cast a brown shadow in the only patch of sun for twenty blocks. He seemed to notice me for the first time; he'd been too busy studying stairwells that no longer existed and secret passages long since stuffed with fill dirt. "Who's this monkey?"

"Curious George," I said. "Mind if I take a hit off that? I'm out of smokes thanks to the inspector."

He turned tired eyes on Alderdyce, who said, "Private cop. He was on the scene of the double homicide."

The Grenadier box came out again. I took one, zipped off the cellophane, and wasted two matches setting fire to it against the wind. It gave me a coughing fit, but the things aren't meant to be inhaled. He offered one to Alderdyce, who shook his head. "I'm working on quitting."

"I'm quitting working; just as soon as we put this scroat in a cruiser. Or a body bag."

Twenty-Five

Alderdyce said, "I vote cruiser. I've got questions to ask."

"I got men to send home all of a piece. Guess which tops the list."

"Your call, Commander. I'm just auditing this course."

The ERT man ran up the antenna on his Motorola. "Snipers, what's your twenty?"

Alderdyce jerked his monolithic head to the side. I fell into step beside him going away.

"I want that Zap," he said, walking with his head down, as if we were bucking a gale. The wind was stiff, blowing steel shavings into our faces, but it was a different storm he was walking into. "Bad enough, almost, to write a couple of letters to police widows. Am I burning out?"

"Yeah. If you're serious and not just flushing out the poison." I took the cigar out of my mouth to spit out a soggy piece of wrapper and never put it back. The burning tip made a bitter hiss when it struck the snow at my feet. "What's new with Guerrera?"

"Nothing's new. Those people have more family than a colony of Mormons, and the ones who aren't related to him wouldn't give him up to God if He showed up with an army of saints. We'd have to turn out every attic, basement, and garage in sixteen square miles just to smell one of his chili farts. This is the Motor City. You know how many garages there are?"

"I'll tell you just as soon as I finish counting all the offensive statements you just made about an honest, hardworking people."

"Oh, go to hell."

"Yeah, I'm sick of it too. But I still think you're barking down the wrong hole with Guerrera. That little prank with Nesto was a Hispanic's idea of subtle. The man who thought it up would find a better way to dump dead weight than stick a needle in him and set him on fire."

"Well, point me to the right hole and I'll bark down it twice as hard."

We were at the barricade. A young uniform with a pubic moustache pivoted a sawhorse like a gate and we stepped through. Another uniform, saggy-faced with eyes fished out of the bottom of a sump, a pale inverted triangle on his sleeve where a sergeant's chevron had been removed, stepped in double-quick to bodycheck a redheaded young thing from Channel Two. She and her cameraman argued with him while we made distance down the street.

"This Mexicantown business has got you in blinders," I said. "The answer's right in front of you, but you're too busy with gangs and cockfights and dope and the revolution that's been going on since the Alamo to see it."

"You can?"

"I'm closer to it. I don't mean that animal you've got cornered up on the second floor. He's still waiting to grow into his great-great grandfather's bandoleers. I'm talking about Molotov cocktails."

He stopped so short I had to retrace two steps to turn around and face him. "What's to talk about? You fill a bottle with gas — cyclostyrene, whatever — stick a rag in it, touch it off with a Zippo, and throw it through a window. You don't need to be Justin Verlander to pull that off."

"So why tape it to a bottle bomb? Ray Charla says if you know a little bit of chemistry and how much air to leave between the accelerant and the cap on the bottle, you can lay it down wherever you want and split. Be eating baklava in Greektown when the stuff goes up in Birmingham. Or Mexicantown."

He realized he was still wearing his bulletproof vest; the weight of it seemed to have just gotten to him. He tore loose the hook-and-loop straps and let it hang open. His shirt was soaked underneath, despite the cold. "You've got a dirty mind. I don't know why it's taken me this long to see it."

"It's a dirty world."

"Only it didn't go down in Mexicantown while the baklava was coming out of the kitchen in Greektown. It damn near claimed the wrong victim."

"Timing. Luck, if you like, because there's no rule of thumb in murder. Turned out okay, though, for the arsonist. The way it went down took away all trace of suspicion."

"You're wrong. You have to be wrong."

"I hope to God I am."

"God," he said. "Who's He?"

"A guy you hang up on the wall and expect Him to stay put."

"So why come to me with it? It's your hunch."

"It's your case."

He reached inside the vest and rubbed the spot where it had hung most heavily. "Run it out. That's what you came to ask. I wouldn't touch it with oven mitts."

I shook myself, releasing a bale of snow from my shoulders. "Nesto set that fire behind Zorborón's garage. He told me this morning."

"Hell, I knew that."

"How?"

"I put Old Man Hanover's iron jockey on his porch roof on Halloween when I was ten. The son of a bitch is eighty-seven years old. He still prowls his front yard with his army-issue forty-five every October thirty-first looking for his shot. Kids are rotten."

"So that's it for Nesto?"

"That's it for Nesto."

"What about Jerry?'

"What *about* Jerry?"

"Nothing, except I think he's ready to talk."

"Why, what'd *he* do?"

"I meant talk, not confess."

"Who're you, Oprah?"

"Go to hell."

"Short walk." He jerked his head toward the duplex.

My hands were numb. I stuck them deep in my topcoat pockets and worked the fingers until circulation stung. "I don't figure you need me for the rest."

"Where you headed, as if I couldn't guess?"

"I'm not going over there yet. I need to hear back on a couple things."

"Shouldn't take long here. I'm getting hungry myself. Molina must be licking the wallpaper right now for the flour. You know how a Mexican knows it's time for his next meal?"

"You know how you can tell when a cop's been using the computer?"

He nodded. "Next time, let's just throw out punch lines."

The charmer came back on the bullhorn, saying something in soothing Spanish. I got in the car, ground the cold engine to life, and pulled into the slick street just as a squad car passed carrying a charcoal grill in its open trunk.

Rosecranz, the little man who lived in the lobby, had unlocked the door to my knee-hole reception room for the odd customer to come in and read my old magazines, just as he had for twenty years, and for twenty years I had yet to find anyone waiting there in the morning when I got in. This time was the same, with a twist: Someone was moving around inside the private office, which I keep locked.

I unshipped the Smith & Wesson once again, stood aside from the frosted glass panel in the door, grasped the knob in my free hand, and went in fast and hard, cocking the hammer for a lighter pull on the trigger in the same movement.

I caught Luís Guerrera in mid-pace. He crouched and spun, a box cutter materializing in his palm as he did so and the blade flicking out like a gas jet. His T-shirt was sweat through and his jeans sagged from his narrow hips, the material heavy with the weight of perspiration and dirt. He looked as if he'd come in straight from a marathon. Which was probably pretty close to the truth.

When he saw who it was he relaxed a little, but the cutter stayed tight in his grip. It went back to wherever it had come from, as quickly as it had appeared, when I uncocked and holstered the revolver.

"Keep away from the window," I said. "Town's full of snipers today."

He sidestepped to put solid wall at his back.

I circled around him and sat behind the desk, giving it a once-over. I never lock the drawers — the safe is a little more secure for hiding the odd crown jewel or fissionable material — but I keep them pulled out at different lengths just in case someone has pawed through them or planted something and didn't take care to put them back exactly the way they were. Ordinarily a cautious character like *El Hermano* would take the care, but in his present condition I doubted he had the patience. He resembled every composite sketch I'd ever seen of a wanted fugitive, with the surprised, put-upon expression the people who designed the Identi-Kits favored. The two long facial scars looked like parentheses.

So far we hadn't spoken. I broke a fresh pack out of the belly drawer, dealt myself a smoke, and skidded the rest across the blotter.

He shook his head. "Never use them. I keep clean."

I grinned, pointing the cigarette in my mouth toward the ceiling, and struck a match.

His whole face turned down in a scowl. "Dirty Mexican; that it?"

"Cut it out." I spoke around the first puff. "If you draw the ethnic card, your own people will cut you off at *los rodillos.*"

"*Las rodillas* means the knees," he said. "You said rolling pins."

"So I'm a lug in two languages. You want to sit down? My guess is you've been working your *rodillas* more than your butt lately."

He shook his head; but he sat, registering surprise when he tried to push the chair back from the desk and it wouldn't budge.

"Bolted down," I said. "I don't like people messing with the feng shui."

"You never stop, uh?"

I stopped. "You were missed at Zorborón's send-off."

"You were there?"

"I don't crash funerals. Cops looked disappointed you didn't show."

"I didn't kill Domingo. He was doing a fair job of it without anybody's help."

"Somebody helped him."

"Who?"

I shook my head. "You came to me."

"License on the wall says you're the detective."

"Whoever it was might've gotten away with it if he didn't try to dress it up with arson. But then it would've been just another OD. It had to look like Seventh Sunday was the man behind the recent rash of suspicious fires in the neighborhood and missed his timing. The M.E. wouldn't have had enough tissue to test for narcotics or it would've been clear he was in no shape to make a bomb. The Arson Squad stops looking when they've got their turkey roasted nice and crisp. But that didn't happen, so the bombing at Sister Delia's stays open."

"Why'd I bother, if all I wanted was to take his place?"

"That's the other theory, but they're not mutually exclusive. If it looked like an accident, you could step right in without being the prime suspect."

"I was in already. You saw him the other day."

"I made that pitch, but you know cops. The plan to hang everything on Domingo fizzled out along with the bomb. That puts you back up top. Like I said, they stop looking when they've got their case."

The smile had died, but its ghost pulled at the corners of his mouth. "You stood up for me, uh?"

"You I don't care about. If you didn't wind up like Siete in a couple of years, some gangbanger — an ambitious Maldado, like as not, as if there weren't enough competition from the Detroit Zaps and the Mexican originals — would do the job. But that wouldn't put the real arsonist out of action."

"You keep talking like you know who he is."

I flicked ash at the souvenir tray on the desk and missed. It broke up and scattered in the current from the furnace blower, which kicked in with a clang and a shudder and the smell of scorched dust. Waited.

He crossed his long legs. That made him look as casual as a panther seated on its haunches. "You should've seen Domingo a few years ago. He was beautiful. Quick, smart — we called him Zorro. Those of us who were born here. They don't know about Zorro in Mexico. It was *El Tigre* brought him down. When the main *hombre* got out of drugs, that made an opening for somebody else to dig in here. Domingo, he liked to know all about a thing before he got involved. What's one little needle prick? Nothing, usually. But he was" — he stumbled a little over the word — "susceptible."

"Well, no one can touch him now. Why come here? You'll get just as much from the cops if you tell them you're innocent."

"I want you to tell them."

"I tried," I said. *"Es no uso."*

"You should stick with English. You sound less stupid."

"I've been told. Why should I be any more successful this time, in whatever language?"

"Because when you tell them I'll be with you." He smiled again when I reacted. *"Es claro, pero no?"*

I nodded. It was clear, but yes.

Twenty-Six

"You can turn yourself in without me holding your hand," I said. "My stock at headquarters isn't that high."

"Higher than mine. I walk in there, what's to stop some rookie from chopping me full of holes? They're all sold on this *excremento* that Mexican gangs aren't afraid of cops. They're liable to think I went there to pick up some notches; that old *macho* thing."

"Could be. But in that case the rookie wouldn't be likely to notice me by your side. My insurance policy has an innocent bystander clause that voids the account. We'd better hold the party here."

"You mean it?"

"The super's getting lazy. He can use shaking up."

"So the answer is yes."

"Sí." I picked up the telephone and called John Alderdyce's cell.

"What's the catch?" said the inspector

once the pitch was made.

"No catch. He wants to close the season on Luis Guerrera."

"So far he's just a person of interest, not a fugitive."

"That's press talk. The Molina thing's got this town strung tight."

"Not anymore."

I didn't ask. I could get the news off the radio. "Guerrera's innocent, John."

"Only if you stretch the definition."

"I'm thinking when you do get him you want it to stick."

"This on the level? No Walker Rope-a-Dope?"

"Nope. Too tired."

The connection broke. I cradled the receiver and got up. "Time to pat you down."

The cutter came back out before I could react, the blade glittering.

After a beat Guerrera grinned. His teeth against brown skin were as bright as UV rays. He executed a reverse border roll, sliding the blade back into the handle as he spun the doohickey and held it out for me to take.

"Graceful." I dropped it in the belly drawer and bumped it shut. "Now stand for the frisk."

He shrugged and leaned his palms against the wall. I slid my hands over ribs and sternum and taut nervous muscle under a thin coating of flesh. It was like searching an Erector Set.

He wasn't carrying so much as a wallet. Where he lived he didn't need one. His credit was good everywhere inside Maldado territory.

I stepped back while he found his balance. "Don't expect them not to rough you around when you get to lockup. Down there they don't sort them out according to who came in on his own and who they had to go out and get."

"I've been through it before," he said.

"That was routine. This time the world's watching. But only as far as Admissions down at County. After that you're no longer in the United States."

"I thought they threw out the rubber hoses a long time ago."

"Where'd a sprout like you hear about rubber hoses?"

"The old man learned English watching old movies. I had to wait till he passed out in front of the set to leave the house without a beating."

"Leave the defense work to your p.d."

"Think I'm lying?"

"They're trying a young puke in Livingston County for beating his girlfriend's three-year-old to death because he peed on his couch, and that little kid still had it better than somebody else. Everybody's childhood sucked. I'm not the one you need to sell."

"I'm not selling anything. I just don't want to get shot down in the street like Jesus."

"Your brother let his *cojones* do his thinking for him. Right now I'm talking about what happens before you're arraigned."

"I never got that far; they kicked me because I wasn't their boy and they knew it. But it can't get any tougher than the neighborhood."

"Not at first, and maybe not at all. Probably they'll just shove you back and forth: 'Stop butting me, punk; you looking for an assault beef?' Playground stuff. Once in a while someone gets the bright idea to dislocate a finger, then pop it back in without leaving a mark. Or they can pull a Hefty bag over your head and tie it around your neck with duct tape. Bend you back over a chair and pour a bottle of Pepsi up your nose. It always seems to be Pepsi, for some reason. Maybe it's a contract thing. Some of the younger cops served in the Gulf and brought back what they learned in the internment camps."

"You trying to talk me out of it?"

"I'm trying to talk you out of coming back here with a half-dozen of your *amigos* when you find out it isn't *Law and Order.*"

"I don't scare so easy." But he was a little white around the nostrils.

"Good; you'll need it. I'm just telling you about things that worked in the past. Local interrogation methods haven't come under investigation lately. They're not likely to change until they do. They don't like gangs downtown."

"Jealous of the competition, I guess."

"The important thing to remember is they'll stop short of crippling or killing. As long as you don't forget that, you won't write your name on something that'll take a lot of sidebars in court to set aside."

"Suppose they slip."

"There's always that."

His mouth tightened a little. It was as close to afraid as he'd shown. Well, I'd laid it on thick; that Hispanic bravado was getting to be as annoying as the same Christmas carol over and over. But I hadn't made anything up.

It was after dark when Alderdyce came, alone as agreed. His narrow-brimmed Borsalino hat and Chesterfield coat were dusted with snow and he looked tired, but that's an old cop trick to make people think they're human. I took out the cutter and held it out. "It's all he had on him. When the case falls apart you can slap him with CCW, put him to work for a couple of months scrapping gum off the sidewalk."

"You won't mind if I go over him again."

I told him to help himself. When that was finished he shook loose the bracelets and read the Miranda in English and Spanish. It sounded more like a threat in the second. I asked what had happened with Antonio Molina.

"You didn't hear?"

"I don't listen to the news anymore. Too depressing."

"He went to a window and the sniper took his shot."

"Dead?"

"Still in surgery; but those boys don't shoot to wound. I've got the department's best interviewer and a steno cooling their jets in the waiting room in case he comes out of the anesthetic. We want his partner."

"He should be easier to take. They wouldn't risk two heavy hitters on a couple of nothings like Django and Berdoo."

"If his own people didn't delete him he'll

be heading due south at speed. We're probably too late already. Molina doesn't come out of it — which he won't, Christmas is for kids — we start over. Including proving there's an original Zap within two thousand miles."

"Most people don't believe in werewolves."

"That supposed to mean anything?"

"*Nada.* Just something Zorborón said."

"I'm already starting to feel nostalgic about the son of a bitch." He clamped a hard hand on Guerrera's upper arm. To me: "Coming?"

"I'm wiped out," I said. "I've got a big meeting in the morning."

"Yeah. This comes from an anonymous tip, right?"

"Sure. I don't like to look at myself on television. *Vaya con Dios, El Hermano,*" I told the prisoner.

He shook his head. "Even when you get it right, it sounds wrong."

After they left I uncapped the office bottle and poured what was left into a glass. It burned going down and soured my stomach, but it numbed the nerve that had been jumping near the bottom. I put away the drinking paraphernalia and went home to finish up the bottle I had there. Since I wasn't looking forward to the next morning anyway I thought I might as well make myself physically miserable as well.

Twenty-Seven

In the morning I left a message for Commander Ray Charla with Arson to get back to me. When the phone rang I had eggs sizzling in a skillet. I tucked the receiver under my chin and flipped them while he read me the results of chemical and microscopic examination of the bill spike he'd rescued from the ashes at Sister Delia's office. He translated the information from the geek as he went.

The next piece of information required more calls. The clerk I spoke to needed authorization I didn't have and couldn't get. The eggs got cold before I tracked down a supernumerary whose job was so close to the subflooring that sudden unemployment wouldn't change her lifestyle. As these things happen, she had access to what I needed; the most menial and lowest paid almost always do. She offered to fax the document to my office, but I said that wouldn't be necessary. I didn't want to put her breach in writing, and in any case there was no reason to bog both of us down in a discussion of why I didn't own a machine.

With a cold egg sandwich floating comfortably in coffee I drove down to Corktown and found a space in front of the square house where the sister lived. The ROOMS FOR RENT signs were still in place, a little more curled at the edges. The same automobiles I'd seen before were parked in the same places, snow piled around their tires; they would move the first of every month when the unemployment checks needed cashing. I walked around a slight dark-skinned girl of about ten seated on the porch steps, preoccupied with the text she was sending, and waited for the hefty landlady to let me in. The next generation will come with thumbs the size of cucumbers. The sun glimmered the color of skim milk behind a layer of clouds as thin as waxed paper and my breath smoked around my ears. It was going to be mufflers with the Easter bonnets again this year.

I found Delia sitting cross-legged on the patterned rug in her room, her bandaged arms rubber-gauntleted to the elbows, sorting Rorschach-shaped scraps of charred paper into piles on a sheet of butcher paper.

The gloves were stained black and there were black smears on her sweatshirt and jeans and the tip of her nose. The unprocessed scraps filled a macramé bag on the floor at her elbow.

"Pull up a chair," she said. "Arson let me forage. If I can restore twenty percent of what I lost from my files, I should qualify for a master's in archaeology."

"That ought to go well with the science degree."

"The girls must love you. You remember everything."

"Some of it comes to me in dreams. Usually when it's too late." *Such beautiful promise. Such profanity.* Why don't Latins rule the world? I sat in the rocking chair. "Been following the news?"

"One more lead story from Mexicantown and they'll have to broadcast it in two languages. The police have Luís Guerrera in custody and a Zapatista named Molina in a drawer in the county morgue."

The TV and radio reports had linked Molina to the murders in the rooster factory — part of a power play, the cops said, to fill the vacuum left by Emiliano Zorborón's untimely death; Roscoe Berdoo and Django would have made inconvenient witnesses. Old Country Zaps were suspected.

The cops were silent on whether Molina had given them any information before he died. *El Hermano,* they said, was being held as a person of interest in the death of Domingo "Seventh Sunday" Siete. The police refused to comment on whether there was any connection suspected with Zorborón's murder and the firebombing of Sister Delia's house of charity.

"How are your hands?"

She held them up in front of her face as if she'd forgotten about them until that moment. "They itch like crazy. That means they're healing. My doctor wouldn't approve of what I'm doing with them, but the sooner I can get my operation back on its feet the better. As things stand it will take months to retrieve what the neighborhood lost this past week. Years, more likely; probably as many as it took to start changing people's minds about what Mexican-Americans are all about. All we needed was murder, arson, and cockfighting to put us right back under that sombrero at the base of a cactus."

" 'Us'?"

She looked up with a smile full of rue. "It went up with the building, but I had a framed certificate from the Mexicantown International Welcome Center naming me an honorary Chicana. Nothing's meant more to me since I took my vows."

"How come?"

"That's an insensitive question."

"So give me a sensitive answer."

"They're a proud people with a rich heritage. They don't let just anyone in."

I said, "They don't need you."

"What?" She sat on her heels, bracing her sooty gloved hands on her thighs.

"Suppose, single-handedly, you turn Mexicantown into the garden center of the Midwest. People will say the locals couldn't have done it without a good old Anglo-Saxon at the wheel. Suppose you fail. They'll say, well, how much could anyone do with such a shiftless people? They've had plenty of that without your help. They don't need you."

"What are you saying?"

"I just said it."

"I should give up."

"That'd be a waste of talent. The world's full of causes in need of a leader. I'm saying you should turn this one over to the people you say you want to help."

"And what if they fail?"

"They fail."

"Just let them drown."

"Or let them learn to swim."

"Pull themselves up by their bootstraps? And where will the boots come from?"

"They're no good if they're borrowed."

"I'm glad to say not everyone is as cynical as you."

"I didn't say they *would* fail. They should have the chance to, all on their own. Or to succeed the same way. It's the only kind of success that counts."

"Who are you, Horatio Alger?"

"The trouble with you earnest types is you get so caught up in the cause you forget you're not alone. You think you're the only one who can save the situation. Little by little, you start to feel contempt for the people you're trying to help. When that happens, the consequences of your actions don't matter. Just the actions."

"Not Horatio Alger. Ayn Rand, maybe; but I don't think of you as having a political opinion of any kind."

I wasn't sure who that was, so I let it slide. "That was a lucky break, getting up to go for supplies just when that Molotov cocktail came through the window."

"The Lord looks after me." She returned to her sorting. "A lot of people in the Order thought I turned my back on Him when I left the Church. I never did; and as it turned out, He didn't turn His back on me either."

"He gave up on Siete in the end."

"Domingo had his chances. We all get plenty, but the well has a bottom."

"The Church says it's never too late."

"That's where we broke. You can't just coast along counting on a deathbed confession to save you in the end."

"That go for Zorborón too?"

"He found the bottom before I came along."

I watched her play her game of solitaire. My legs would long since have gone to sleep in that position, but she'd never had a bullet in one.

I said, "It's a wonder you waited as long as you did."

She turned over three more scraps of half-incinerated paper, rejected one as unreclaimable, and stacked the others before looking up. "Waited?"

I shifted gears again. "I looked up your school transcripts."

"I could've saved you the trouble. All you had to do was ask. I didn't make the dean's list."

"You didn't have to. You mentioned you'd studied science at the University of Detroit before you decided to become a nun. The people in charge of Records wouldn't give me the time of day, but a party whose name

I wouldn't mention in interrogation is longer on talent than discretion. Chemistry was your interest, two semesters. According to Ray Charla, anyone with rudimentary chemistry training could have mixed up enough cyclostyrene to blow up the City-County Building."

"Someone blew it up? I guess the doings in the neighborhood shoved that one right off the front page."

"Now you're just vamping. Not like you."

She arranged what she'd stacked into a jigsaw puzzle. Her concentration seemed to have deepened.

"It was that second bottle did you in," I said.

She gave up then, pushed the papers away from her, and sat back once again on her heels. "It's been a generation since catechism, and you're no good at making up riddles anyway. Your mind's too direct."

"So is a turtle's. He gets there eventually."

"Does the same go for this conversation?"

"Charla found what was left of two bottles close together in the rubble in your office. Someone filled one with super-accelerant, the other with common drain cleaner and aluminum foil. MacGyver would've been proud."

She scratched the side of her jaw, leaving

another streak of black. "You don't have to spend much time at street level in this town to know aluminum foil and drain cleaner makes a dandy low-grade bomb. You sure don't need a knowledge of the table of elements."

"You also don't need to risk throwing an explosive device through a window and maybe being seen. Anyone could figure how far to fill the drain-cleaner bottle to leave enough air for the bomb to go off on delayed-action. Then all he'd have to do is tape it to a bottle of gasoline or charcoal lighter fluid — or cyclostyrene — plant it near enough to a window from the inside to make it look as if it had been thrown through the glass, and make arrangements to be out of range when it went off. The blast would blow out the window, and with all the ash and debris lying around afterward, it'd be almost impossible for even an arson expert to say whether the window shattered from outside or inside. There'd be plenty of glass fragments on both sides and not enough difference to make a case against the so-called victim.

"You were the only witness to the bombing," I said. "No one else saw or heard anything until the fire broke out. The entire police theory was built on what you gave them."

She was a rock under pressure; but then I said before it takes a strong constitution to live in a world of confessions and still maintain equilibrium. "The witness lied. Pretty theory. Too bad it depends on the person who set the bomb coming away unscathed." She held up her hands, bandaged under the rubber gloves.

"Minor burns. Even the EMS attendants didn't put up much of an argument when you bailed out of the stretcher. Just how much air to leave in the bottle depends on variables like humidity and temperature, which this time of year is a crapshoot. You timed your run well enough to avoid serious incineration, but you were a half-second off to keep from getting a piece of it. My thought? It blew up just after you finished planting it, when your hands were still inside the edge of the blast. That turned out okay for you, because it went a little more toward eliminating you as a suspect. A crime-scene purist might question the splash pattern; but who around here would consider Sister Delia a suspect, knowing her dedication to the citizens of Mexicantown?"

"So I'm a fraud. What's my end? Munchausen by proxy? Set myself up as a hero so I can warm myself in the glow of public adoration?"

"Not you. The dedication's real. You applied yourself to the task of ridding the neighborhood of its bad element. It's why you made yourself out a gang target, so it looked like the bad element wanted to knock the mortar out from under the cornerstones. First you sacrificed the paint job on your car, posing as a victim. Penny-ante stuff, not meant to draw much attention at the time — wouldn't do to spark an official investigation too soon — but torching your office nailed it tight, and right on schedule. After that, no one in the world would suspect you of killing Zorborón."

She laughed; I wish she hadn't. It had the shrill edge of hysteria, like rats fighting between walls. "How'd I do that? I forget."

"A garage is a noisy, public place, people coming in and going out through the bay doors without the employees taking much notice because of the traffic volume. You wouldn't have needed much of a disguise — a cold spring makes anyone in a stocking cap and a bulky coat invisible — maybe you didn't bother. You can get too clever with that kind of thing and draw more attention to yourself.

"Anyway, no one paid much attention

when you let yourself into *El Tigre*'s office and shot him between the eyes. That doesn't take much skill at close range, especially when he wouldn't be expecting Sister Delia to give him anything but a good tongue-lashing, and he was used to that. He trained as a boxer, so his reflexes were better than average, even allowing for middle-age slowdown. And he was a cautious man by virtue of his profession. But the worst he had to fear from you was a picket line, he thought. And so he was sitting comfortably behind his desk when you put a bullet in his brain.

"The noise was no problem," I said, "not with one of the Tijuana twins banging the bejesus out of a hunk of metal on the workbench and the other using an air wrench. I never got a good look at that gun you showed me. Not a big caliber, I'm guessing. You bought it for your personal protection, not to hunt elk."

She stopped laughing as if a breaker had been tripped. She was still kneeling with her weight on her heels and her hands on her thighs, as if she'd been interrupted in the middle of planting petunias. She dusted off her rubber-encased palms and let one drop inside the macramé bag, rustling among the charred papers inside. She put all her attention to it as if the next piece she excavated would unlock the key to her whole filing system. "Proof?"

I stroked the arms of my chair, watching the movement inside the bag. "Ray Charla found the tool you used to scratch those naughty words and pictures on your car. The paint chips should be easy to match."

Her hand stopped groping.

"You overdid it with Siete," I went on. "In six months, maybe less, he'd be no one's headache but the coroner's. But you thought you needed a fall guy — two, counting Luís Guerrera, the obvious choice based on gang ambition — and it took two more obstacles out of the way between Mexicantown as it is and the one you had in mind. Did you help him along with that shot of black tar heroin, or did he provide it himself? It won't matter to the judge or jury, but it's a hobby of mine to tie off all the broken blood vessels."

"I suppose someone's recording all this."

I shook my head. I kept my eyes on her bag. "I'm allergic to adhesive tape. Anyway, the cops have all the evidence they need. The Molotov cocktail with a time delay — you're well-known here, if you bought the ingredients locally, some clerk will remember — the paint scraps to lay the deal off on the young werewolves; I don't know if the cops will ever be able to tie you to Zorborón tight enough to make a case, but those forensics types are clever. They can match one exploded bomb to another well enough to say it was the same party both times. The rest is courtroom pyrotechnics."

She shook her head, an eminently sad gesture that reminded me of Zorborón just before he'd ordered Nolo Suiz to wring a rooster's neck. They were the same person, chained to a set of values created by themselves. "All this for a better world."

"Worse has been done for less. Zorborón out of the picture, *El Hermano* too, the Maldados and Zapatistas neutralized; they hanged John Brown for insurrection, but he's a hero to the anti-slavery movement. If I were you I'd retain Rafael Buho. He's a good lawyer, just unscrupulous enough to know how to put virtue to good use. By the time he's finished you'll look like Delia of Detroit, the patron saint of immigrants and hopeless cases."

"I never wanted that. If I were successful and no one remembered me, that would be all right. A lot of good has come from bad. Christ knew that. Whether the good was good enough is up to Him to decide."

The world kept turning, as it will. Little pieces of something clinked musically on the roof, like a chandelier shedding its pendants; freezing rain. The police cruisers would need to slow down on icy corners.

"He was dead when I got there," she said, "Siete was. Anyway, he wasn't breathing."

I wasn't either. I hadn't realized I'd stopped until that moment. I took care of it with a long intake followed by a gust of pent-up air. But I kept my eyes on that bag.

"It didn't matter," she said. "I was pretty sure I'd find him passed out; that was his natural state near the end. If Guerrera was there, or anyone else, I'd have called it off and tried again later. As the angel of Mexicantown I didn't need an excuse to visit anywhere in the neighborhood. I might even save a soul, and who's to know what I was carrying in my bag?" Her hand came out of it wrapped around a pistol no larger than a novelty cigarette lighter.

Size didn't matter: the same .25 caliber had been enough for Zorborón. A professional would have ditched it, but murder is almost always committed by amateurs, and who would have frisked her?

"Don't bother to get up," she said. "I'm no lady."

I sat gripping the arms of the rocking chair while she gathered her legs and pushed herself to her feet.

"Make yourself at home — please. Count to ten slowly before you leave. I'll be counting on the other side of the door."

"Pure pulp," I said, "and from a saint. There must be something better in the New Testament."

"Try quoting it in Mexicantown. See how far you get."

"You took the words right out of my mouth. Where does the angel of Mexicantown go when she's on the run?"

"Call it animal instinct. I'm not a martyr, no matter what you might think."

I tightened my grip to steady the rocker and rose.

The little square pistol followed me. "Don't get up, I said."

"I'm not Zorborón or Siete, Delia. So far everything you've done you did for what you saw as right. Why be inconsistent now?" I held out my hand for the gun.

She was bolted to the floor, the semiautomatic grafted to her hand. With her clothes and face smudged she looked like a grown-up Little Orphan Annie, if Annie had wandered into *Dick Tracy.*

I kept my right hand where it was, palm up. That was my gun hand; but the Smith & Wesson was behind my right hip bone. I might as well have checked it at the bus station. The first time I needed it, really needed it, it was out of reach.

I was watching the hand holding the pistol, not the woman who belonged to the hand. Against the advice of TV detectives I ignored her face, her eyes. She wasn't gripping the trigger with her eyes. I was watching when the rubber covering her index finger creased at the joint, applying pressure to the trigger.

Twenty-Eight

Despite its larger size, a .25 doesn't pack the same punch as a .22; it all has to do with percussion and velocity. Aiming is mostly a matter of luck because of the lightness of the frame and a design intended more for easy concealment than target shooting. Any ballistics expert will tell you your chances are better standing still and taking the bullet in the body than making a rash move that might put it in your eye or nick a major artery.

Any ballistics expert, that is, who has never faced one in the hand of a killer who's struck twice and hasn't anything to lose.

I lunged toward the weapon, grasping at her wrist to jerk it up; but I chose the wrong leg to propel me, the bad one, and lost a tenth of a second I couldn't afford. A slug needs a lot less than that at close range. I was six inches short for the time. A lifetime.

The Lord had switched sides. She didn't

squeeze the trigger.

She flinched at the sudden movement, but her finger loosened — deliberately, I thought later — and I scooped the pistol out of her hand with no resistance on her end.

For a while I stood there, breathing as heavily as if I'd run a marathon, the small flat gun lying in my palm like a compass. She seemed not to be breathing at all. There was no expression on her face and nothing behind it. I watched her pupils contract as if she were on a heavy-duty drug. For a moment her arm stayed where it was, bent at the elbow with her hand gripping a phantom weapon, then slid slowly down to her side.

The physical threat was over; now came the chaser. I was looking at her face now, at the blood sliding out from under the skin in a flat sheet, and anticipated the moment when it stopped supplying oxygen to her brain. I dropped the gun into my side pocket and stepped forward in time to catch her. She was a tall woman and strong-boned; a disc jinked in my back and the tendons strained behind my knees, but I kept us both off the floor. I lowered her to the rug. She was as gray as ash. I inventoried her vital signs. They were all in place.

I took out the pistol and sniffed the barrel. It smelled like a spent match, a little stale after a couple of days. I sprang the clip. Two gone, counting the one that jacked itself into the chamber after she shot *El Tigre.* I put it back together and returned it to my pocket.

Standing there with my feet straddling her I got out my cell, dropped it, and picked it up. I cleared the screen twice before I got the number right. Now that the thing was finished I had trouble focusing on the numbers. My fingers were as nimble as hooves.

Alderdyce answered as politely as always. "What now?"

"Did I interrupt your devotions?"

"Just speak."

"It was Sister Delia."

"Who says?"

"She does." I told him the rest.

"The fuck you say."

"We already talked about it."

"I was counting on you being wrong."

"Me too."

"I never thought she'd pull a gun."

"Me too."

"But I wouldn't think she'd miss."

I started to say, "Me too" again, then started over. "It turned out she cares a lot more about protecting the neighborhood than herself."

"Dumb luck."

"The only kind I ever have, not counting bad."

"Twenty-five, you said?"

"Yeah. One fired. My prints are all over it, but I didn't touch the shells."

"How is she?"

"She pulled a faint. Beat me to it."

"Ambulance?"

I looked down at her. At that moment she stirred, drawing an arm across her face. A sigh slid out. It was that moment of awakening when all was sweet and fresh; then you remembered. Her breath caught at that point of fracture. Her head came up, the eyes clear and fixed on mine. No hostility there, or fear. Nothing there at all.

"Squad car," I said. "She doesn't like ambulances."

"Lucky break, considering how she treats things she doesn't like. Hell," he said then. "Now I've got to kick Guerrera. I can't make a suspect stick."

"This one will."

He went away for a moment. Information got exchanged almost out of earshot. Then his voice came back strong. "That was thin even for a hunch, having Charla test that bill spike."

"Thinner than that. The lab didn't find

anything on it worth reporting. I never told Delia what it was they tested. For all I know she scratched her car with a bobby pin. Who keeps track of bobby pins?"

"Only you would try lying to a nun."

"I'm not Catholic. As far as I'm concerned it's the same as lying to the police."

A short silence on his end, scratchy with office static. "Job's over, Walker. Give it a little time before you shove the thorn back into the lion's paw."

As I put away the phone she started to sit up. I stepped clear, then helped her to her feet and over to the rocker. She wasn't as hard to transport when she was helping. She looked up at me, her fists closed on the chair arms. Her pupils were back and her color was normal, not counting the purple depressions like bruises under her eyes. "That was the police?"

"John Alderdyce. You know him."

She unclasped a fist long enough to make a gesture as meaningless as what I'd said. "I heard what you said. Was it the oldest trick in the book?"

"Depends on the book. Mad?"

"Disappointed. Talk around the neighborhood is Delia knows the street. I used a paper clip," she said. "One of the big ones. I don't know what I did with it afterward.

Threw it away, probably. If I'd paid attention I wouldn't have fallen for that stunt."

"Plenty more where that came from."

She looked down at her hands and seemed to realize for the first time she was still wearing the filthy gloves. She stripped them off. They made a nasty sound, like someone being scalped. She let them fall to the floor in a heap, flexed her fingers where they stuck out of the bandages. The gauze looked clean. "What's next?"

"A drink, if you've got one."

"I meant for me."

"So did I."

"Tequila. In the wardrobe."

"Tequila, seriously?"

"What did you expect here? I survive on the barter system. You never know what you can get in a trade. Medical supplies, for instance."

"Liquor counts."

The bottle of Cuervo Gold stood in a corner behind dresses and slacks on hangers. It was nearly full. I looked around. "Glasses?"

She shook her head. "Dixie cups in the bathroom down the hall. The landlady keeps a nice antiseptic house."

I didn't want to leave her. "Any strong

opinions about drinking straight from the bottle?"

"You know my strong opinions."

I uncapped it and handed it to her. "No circus like with Molina," I said. "No TV cameras, at least not tonight. No one's going to look good in the headlines on this one."

She looked at the bottle as if she'd never held it before, then tilted it up; coughed a little, made a face, and swigged again. She wiped her mouth with her sleeve, leaving a black streak across the lower half of her face. She saw the mess then. "Let a lady spruce up for her perp walk?"

"There a window in the bathroom?"

"Yes."

"Sorry." I gave her my handkerchief.

"There's a hand mirror on the dresser."

I found it on the chipped marble top, an antique in a yellowed celluloid frame with a fat handle, the initials C.S. on the back. For the first time I wondered what Delia's name was before she joined the Order. She wet a corner of the handkerchief with tequila and scrubbed at the streaks on her face. She combed her short hair with her fingers, gave me back the mirror and handkerchief, and passed over the bottle. "Gift from a neighbor," she said. "He thinks Cana was Cancún and Jesus turned the Gulf of Mexico into tequila."

"Who told him that?" I tossed aside the hanky and drank. It tasted no better than the last time I'd tried it, but taste wasn't the object. Just for the hell of it I looked at myself in the hand mirror. Some stains don't wipe off.

"It might have been me," she said. "The Church doesn't swing the weight here it does back home, not with the second generation. A kid who can't pick out Israel on a map needs a connection he can understand. How long will I be in prison?"

"Ask Buho. When I recommended him I meant it."

"I know him, too. Another vulture."

"You know everybody. Don't knock vultures. I'm sort of related to them."

"We were talking about prison."

"You were talking about prison. You may never see the inside of one. Whether you even stand trial may not have anything to do with whether you plead guilty."

"You mean I'm incompetent."

"I'd never call you that."

"Crazy."

"Sister, you're buggier than a Salvation Army mattress."

"That's cruel. Even if I did point a gun at you."

"You firebombed two places, committed one murder and may have committed a second, in order to save the neighborhood you set on fire. You tell me."

"How can I, if I'm crazy?"

"Yeah, that's a poser."

"Amos?"

"Still here."

"I couldn't shoot you."

"I know."

"Did you know before?"

"Sure."

"You're lying. I can always tell when someone's lying."

"You can take the nun out of the Church." I wet my lips. They were dryer than usual for early spring. "You almost took me out with Siete."

She paled again, and I thought she was going to pull another faint. But at least this time I wouldn't have to catch her.

She didn't. "I never intended anyone else to get hurt. I overcompensated after the last time, left too much air in the bottle. Making this one took twice as long because of my hands. If I'd thought —"

"You didn't. I said you were buggy. Anyway it takes three times to make a pro."

"Who says?"

"I just did. I say a lot of things trying to sound like I know what I'm talking about. Maybe it takes more. Maybe there's no set number; formulas are for math. It's the only true science. But most amateurs never make it past three."

"Who would ever want to go pro?"

"You'd be surprised. The health plan sucks, but you can't beat the hours."

She hugged herself. If anything the room was overheated. You never know when shock will hit or what form it will take. I had to keep my hands in my pockets to stop them from shaking. "I love these people," she said.

"They love you back. We'll know how much when they total up the Sister Delia Defense Fund."

"What good will that do them?"

"Not a damn thing, except make them feel good."

"What will happen to them?"

"Somebody else will come along. Maybe another you, only more patient. Maybe a scam artist."

"Encouraging."

"You want a pep talk, don't call a detective."

We stopped talking for a while. Somewhere in the building someone was watching a movie, a romantic comedy, from the tired oldies on the soundtrack. It was dark outside the window. From my angle the lights of the city made soft colors against the frosted glass, like tethered balloons. As if a party balloon stood a chance in Detroit. I heard a siren, frowned; I'd expected discretion, if not mercy. The noise swelled as it passed under the window, brazen and hollow at the same time, and receded behind the wall of a building on the corner; subsided, like a bad headache. It belonged to someone else's tragedy.

When I looked back at her she was smiling faintly, like a ghost remembering. "I'd do it again, you know."

"I know. Have another drink."

TWENTY-NINE

Roscoe Berdoo and the *mestizo* known only as Django found local fame, however briefly, after their encounter with Antonio Molina; the "Berdoo-Django murders" had a wizard cadence that rang solidly in headlines and TV news teasers for a week or so before Molina's death kicked it to the other side of sports and weather.

The suspect's deathbed delirium gave the cops the name of a small-time operator from Tijuana ("You want to meet my seester?") who moonlighted behind the wheel and on impromptu loading docks for the Colombian/Mexican drug cartel and who was just the kind of monkey who'd drive a Wonder Bread truck and load it with caged roosters while Molina took care of the personnel inside the warehouse. His description and mug shot from an old arrest for solicitation were faxed to the U.S. Border Patrol and officers on both sides of the border, but when he didn't turn up after two weeks it was assumed he'd slipped across before the bulletin went out.

"Depend on it," Alderdyce said, "a constable in some village made up of a gas station and three house trailers up on blocks will shoot him driving away a stolen car without paying for his gas. *La Ley de la Fuga,* they call it down there: the Law of Flight."

"Think it'll be that random?" I asked.

"I have to believe there's *one* honest man in a uniform there."

But the man never got that far. A day or two later, morel hunters prowling a swamp in Macomb County found a badly decomposed corpse tangled in rushes; for a while it was thought to belong to a father of three who'd disappeared weeks earlier after being diagnosed with severe clinical depression. On that theory, the fact that ligaments had been severed in the man's throat suggested suicide with a knife or razor. Then a medical examiner with time on his hands became curious about the dental work, and traced a number of mercury fillings banned from the United States for years to a dental college in Nuevo Laredo, Mexico, whose students practiced on inmates in the local jail. Records were examined. The dead man was Molina's partner, who'd drifted away from the bread truck after Molina sank it in the swamp with him inside.

"Right back where we started," Alderdyce said. "Worse: It'll take three rolls of the dice just to get to Square One. We know even less than we thought we knew when this thing started to go down."

"It's not that bad," I said, bracing myself against the dash. We were driving to Beverly Hills, the inspector at the wheel of an unmarked car he'd signed out from 1300. He drove like a cop, as if the laws of Man and Nature didn't apply to him. The ice storm had turned trees into fine crystal and the asphalt into a sheet of polished black ceramic. Turning a corner involved both lanes and a piece of the curb on the opposite side of the street. "We didn't know the original Zapatistas were involved when it first went down."

"We don't know it now. We *know* it, but not to count on INS and DEA and the FBI. They don't make a move without solid evidence, and we don't have the budget."

"You might want to pull your foot out of the firewall. This is a school zone." We were approaching Chata Pasada's neighborhood and the home of Alderdyce's son and Nesto.

He maintained speed for a hundred yards, then let up on the accelerator as if it were his idea. The tires continued to turn at the same rate of speed for fifty yards after that. There was no friction. "This whole Zap thing's got my gut tied up in knots."

"You? You're the loosest guy I know."

"Thank you and go to hell. They're a big-time operation down there. I mean the drug smugglers, not the revolutionaries whose name they stole: Al-Qaeda and the Mafia wish they were as well-organized as this outfit. But to make a move this far north needs financing."

"They blow their noses in hundred-dollar bills."

"That's the problem. They deal strictly in cash, bales of it, truckloads of it, and spread it around thick enough to buy the Vatican; it's no wonder even a Mexican cop with delusions of honesty won't move against them when everyone's involved from his sergeant on up. It's got to be cash, and up here the supply line's too long. Anything can happen to a shipment of untraceable bills between here and the border. They need someone local with the connections to make it portable."

"Someone like who?"

"Someone with the organization in place to launder money, turn it into stock certificates and municipal bonds, merchandise you can move overnight by the warehouse load, and squeeze juice back out of it in the form of clean cash. Pick up a phone, send an e-mail, and arrange to have it delivered by Brink's, washed in the blood of the lamb. Not just make it *look* legit. Turn it into the real thing."

"That's way out of Luís Guerrera's league," I said. "Zorborón in his prime couldn't swing it."

"We have to look outside Mexicantown, and probably outside Mexico. Bribe and kill, that's all the Zaps know. They haven't needed to know anything else until now, and they're not patient learners."

"It needs Wall Street."

"It needs someone who can work Wall Street. Personally I don't think the Suspender Boys have got the balls for it.

"Normally it wouldn't bother me," he said, "except for this itch I get between the shoulder blades that tells me it's in my jurisdiction."

We pulled into the driveway. The garage door was open, with two vehicles inside. His son was home.

Chata was expecting us; Alderdyce had called before picking me up at my office. She wore a plain blouse tucked into a dark wool skirt and her hair was loose to her shoulders. She led us into the living room, where her brother was sitting on the sofa in a crisp white T-shirt and clean jeans. He'd had a haircut. He looked oddly younger without the curls; with that slight build he could pass for fourteen. I saw Rafael Buho's hand in that. The boy was leaning forward with his hands folded and dangling between his knees. They looked large and clumsy at the end of his slender wrists. His growth spurts would be worth watching in stop-motion photography: first the feet, then the hands, then the head, then the feet again.

His sister sat close to him. We sat in the other chairs. Alderdyce said, "Just because Zorborón isn't here to press charges doesn't mean you don't have to answer for setting that fire. There was a mechanic working late that night. If the fire had turned into anything, this conversation would be taking place in court."

Nesto said something too low to catch. The inspector told him to speak up.

"It was just trash."

"Not the point."

"He wasn't trying to hurt anyone," Chata said.

"A judge will understand that, or he won't." He kept his eyes on the boy. "It's your job to convince him. That tattoo won't help. It's a red flag downtown."

Nesto rubbed the hand where the tarantula had healed.

She said, "We'll have it removed."

"Good. A long painful procedure should prepare him for what's coming."

"What do *you* say?" Nesto was looking at me.

"I'm just here for the ride."

Chata said, "Please."

"I'd feel better if your husband were in on this conversation. Where is he?"

"He's sitting at the table in the backyard."

Alderdyce said, "Drinking?"

"No. That isn't his problem. You didn't see him at his best the other day. I'll get him."

I waited until she was gone, then leaned forward and looked at Nesto. "You'd have saved two lives if you'd given the cops a description of Antonio Molina at the chicken coop."

He straightened suddenly, drawing his hands onto his knees. "I told you I didn't see anyone."

"You also said you didn't see a truck. I'm getting so I don't even bother to listen to your first answer.

"You were afraid," I said. "I knew at the

time it was a stall, but I didn't press it. I gave you a few days to put it all in perspective. That was a mistake."

"It sure was." Alderdyce looked stonier than usual, and usually he could outstare the *Thinker.* "I don't give a rat's ass about Molina and his junior partner, but if I'd had to write a letter to a cop's widow after that standoff later, I'd've made you deliver it in person."

"But I didn't —"

"Stop it," I said. "The clock's against you. Those guys were experienced crooks, small-time or no. You might have ducked out without being seen by one, but there were two, and they were using that door to move out the fighting cocks and looking over their shoulders expecting an official visit. There was only one time they might have been distracted long enough for you to chance it. That was when Molina was busy killing Django and Berdoo. Even if they weren't, there wasn't a fear in the world that would keep you in the building after that."

Alderdyce said, "I'm not turning you in for withholding evidence. What's the point? The killer's dead. I'm turning you in for malicious destruction of property."

Nesto started. But Jerry's father went on before he could say anything.

"It'd be better if you went in voluntarily. You'll have your community service in before summer vacation."

"But there's no point in that either!"

"You might change your mind about that sometime. If you don't, the hell with you."

The boy slumped back into his earlier position. He looked at the floor, said something I didn't catch.

"Speak up!" Alderdyce barked.

"I said okay."

The back door shut with a bang, bringing a harplike tinkle of icicles tumbling from the eaves. I stood.

"There's a burned-over lot across from Holy Redeemer needs a building for charity to work out of," I said. "Know where we can find a carpenter who works for nothing?"

Nesto's head came up with a grin on the front.

Alderdyce looked up at me from his seat. "Where are you going?"

"Out for a smoke. Your son's coming in."

I never knew what they talked about. The inspector didn't volunteer anything and I didn't ask. They weren't alone together long enough to work out a lifetime of friction, so maybe it was just a cold polite conversation with nothing to show for it. Anyway I never saw any of them again. Except Alderdyce, of course.

THIRTY

A week or so later, with the weather warming up, I prised open the window to stir the sludgy air around the office and picked up the phone. I'd had my arms to the elbows in stale files all day. I was happy for the interruption and answered cheerfully.

"I've caught you in a good mood."

It was a husky velvet voice, a female contralto, without an accent, not even American. I caught a chill from the window just then and swiveled my chair to turn my back to it. Then I decided having my back to a window wasn't a good idea while I was talking to the person who owned that voice, and rolled out of the line of sight.

I said nothing.

"You've cost me a great deal," the woman said. "I had time and money invested in Mexicantown. It isn't as if I can write it off my taxes."

I found my voice. "Where are you calling

from?" The connection was too clear for comfort; none of the hisses and gurgles of a trunk call from overseas. We might have been in the same room. Even the same country was too close.

"I think something may have to be done about you, Mr. Walker. Not now; now's officially then, thanks to you. But next time maybe."

"I'm open to a retirement package."

"Not you. A very disagreeable man I did business with once had a favorite aphorism: 'If you can't bribe him, kill him. If you can't kill him, promote him.' Meaning kick him upstairs out of the way. The man died in a Death Row infirmary, but the principle was sound. You won't bribe, and you're in a profession with no hope of advancement."

"I'll remember the advice," I said.

"I felt sure you would. Good-bye, Mr. Walker."

"Good-bye, Madame Sing."

I could still hear that voice purring in my ear after the line went dead.

Charlotte Sing was an international criminal; but anyone who picked pockets in Detroit and Windsor could claim to be one. She was wanted on three continents, all capital crimes, and a couple of them had pulled me out of my orbit into hers. But three times doesn't make you a pro, it just reduces your odds of survival by 30 percent — more in her case, because she didn't live by the law of averages any more than she did all the others.

What her interests had been in the Mexicantown business I couldn't guess and didn't want to know. What I wanted was to get drunk: loud, silly drunk, singing and all. But I was out of liquor, and I was glad. Now even more than ever I needed to maintain my edge.

ABOUT THE AUTHOR

Loren D. Estleman has written more than sixty novels. He has already netted four Shamus Awards for detective fiction, five Spur Awards for Western fiction, and three Western Heritage Awards, among many professional honors. *Burning Midnight* is the twenty-second Amos Walker mystery. His recent novels include the Valentino mystery *Alone,* the historical novel *Roy & Lillie* about Judge Roy Bean and the famous actress and celebrity Lillie Langtry, and *Infernal Angels,* the twenty-first Amos Walker novel. He lives with his wife, author Deborah Morgan, in Michigan, where he has recently completed *The Confessions of Al Capone,* an epic novel of the iconic American gangster.

The employees of Thorndike Press hope you have enjoyed this Large Print book. All our Thorndike, Wheeler, and Kennebec Large Print titles are designed for easy reading, and all our books are made to last. Other Thorndike Press Large Print books are available at your library, through selected bookstores, or directly from us.

For information about titles, please call:

(800) 223-1244

or visit our Web site at:

http://gale.cengage.com/thorndike

To share your comments, please write:

Publisher
Thorndike Press
10 Water St., Suite 310
Waterville, ME 04901

DATE			